A little of Chantelle Rose

Cristina Hodgson

*"An extremely witty romance with a twist
and refreshingly different. For all the "roses"
that know the only spike should be a stiletto, here
is a new heroine to escape with. Chantelle Rose
is like chocolate something to devour in one sitting...
the perfect date night book when you're not out
on your own adventures."*

Camilla Morton,
International Bestseller of
"How to Walk in High Heels"

Discover us online:
www.crookedcatbooks.com

Join us on facebook:
www.facebook.com/crookedcat

Tweet a photo of yourself holding
this book to **@crookedcatbooks**
and something nice will happen.

To my mum, dad and brother.
Everything I am, you helped me to be.

Acknowledgements

There are many special people I would like to thank who have formed part of my journey. It's actually hard to express in words (contradictory as that sounds coming from a writer) how grateful I am to be given this opportunity to present my debut novel. For this, I would like to firstly thank my publisher, Crooked Cat, for this amazing opportunity. To Laurence and Stephanie who are the team behind this unique publishing company, and who have created a wonderful community of "Cats" who have become my writing family.

To my brilliant editor Sue Barnard. I write to express what's burning inside me. You edit to let the fire show through the smoke. Thank you!

To all my amazing friends from childhood, through School and University. A special thank-you to each and everyone of you. Impossible to name you all here, but you know who you are!

Some friends, however, are like stardust on a dark night, leaving a magical trail in their wake, and as if touched by magic come into your life and stay there. To Alice, Dush, Suzanne, Aimee, Steph M, Steph R and Sara, thank you for your friendship and unconditional support and for so many special moments. Here's to many more.

To MG, for giving me a chance many years ago. For believing in me then and now.

Finally, to Fran and to my two beautiful children, without whom this journey would have no meaning...

About the Author

Cristina Hodgson, mother of two, born in Wimbledon, London, currently lives in southern Spain. Cristina had a long career in sport, reaching national and international level and still actively participates in Triathlon races and enjoys outdoor activities. In her spare time she also enjoys reading and writing. She won a sports scholarship to Boston College. After a period in Boston, she returned to the UK and graduated from Loughborough University with a degree in Sports Science.

A Little of Chantelle Rose is her debut novel. Amazingly, it has nothing to do with running!

You can find out more about Cristina Hodgson at **www.cristinahodgson.com**

A little of
Chantelle Rose

Prologue

"CUT!" called the director. "Lunch break."

Thank goodness for that, I thought, as I eased myself of this really stiff, hard- backed stool where I'd been sitting all morning. My legs felt numb, with pins and needles in my feet. Any attempt at walking at this point meant a shuffle across the set towards the canteen in the most unglamorous manner. What on earth had possessed me to be an extra in this gangster film? I sighed. I'd been here since 6am, rushed through hair and make-up, landed on this stool by 7am and had been sitting here ever since. It didn't help that the rickety old stool had joint problems and creaked and squeaked every time I so much as breathed in, much to the despair of the director who kept sending me death looks throughout the morning.

"The mikes are latest technology, my dear," he'd said. "Very sensitive. So please *KEEP STILL!!!!* Thank you darling." Which was actually, I think, my cue to get up and leave. But instead, much to my bewilderment, I'd remained like a dumbfounded child.

I glanced at the mirror as I moved through to the canteen area. What I saw was not a pretty sight. I looked like I'd run my hand over an electric fence. My frizzed-out big, sooty-black hair, never the best even on a good day, had suffered an hour of backcombing which had left it standing on end, and a whole can of hairspray had finished the job off. Quite effectively too, as six hours later there wasn't a hair out of place. Or in place, if you see what I mean. And as for the make-up... Purple lipstick (which, believe me, does not go with my skin type), and sparkly, sparkly eye shadow... Well, *Monster High* springs to mind. This is not the appearance I'd

3

expected after sixty whole minutes under professional hands. I looked better after a night clubbing to the wee small hours.

What was I doing here? I had been brooding over this question all morning, and I had the spiel ready for anyone who asked: "*Well, I just thought it would be great to meet the stars...*"

Or: "*I just wanted to live the experience...*"

The truth is, I was just desperado for money, and, what the heck, the pay wasn't bad. Actually it was a snooty accountant "ex" of mine who got me into it – although he meant it as one of his typical put-downs. He saw an ad in one of the local weekly rags which said that a long-running TV series – and as near porn as British TV is allowed – was looking for extra "extras". He sent it to me with a stick-on note from his snotty City firm. He could have simply texted me and saved the first-class stamp, but then that would have been way too "normal" for him. His note candidly read: *You're good at acting... and deceiving... and lying. Why not apply?*

Bit harsh, I thought, but I'll show you. And, anyway, something devilish inside me said, *This could be fun. And money, too!*

I rang the number and a nice-sounding lady (who I later found out was actually a man… Well, you know…) told me to send a photo and they'd "let me know." And that was that. Nothing. But nine months later the nice-sounding "lady"(who, I must say, was really nice – and, as my snooty ex would have said, "as camp as a row of tents") telephoned and said they were making a low-budget full-length gangster film, and I had one of the faces they wanted.

They were shooting sleazy bar scenes. Bloody cheek. I didn't think I had a sleazy-bar-type face, and was tempted to tell them to shove it. But, then again, I thought, it might be wicked fun. And, of course, there was the money…

I skived off work for the day. Which is, in short, how I found myself looking like the "tart" they'd had in mind from the start.

I didn't realise how hungry I was until I entered the

canteen area. There was a really long queue at the healthy food option, and I hesitated for a moment. If I joined that queue, the chances were that by the time I got any food on my plate it would be time to get back to the set. I like to watch what I eat, but not eating at all didn't seem a good idea either. If my stomach started rumbling during the afternoon takes and the mikes picked up on all the noise, I think I'd be personally assisted off the set by the director himself.

There was nothing for it. I made a bee-line for the hamburger stand and piled my plate with chips, ketchup, and the works.

I felt a bit out of place; everyone else seemed to know one another.

"Dah-ling, it's so wonderful to see you again! Cynthia, isn't it?"

I was also snatching comments like "Well, my agent tells me..." and "My personal trainer..."

None of this held much interest for me, as much as I tried to be intrigued by what agents and personal trainers had to offer. I was more concerned about juggling my mountain of food and my large coke with its feathered straw while at the same time attempting to perch myself delicately on a lop-sided bench. The furnishings on this set really did leave much to be desired.

Finally settled, and at the same time feeling a bit guilty about all these calories I was about to get my digestive system to try to break down, I heard a small sharp cry to my left. I looked up and saw Susie, one of the ladies in the make-up department, dashing towards me with her make-up bag swinging on her arm, and looking like one of the medics in *Grey's Anatomy* out to save the world. She paused by my side, and to my amazement snatched the burger right out of my hands. The burger sailed through the air and narrowly missed the film director as he walked past. I thanked my lucky stars that he was completely unaware that he'd almost got mayonnaise all down his Armani suit.

I turned my attention back to what I assumed was a sun-stroked crazy woman who'd blagged her way to becoming a make-up artist. This would actually explain my "sparkly, sparkly" eye-shadow.

"Dah-ling!" she exclaimed. "Like this!" She then dug into my still untouched plate of chips, picked one up and opened her mouth so wide that I could just about make out her tonsils. She placed the chip onto her tongue with delicate fingers, making sure not to brush her lips or lick her fingers. This, I reflected in part admiration, must have taken some practice.

"You mustn't smudge your make-up," she went on. Then, like a mother hen, she peered over at the other members of the cast, searching out others in need of her attention. In a flash she was gone, bags swinging.

Right... I picked up my plate of chips. I had the solution and promptly made my way to the Ladies room, where I proposed to wolf down the remainder of my food out of sight of the beady eyes of Mother Hen.

I stood in the washroom, avoiding the mirror because I really did look something shocking, and finished off my lunch. I was given a couple of suspicious looks by some of the other girls who'd entered the Ladies in order to preen themselves. I just winked at them and went on eating. I'm not sure if the looks were aroused by my metre-high hair or my choice of lunch location, or that, despite all the food piled on my plate and my apparent unhealthy appetite, I managed – though God knows how – to stay relatively slim. And in that tight-fitting red catsuit I'd been given to wear, my figure was highlighted all the more.

Lunch over, I slipped out of the toilets and meekly sought out Mother Hen, bracing myself for her disapproving glare. Though, when I finally found her, she just clucked over me in a disappointed tone, but didn't seem the slightest bit surprised to find me lipstick-free. She got right into re-applying all my make-up, and as I moved back onto the set, I felt I had a brick wall of foundation applied. To my horror she even got out the shiny eye shadow again, despite my moan of protest.

I got told by one of the crew that the director wanted to

see me. In a panic I walked over to where he was with the "hot stars" of the film, thinking I probably did get mayonnaise down his suit and he's going to charge me for the dry cleaning.

"Turn around," he instructed as soon as I approached. Bemused, I turned, feeling like a fool, and blushing as red as my catsuit.

"Cute tight ass," he said, though not to me, rather to the gang around him. I felt my skin crawl and flush even redder. What with the red outfit I was wearing, I felt I was glowing as bright as a light bulb.

"Excuse me," I stuttered as I finally got my voice back.

"Come and see me after today's shoot and we can talk business," he replied.

Bet we can…! But I didn't think it was talking he had in mind. Warning bells rang, and escape plans shot through my head. But before I could leg it off the set, I was taken by the arm by the owner of the only friendly face there seemed to be around, and was led right to the front of the set.

"Just stand here," I was told. I remained frozen to the spot – not because I wanted to, but because my legs refused to obey my brain's instruction to run. I was still stunned by the comment I had just heard. Once again I wondered what on earth had possessed me to agree to this idea of being an extra.

Suddenly the whole place seemed to go mad. People started crowding around me with lights, light-meters and clipboards. Others were shouting to technicians and floor crew, whilst Mother Hen attacked my hair and my face – again! I was pushed and shoved and manhandled, shoulders pulled back, bust out, red catsuit smoothed over bum, hips twisted.

Silence.

In this scene, I was told, I was going to be "in shot." I was rigid with fright. My only relief was the thought that at least I wasn't an extra "extra" any more.

There was a really hot camera light focused right to one side of me, and I wondered how long it would take for me to sweat off all my make-up. I was handed one of those small battery-powered pocket fans to keep the sweat beads from gathering whilst I waited. Then I was given instructions that "Craig" (the star of this really tawdry gangster movie I'd got myself into) would walk past me, which is when I would have to "hold it" as the camera would zoom in on me. The one comfort I had was that with my hair all buffed out and the mountain of slap I had on, no one would actually recognise me when the film got shown on the big screen.

"ACTION!"

The shout brought me back to reality, if you could call this madness reality. I'd been given strict directions not to look at the camera, and to act surprised when Craig sauntered past me. I don't think I could have acted more startled if I'd tried, for Craig didn't just meander passed me. He halted by me with a loud "HI SEXY," grabbed my arse and planted a kiss full on my lips as the camera zoomed in for a real close-up. Furthermore, for some reason known only to the director we had to repeat this scene at least fifteen times – and with each re-take, Craig's hands lingered on my bum and his lips on mine a little longer.

"Don't know about you, Kiddo, but I love this scene," he'd whispered as he'd moved back for the thirteenth take. I don't know what offended me more, being called "Kiddo" by someone who was (mentally at any rate) several years younger than me, or with his over-familiar manner with my body parts.

By the end of the day, and – mark my words – it had been a long day, I was exhausted. The last thing I wanted was to "talk business" with Mr Director. So cash in hand I made a quick exit, hopped into my Mini (not one of the nice spacious modern ones, but the classical model – in other words, a real haggard old banger), and once safely inside I whooshed off, leaving behind a black cloud of exhaust fumes.

Chapter One

I'd almost forgotten most of the details (the waiting, the boredom, Mother Hen, the panic, the horror, the shame, the chat-up) until months later, when I actually found myself watching the film, *The Business*, in the cinema. Then all those memories came flooding back. What's more, my thirty seconds of fame seemed to last a lifetime as I watched from the plush and comfy cinema seat, which I just wanted to sink into and curl up in shame. Not only did the camera take a close-up of my face as Craig's lips clamped down on mine, it then panned out and took a shockingly close look at my bum, and I realised that the clingy all-in-one catsuit was totally transparent. Peter – my boyfriend of two months – let his hand go limp in mine as I also grasped that, despite the big hair and that scary amount of make-up, the girl on the screen was obviously me. And, to put it mildly, I came across as a real tart.

I got stared at as I walked out of the local cinema, but probably could've got away with denying the whole thing, had it not been for the fact that they'd even used my name in the closing credits. Peter refused to budge, not having said a word to me until he could confirm that *The girl in the bar* was *Chantelle Rose* – in other words, ME.

"I'm an extra in this film" I'd casually remarked to him, as we'd queued up for the tickets earlier on in the evening. He'd looked at me in amazement; he obviously hadn't believed me. Well, he believed me now!

As soon as we left the cinema, he just exploded. We hadn't been together long, but he was the real jealous type. Having just witnessed his girlfriend expose her behind to the whole world in a cheap film – and one that was actually

9

becoming a box office hit – was just too much for his ego.

"Christ, Chantelle, you said you were an extra in the film. You never told me that you were a... a... a *hooker*," he spluttered, quite loudly. The people around us hushed in expectation.

"Hooker!" I actually snorted out loud at the notion. "In that case," I continued, as sweetly as possible, "you'll find that you owe me a hundred quid, and that's just for tonight's pre-dinner rendezvous. I'll send you the bill sealed with a kiss, Romeo..."

As I walked off, I heard someone say, "Is this some sort of sketch to the sequel?"

I found myself heading towards Tammy's house. She'd been my best friend since I got out of nappies and became aware that I'd actually found someone who truly understood my babbling baby talk. And still does.

"Peter is a real geek," Tammy stated, after I'd told her what had happened.

"Thanks Tammy," I replied sarcastically. "It's not what you've been telling me over the last two months. What were your words? *He seems a fine lad*." This, I then suddenly realised as I started laughing at my own ignorance, was Tammy's way of saying *Girl, he's a real nerd*, and I was just too desperate at the time to cotton on.

"By the way," she continued, "I saw you in the film last night at the cinema…"

"And…"

"And you looked a right slapper." She doubled over with laughter at the look of dismay on my face.

I threw a pillow at her that I'd snatched up from her bed. She's got one of those huge plush en-suite bathroom-bedrooms. The only downbeat point is that the room is in her parents' place – well, mansion really – where she still lives. Tammy's family are loaded, and the only reason she doesn't move out is because with the live-in maid, she gets out of cooking and having to do her own laundry.

"Let's do something fun this weekend," she suggested. "I've still got some Rural Inn vouchers to use up. We could get out into the country and have a real girly weekend like we used to. You know, midnight feasts, make-over sessions... And I'll let you drive."

This was her ultimate selling point. Tammy, for her twenty-first birthday, was given, tied up with a big pink bow, a real sleek Jaguar. One of those really flashy cars, which aren't actually of any practical use whatsoever, because the only thing they're made for is to reach 180 miles per hour in the blink of an eye. But, of course, if you do get to that breakneck speed you get fined big-time by those hidden speed cameras which seem to be everywhere. Why these cars are made is beyond me. To show off, I guess. I always thought I'd get a big monster van if I had the money, one I could live in if things got really rough. But the idea of being able to sit behind the wheel of Tammy's fab electric blue Jag, knowing I could outrun any chauvinistic male driver I came across on the road (which is daily becoming the front-line between the battle of the sexes), was just too great an opportunity to let slip.

So, of course, I agreed.

Speeding out of town in the blue Jag and into the countryside, I did put my foot down just a couple of times simply to piss off a number of executive macho men. Before we knew it Tammy and I had reached our rural destination, a quaint little cottage. But what had happened to the supposed Rural Inn? There was a big *For Sale* sign up outside, I noticed, as we walked up the crazy-paved garden path that led to the front door.

Wow! That front garden was a real dream garden. To the right of the crazy-paved path was a large oak tree that branched out sheltering a quaint wooden love seat that swung ever so slightly in the gentle breeze. There were roses all around the perimeter of the garden, of every shade of pink, orange, red and yellow. I imagined fairies sheltered in the tall grass as they hopped from one bluebell to the next on their way around. The air was rich with lavender and rose. There was a carpet of lush green grass all around what had just become the cottage of my dreams. And ... Snap out of it.

What with fairies and all, I was in danger of turning into a real sentimental old daydreamer.

"If I won the lottery I'd buy this place," I admitted out loud, though more to myself than to Tammy.

"Bit of a country lass, are we?" she remarked, eyeing me as if I was some kind of freak. Tammy could never live without her city comforts, but for me it would've been a dream come true. If I were to leave Tammy just 50 metres from this garden path she would manage to get lost for sure. On the other hand, place her in the middle of any city in the world and she would find her way around by instinct, following scents of Chanel, fine leather and exquisite cuisine, until she made her way home with a mountain of shopping bags and luggage.

I knocked hard on the solid oak door and thought that we'd somehow got the wrong place as the knock echoed around the obviously empty house.

"Good afternoon ladies," called out a loud masculine voice from the front of the driveway. Tammy jumped. We'd both been caught off guard, but Tammy, who can be a bit over the top at times, grabbed hold of me like a frightened three-year-old. We both turned and Tammy let out a small gasp and further tightened her grip in my hand.

Before us was Mr Diet Coke. He honestly did look like one of those male models used in the sexy, steamy diet coke TV adds. You know, the one that has the guy naked to the waist, pausing over his labouring job as six or seven executive women practically fall out of a window in a high-rise office block just to get a glimpse of him.

I didn't realise men as good-looking as this existed in the real world. Having said that, there was something about him that looked familiar, though I just couldn't put my finger on it. I was sure I'd seen his face somewhere before. I lowered my eyes as subtlety as possible to take in his six-pack, which seemed as if it had been tattooed on his exposed hair-free chest, which glistened slightly with perspiration. He had a three-day stubble on a strong but nicely-set jaw. His dark locks flopped onto his face in a charmingly boyish gesture, and even from where I was standing – at the other end of the garden from where he sat poised on a huge and high-spirited black stallion – I could see he had clear sky-blue eyes.

I was suddenly aware that Tammy was still holding my hand, or rather, squeezing the blood out of it, and under my breath, for her ears only, I hissed sharply, "Let go. He'll think we're a right pair of dykes." Not that there's anything wrong with that, of course. Nevertheless, at this precise moment I didn't want Mr Sex to think I was a raving lesbian.

I could feel his piercing blue eyes stare at me as I untangled my hand from Tammy's.

"May I help you?" he continued, as his horse starting nervously pawing at the soft earth below its feet, looking like it was going to charge right at me. I reminded myself, as I tried to keep calm, that as far as I knew, it was bulls that charge. In a voice that sounded really cool and blasé (as if, despite being totally lost and looking at the best-looking guy I'd ever seen, I was totally in control), I said, "We're looking for the Rural Inn and thought that this was it. Maybe you could guide us in the right direction?" In fact, I added to myself, you could probably guide me anywhere.

"I thought so," Mr Diet Coke answered. For a split second I assumed he'd read my mind, and slated him as a cocky big-headed idiot. I immediately retracted this thought as he continued, "Most people stop here thinking that this is the rural accommodation, when, in fact, it's still another ten miles down this country lane. You can't get lost. It's straight on. Four miles before you reach it you'll come across a crossroads with a sign to a nature reserve to the right, and on the left is a track that leads to the river."

"Oh thank you," Tammy called out, all husky-voiced, as she scooted up the garden path in an attempt to get a better look at the tall dark stranger. I inwardly condemned her *un-cool* approach.

"I'm Tammy," she cooed. "And she's Chantelle," she added, with a nod of her head in my direction.

"I'm Robbie," he answered in a smooth, seductive voice as he looked straight at me. I felt like melting on the spot.

"Enjoy your stay in the area," he added, before he kicked the black stallion and in a flash was gone in a hair-raising gallop down the country lane. Tammy and I were left weak at the knees.

"Was he lush or what?" Tammy blurted out as soon as Robbie was out of sight.

"Not bad." I said trying to sound cool, calm and collected.

"Not bad?" she mimicked. "Just look at you! You're all red and flustered."

I'm not am I? I panicked, all sense of composure and calmness lost as I rushed towards the car door mirror to view my reflection.

"He was giving you the real *Give it to me baby* look before he galloped off into the horizon." Tammy smirked.

"No he wasn't," I said, well aware that I was glowing bright pink. "He was giving me the *She looks like that slapper from the gangster film* look."

"Why, missy," Tammy observed archly, "I do believe you've fallen in love at first sight."

"Give over," I groaned as I handed her the car keys. "I'll let you drive the last ten miles," I added, in an attempt to change the conversation. Though the reality was that, for some reason, I didn't want Robbie to think I owned this really expensive, totally unpractical blue Jag – a complete misfit with country living. The likelihood of seeing him again was minimal, but just in case….

As Tammy continued the drive down the country lane I found myself feeling ridiculously happy, which was why, when we arrived at the crossroads and Tammy suggested driving down to the riverbank for a better look, I agreed. At any other time I would have told her she was crazy to drive her precious blue Jag down a muddy track just to go check out some random river. But I was miles away; I was letting my imagination run wild with thoughts of how Robbie would call at the Rural Inn for me the following morning astride his black stallion and ask me if I'd like to go riding with him out into the woods…

So by the time I was brought back to reality it was to realise that not only had we arrived at the river bank, but that Tammy had managed to get her lovely sleek electric blue Jag – and us – stuck in the mud.

This, believe me, was not hilariously funny. The Jag, which being a sports car is low to start with, visibly started sinking. When I finally got my act together to get out of the car, it was to find that the doors were jammed shut, the mud having crept right up the sides of the vehicle.

Quickly I pressed the button to open the window and started to squeeze myself through the window frame. Tammy gave me a huge shove on my behind to help me through. Miraculously I made it outside and onto my feet, which required some bodily contortion to avoid landing head first into the mud. I squelched to the front part of the vehicle.

"Put it in reverse," I called out, thinking we still had a chance of shifting the Jag out of the mud pit before it was completely swallowed up. Tammy obediently crunched into reverse gear and put her foot down to rev the car out. Wheels started spinning and mud sprayed everywhere as I pushed with all my might (which is not much) on the front bonnet. But it didn't take an Einstein to calculate that the electric blue Jag wasn't going anywhere. It was completely stuck in the mud and not quite so blue anymore. Meanwhile, Tammy had gone as white as a ghost at the probable thought that her dad would've freaked out if he could've seen us – and that she was on the verge of facing the consequential humiliation of being grounded at the grand old age of twenty-four.

Dusk seemed to be closing in thick and fast and it became obvious that we'd have to walk the remaining four miles of our journey to fetch help. And, as can only happen in a typical British summer, a thunderstorm broke and it started pelting down.

Tammy at this point had managed to get herself stuck in the window of the driver's seat in her attempt to escape the drowning car. I slopped my way over to her, amazed that my chic and flimsy flip-flops from Selfridges actually remained on my feet instead of being sucked into the mud. Having reached Tammy I grabbed hold of her hands and yanked hard as she wriggled her way out of the car. With one last heave she popped out like a champagne cork, all nine stone of her, and she collapsed on top of me in the brown, sticky mud.

Tammy's face was right above mine. It was lucky really that she hadn't head- butted me. I could hardly breathe, having already been totally winded by the fall.

"I hope I'm not interrupting anything?"

The familiar masculine voice sent me cringing. It was Robbie, and I truly wished I was anywhere else on earth at that moment. Now he must surely think we're a pair of dykes frolicking around in the mud together.

In a flash he'd dismounted his stallion and was helping Tammy to her feet.

"I thought I told you to keep straight on."

"I know, I know," I could hear Tammy saying. "But I just wanted to drive down to the river bank to take a look."

Robbie then reached down for me and took my hands in a strong firm grip as he effortlessly got me to my feet. Humiliated, I could see that he could hardly suppress his laughter; his sparkling blue eyes twinkled with mirth as they looked me up and down. Moreover, I could tell what was going through his head: *Typical bloody female drivers.* Which is just so untrue. I wanted to say *I'm a good, sensible driver and would never have let Tammy venture down this mud track if I hadn't been mooning after you.* But I was just too embarrassed to even say "Thank you."

"You girls remain here and I'll go and fetch some help. Try to keep out of the rain or you'll catch your death of cold."

Yes dad! almost slipped from my lips, and I had to bite my tongue to stop the words coming out. In any case he was way too sexy to be my dad. Up close I calculated he must have been in his early thirties, seven or so years older than me. He must have thought I'd just hit my teens or something, going on the rather immature first impression I was giving him. But like two obedient kids, Tammy and I nodded our heads in meek agreement, and in a flash Robbie was gone, the only sound being the clattering of hooves in the distance mingled with the pitter-patter of falling rain.

Tammy took hold of my hand and squeezed it as she turned to me. "Sorry to get you into this mess."

As I turned to face her with a casual "Don't worry," she let out a loud gasp.

What? What's wrong? Is my nose bleeding? I panicked as I instinctively reached up to check that my nose wasn't spurting blood and peered towards the dirty car window to see if I could see my reflection there. Then it was my turn to let out a cry of horror. All I could see were my bright honey-coloured eyes staring back out of a mud-covered face. I looked like I'd gone real nuts with an organic mud facemask and had applied it all over my face and right into my hair, which was plastered down with big globules of stinking muck. I took in a deep breath from the shock horror of seeing my reflection, and realised, on taking that deep breath, that the mud was really pongy – somewhere between whiffy pond water and seaweed.

"Just great," I exclaimed, "I've just gone and met the guy of my dreams, and I look like this! Shit!"

Tammy grinned. "I knew you thought he was lush."

At least an hour had passed and it was deathly dark in the middle of the woods in No-Man's-Land. The rain, at least, had petered out.

"What if he's not coming back?" whimpered Tammy, obviously worried that we'd been left for good in this creepy wood next to a stinking pond and would have to sleep the night squeezed into the Jag – and that was if we could get back in. I didn't think that Tammy had ever slept in anything so small; her nursery cot had probably been more spacious than the Jag. Not that the idea of trying to get back into the drowning car was a wise one. Being buried alive was not the most astute plan.

"Don't worry," I responded, trying to remain calm for both of us. "He'll be back. And he'll have one of those digital cameras to film us, and YouTube it around the globe. He's got money to win out of this. Oh yes, he'll be back."

Then, right on cue, I could just make out the throttle of a tractor somewhere further up the lane, heading in our direction. The lights of the tractor were soon upon us.

I'd tried to remove as much mud from my hair and face as possible, though with little success, so I hid behind Tammy and out of the glare of the tractor lights as it approached, thankful that it was really dark and that I could blend slightly into the shadows.

Robbie hopped down from the tractor cab with the grace of a ballet dancer (those looks and grace, plus my luck, probably meant that he was gay!) as the driver hauled the tractor to a stop.

"Doing a bit of rally driving, were we, ladies?" he called.

I had to clamp my mouth shut in order to stifle a smart comeback. I realised that this was our only chance of getting the Jag out of the mud, and I was wise enough not to be rude and have our Good Samaritan turn on his heel and leave us in the dark again.

Tammy's upper-class education came shining through, as it always does in moments of crisis. She rushed forward to greet the tractor driver, eyelids fluttering and head-to-toe grace and good manners.

"Oh, thank you so much for going out of your way to help us out of this mess. I couldn't be more thankful. You're real gentlemen, both of you," she added, directing her fluttering eyes now at Robbie, voice huskily pitiful as she blushed in modesty. I wondered how she put on this big ultra-feminine act. She was like a reincarnation of Scarlett O'Hara.

"I'm Tammy," she continued as she delicately offered her hand to the driver.

"Ray," the driver said as he jumped down from the tractor. Taking Tammy's hand in his, he bowed slightly.

She's got him round her little finger already, I thought.

"And you must be Chantelle," Ray added as he looked in my direction. I winced. God! I'm going to be known in these parts as the girl who took a mud bath down by the river.

Robbie and Ray fastened the Jag to the tractor and hauled it out of the mud. To everyone's amazement the car actually started – a huge credit to the Jaguar engineers – although it was filthy, wet and really reeked; not quite like the Great Stink, but almost. We made it, thankfully, to the Rural Inn without further incident. Robbie and Ray followed behind.

Why did I keep on thinking of Dixie and Trixie? Weren't they the two cartoon characters under suspicion of being gay? Or was that Noddy and Big-Ears? Or maybe I was just getting confused with one of the TellyTubbies.

"I think they're gay," I observed out loud to Tammy.

"You think any good-looking guy is gay."

"That's probably because they usually are."

"Ok, let's bet on it. I bet fifty quid that they're not gay."

At this time fifty quid was a lot of cash for me to lose. But what the hell, we were only in the area for a couple of days, and neither of us were going to be able to prove anything either way. So I held out my hand, which Tammy took in hers, sealing our little gamble.

As soon as we reached the Rural Inn, which was quaint but not as beautiful as the dream cottage we'd come across earlier in the afternoon, I rushed inside avoiding the startled (not to say horrified) looks of the reception team. When I made it to the room Tammy and I were to share for the weekend I dived into the power-shower to scrub off all the dry and cracked mud that encrusted every part of my body. Brown rivulets rolled down my skin and it was a good while before the water ran clear. Finally cleaned up I wrapped around me the one and only towel, minuscule I might add, and stepped out into the bedroom, making a mental note to complain to reception that one tiny towel just wasn't good enough. And there by the door to the room, which was wide open, was Tammy, once again doing her Scarlett O'Hara impression.

"Thanks for helping me bring the bags up and, of course, for getting us out of that mess Robbie."

Robbie, meanwhile, having heard me open the bathroom door, was looking straight in my direction. Thank God I'd waxed my legs last night, for that ridiculously small towel wasn't doing a very good job of covering me.

"See you tomorrow then," continued Tammy as she closed the door, totally unaware that I was half naked behind her. Robbie, before having the door closed on his face, just gave me a good look up and down, with no attempt to hide the amusement on his face.

"What's that about tomorrow?" I weakly asked as Tammy turned to face me.

"Oh! So that's what he was looking at," she observed, seeing me in my birthday suit sparsely covered by the mini-sized towel.

"I've just arranged for Robbie and Ray and you and me to go out tomorrow lunchtime for a picnic."

Ding Dong. Round One to Tammy. She's really taking this bet seriously – and by God was my heart racing. For the first time I was glad that Tammy had got the car stuck in the mud. It had been the best thing she'd done in ages.

Chapter Two

But before lunchtime came around the following day, Tammy and I were actually speeding back towards London.

"They'll think we've stood them up," I said, for the umpteenth time.

"No they won't," Tammy reassured me, though I could tell she felt just as bad as I did, especially after going down to breakfast and finding her Jag sparklingly clean and blue once more. There was a note on the bonnet: *Having always wanted my own Jag, I've gone and made the most of it and cleaned yours. See you ladies at lunchtime. Ray.*

"I'd left him the spare set of keys" explained Tammy sheepishly. "I didn't really expect him to clean it, at least not so quickly. Anyway, I'm sure that nice-looking girl in reception will pass on our note of apology and explanation. And will you please sit still missy? I'm not going to drive any faster just because you're jiggling all over the place as if you've got ants in your pants."

Much to Tammy's exasperation, I couldn't keep still. In fact I hadn't been able to remain calm or think straight since ten o'clock that morning. That was when I'd received the phone call.

I'd been offered the chance of a lifetime, and there was no way I was going to let the opportunity slip.

I was more excited than a four-year-old on Christmas Eve. I just hoped the phone call wasn't a hoax, because it all just sounded too good to be true.

I'd been offered the chance to earn one million dollars!

The actual details of the film contract I'd been offered were all very vague in my head. After hearing *one million dollars*, I think half my brain cells died from sheer excitement.

It had been arranged for me to dine that very evening at the Ritz with a Mr Guillem, an agent who had contacted me that morning. So that's why we found ourselves speeding back to the city. Tammy was driving, because in my state of nerves I would have probably crashed the car.

"What am I going to wear?" I wailed as it slowly started to sink in that I was to have dinner that evening in one of the most expensive and snooty hotels in London, and I had nothing remotely appropriate to wear. The only semi-respectable little black dress I owned had a very inelegant deodorant stain on it. Also, I realised with a gasp, I couldn't possibly pull up outside the Ritz in my psychedelic green Mini with its huge dent in the bonnet and designer scratch marks all down the right hand side.

Tammy, of course, knew all about dining at the Ritz. The first time she'd been taken there was at the age of five for her birthday celebrations with the fun old gang of her parents, grandparents and elderly aunt and uncle. Say no more! It amazes me that we ended up in the same nursery despite coming from totally different backgrounds. Tammy's father, however, thought that mixing with "ordinary" children – at least during nursery age – would do Tammy good, spur her on, and develop her social and survival skills.

His little experiment almost got her killed. If it hadn't been for the fact that I loved beating up and chasing off all the kids who took to pulling at Tammy's fancy dresses and extravagant silk bows that always decorated her long pigtails, I don't know how she would have survived. I was such a rough little tomboy, and truly believed I was Luke Skywalker, protecting Tammy with my light sabre.

And now, the time had come for her to rescue me. "You've got to come with me, Tammy," I pleaded. Or rather, ordered.

"Darling, of course I'll go with you. I couldn't let you go by yourself. It would be like sending a child into a lions' den. It's silver service, my dear. You wouldn't know which fork to pick up first."

***

As we pulled up outside the Ritz a bellboy rushed forward to park the Jag for us, and I nervously moved to step in line with Tammy as she strode confidently up the stairs to the main entrance.

"Stop fidgeting," she hushed in my ear. "You look fab." I did, too; that impromptu mud mask I'd applied down by the river yesterday had done wonders. I had a healthy glow about me, and even my hair was remotely under control.

The hotel doors were held open for us.

"Good evening ladies," the doorman announced, in the poshest accent I'd ever heard. It even beat Tammy's dad. I wondered if the job qualifications had specified *posh voice essential*, or if the training for the position had involved intense elocution lessons.

As we moved into the lobby I gasped out loud, and let slip the most unrefined *Bloody Hell!* The exquisite surroundings almost swallowed me up. I felt totally out of my depth, and I wondered why on earth I hadn't insisted on meeting at Pizza Express. I didn't even need to read the menu there.

We were greeted and escorted to the Rivoli Bar, where the walls are panelled in polished Camphor wood veneer enriched with Lalique glass panels and gold Keystone nuggets. Not that I actually knew this, of course, but Tammy kindly recited all the details. All I was able to comment was, "Got a bit of Art Deco going, hasn't it?"

I was so nervous, and relieved that Tammy was with me. The people around were extremely well-dressed; diamonds glinted in the light, and the air was heavy with expensive perfumes. In fact as I breathed in the perfumed atmosphere I was aware that it was making me feel a little woozy; quite sickly actually. Together with all the rush, the heady scent and my jangling nerves I could feel a dizzy spell coming on – just as I heard behind me a smooth, confident voice with a hint of a French accent.

"Miss Rose? So pleased to meet you. I'm Frederic

Guillem."

As if on cue, like in one of those horrid and embarrassing dreams where you find yourself walking down Oxford Street totally starkers, I felt my vision blur and fainted flat on my face.

I came around minutes later, probably thanks to the freezing cool pack that had been placed on my forehead. I wondered for a while what I was doing lying down with my legs raised on a chair. As I remained slightly dazed I could hear a distant voice saying, "Is she always this dramatic? Bit of a Drama Queen, is she? I must say she'll fit right in…"

What the hell is the guy going on about? Grimacing, I put my hand to my forehead to remove the freezing ice bag. What with the rain last night and now this, I'll come down with flu in the blink of an eye.

My mind was still in a bit of a blur. What the hell was I doing in such a finely furnished bar? Then I noticed the dress I had on. I'd a vague notion that it was Tammy's, because it was way too flashy to be mine, and with the long slit all the way up the left leg and my legs raised I suddenly realised that I had my g-string exposed. Then Tammy's voice beside me brought me fully back to where I was like a steam train. Mortified I grappled to stand, trying to do so as elegantly as possible although in my three-inch heels it was nearly Mission Impossible. Finally on my feet, wobbling all over like I'd had one too many Bloody Marys, I cringed. I bet I'm the first person ever to faint at the Ritz. I was relieved to notice, however, that everyone else in the Rivoli Bar were engrossed in their own little word, all politely ignoring, in true British style, the fact that I'd just fallen flat on my face and had exposed my underwear for all to see.

I found myself towering over Mr Guillem, a short, stocky middle-aged man dressed in a fine beige silk suit which would have cost him more than I earned in a whole year. His dark brown eyes danced merrily as they looked me over, though his voice was soft and there was a hint of genuine concern as he pulled out a chair for me.

"Do you feel alright, or would you prefer to postpone the

meeting for another time?"

"No," I said quickly. "I feel fine. I honestly don't know what came over me." I flashed him one of my brightest smiles, thinking I had to win him over quickly before he concluded that I was a right nutter and I could kiss the million dollars goodbye.

Totally at ease, Mr Guillem, with Tammy and me on either arm, waltzed us through to the restaurant like a real sugar daddy. Judging by some of the looks we were getting as we passed, I clearly wasn't the only one to think this.

A four-piece band had struck up as we walked into what has to be one of the most magnificent restaurants in the world. We sat down for what I discovered would be a multi-course meal and I began to have images of me exploding out of the tight-fitting dress I was wearing. Tammy, who was sitting opposite me with Mr Guillem to my left, winked at me as she picked up the first fork. I followed suit.

The meal, though a superb blend of classical cuisine, was totally lost on me as I struggled to keep track of Mr Guillem's contract offer and at the same time played *Simon Says* with Tammy, copying her every move. Sitting still and tall, back straight, bust out, elbows off the table, sipping delicately – without slurping – at my wine instead of gulping it down as I usually did, I elegantly pressed the napkin on either corner of my lips after every other dainty and minute bite.

By the end of the meal I'd signed a pre-contractual agreement (whatever that is), and nodded politely as Mr Guillem took my hand in his in a warm firm hand-shake.

"Well, Miss Rose," he said, "I'll be seeing you shortly then. My secretary will be in contact with you with your flight and accommodation details. I'm truly looking forward to our project and business plans ahead. I'm going to make you a star!'"

I had to lean on Tammy as we waited outside to pick up the car thinking I was going to faint again. I was really giving my blood pressure a hammering.

"Do you think he's a bit of a con-man?" I asked Tammy.

I'd learned during the evening that Mr Guillem was supposed to be one of the leading and most sought-after movie agents. During the meal he'd told us the most unbelievable story. He'd been asked by Lionel King, his top star and the biggest name in Hollywood to date, to watch *The Business* and observe the girl in the red catsuit – and offer her a role in his next big production: an action-packed, multi-million-dollar-budget film.

"'I want that girl,' he said. And what Mr King wants, Mr King gets." Mr Guillem beamed as he'd patted my hand like a kindly grandfather. "You see, darling, Mr King says you've got a million-dollar asset."

Eyes wide, smile frozen, my mind boggled. *Did he say "asset"... or "ass"?*

"His credentials all looked in order," Tammy replied, "and he's obviously used to pulling off important deals. He's got that superior look of confidence about him that's obviously not from his dumpy, chunky size. Anyway, there's only one way to find out…"

Chapter Three

Ten days later I found myself flying First Class over the Atlantic. I sat back in the sofa-like plane seat and tried to let myself relax. The last ten days had been manic. What with cleaning up my flat, sorting out my visa, giving all my beloved plants to Tammy... Which, thinking about it, was probably a mistake – Tammy would never even remember to water them, let alone talk to them.

The best moment had been the Monday morning after my meeting with Mr Guillem, when I waltzed into work, deliberately arriving one hour late. I worked in *Café Cappuccino*, a coffee shop down the road from where I lived, where I worked my socks off all hours of the day and night and most weekends. It was beyond Tammy why I put up with the crappy job, with its shitty pay and totally chauvinistic slave-driver of a boss. And it was beyond me to be able to explain. But that Monday morning I felt on top of the world. As my boss started having a right barney at me for being late, I picked up a tray laden with steaming coffee cups and just let it slip ever so accidentally to the floor. He went a deathly shade of yellowy-grey, and for a panicky split second I thought he'd have a heart attack. But he recovered in a flash, calling me obscene names and threatening to take the broken mugs and spilt coffee out of my wages.

I smiled sweetly.

"Go fuck yourself, you and this fucking job."

And with that I turned on my heel and left. Well, fled is probably the correct term: I really didn't want to hang around for his reaction once he'd recovered from the shock at what I'd said, right in front of his customers. But I did notice, as I made my quick exit, the little old lady who was always in

Café Cappuccino for breakfast turn purple as she choked on her muffin, no doubt flabbergasted by my language.

Champagne was offered around by the flight attendant, who looked like she'd just stepped out of primary school, whilst I settled down and browsed through the choice of interactive entertainment. To my horror, *The Business* flashed up on the film list. I desperately tried to sink further into my swanky First Class seat, hoping to remain unnoticed by my fellow passengers, especially dismayed on observing that several had opted to watch it. In a flash I fished out the sleep mask from the gift bag given out at the start of the flight. It was more like a first aid travel kit that had everything in it bar the kitchen sink. So with the big black mask on cutting out the light and my view of the other passengers, hoping with childlike naïvety that as I couldn't see them they couldn't see me, I settled down, and for the first time in ten days felt sleep overcome my exhausted body and mind.

***

I woke all hot and flustered. I'd had one of those really sexually-charged dreams, Robbie being at the centre of my fantasy. As I shifted in my seat to shake off the tingling sensation that enveloped my whole body, I caught the guy sitting in the aisle opposite staring right at me. I wondered if I'd cried out loud in orgasmic delight whilst dreaming, or if he could have recognised me from *The Business*. Rudely I turned my back on him. Either way, I didn't want to know.

It was a real bumpy flight over the Atlantic, a bit like a never-ending roller-coaster ride. I'd flown over the Atlantic before, but to east-coast Florida, and that journey stands out clear in my mind. Not so much for the bumpy ride on that flight also, but rather for the fact that the "new friend" I'd made on the flight – one of the many new friends that I kept picking up, as only children can – threw up all over me in a severe attack of motion sickness. What did I do? Well, with the smell of vomit right up my nostrils, I threw up all over her, too. Looking back with humour at the incident, I imagined that we must have looked like two possessed little devils having a puking contest.

I remember that holiday in Florida very clearly. I'd gone out with my parents. It was to be our last holiday together as a family. I was too young at the time to truly understand, but as I chased around Disneyland after Mickey Mouse and Donald Duck to have my photo taken with them, and got soaked to the bone by Shamu the Killer Whale at Sea World, my mother, sweet and gentle to the end, was dying of cancer. My father, who'd been totally devoted to her during all their years together, never got over her death, and eighteen months ago, after suffering for fifteen years with a broken heart, passed away too. I was the only person not to cry at his funeral, as I knew that at last he'd stopped suffering and that finally Mum and Dad were together again.

I'm aware that this is the reason why none of my relationships with guys last more than a few months. It's simply because I always compare what I have and feel to what I witnessed with my parents. As it never comes close, I keep searching. It's almost as unrealistic as hunting for a pot of gold at the end of a rainbow.

Twelve hours later, thought it felt more like at a week had passed since I'd left England, I arrived in sun-kissed California. I got the whole body search and had all the items of my luggage turned upside down as I went through passport control and customs. I wondered, not for the first time, what it is about me that made people automatically assume I'm either a fully-trained terrorist or some kind of drug pusher. Ever since I'd started travelling without my parents I'm always given the whole once-over. I'm obviously the kind of person who's described in airport anti-terrorist classes as the type to have on their A-list of suspicious-looking passengers. I put it down to my frizzy black hair; they obviously think it's a wig and that I'm in disguise.

Finally released from the bombardment of questions of *What? Why? Where? Who?* thrown at me with reference to my visit to the States, I walked through customs and out to the arrivals lounge. There was a mass of people milling around, and I suddenly realised that I'd no idea who was picking me up or where I would be taken. Visions of an evening newsflash screaming *YOUNG WOMAN KIDNAPPED AND TAKEN HOSTAGE AS SEX SLAVE* raced through my mind, and not for the first time I wondered what the hell I was letting myself in for. I'd thrown myself head-first into accepting this crazy project without really knowing what I was getting paid to do.

What I did know was that ten days earlier, leading a perfectly normal if rather boring life, I'd come across the house of my dreams. Now, given the opportunity to earn more money that I'd ever thought possible, I planned to buy it and set it up as a little rural getaway. All right, I'll be fair, I won't kid anyone – though I wince to admit it – I hadn't just fallen for the house; I'd fallen head over heels for Robbie too. I couldn't stop thinking about him. He was the first person I'd ever come across who'd had that overwhelming effect on me – not counting ET. I'd a real obsession with him when I was around seven, and then there was Kermit the Frog from *The Muppets* who'd been my hero in my earlier years, too. But then, neither of those were real people.

Wondering what my next move would be on finding myself abandoned on the other side of the Atlantic, I bumped straight into someone holding up a banner which had **MISS ROSE** written in huge letters. I would have spotted it a mile off if I hadn't been daydreaming over Robbie.

"That's me," I said meekly, realising I'd winded the poor fellow with my trolley. He was an elderly chap fitted out in a flashy chauffeur's uniform, and I wondered if he didn't feel dead embarrassed having to walk around in public with that outfit on. But I kindly kept my thoughts to myself as I held out my hand to shake his. I was quite relieved to find that his grip was as weak as mine. At least if he tried to pull something funny on me in the car I could probably out-fist him.

I sat back as we drove through the sprawling city of Los Angeles, thinking that this all had to be a dream and I'd wake up with a jolt. I was sitting in a whopping huge white limo which was larger than my bedroom back in my flat in London. It was kitted out with all sorts of gadgets which I didn't dare play with, thinking I'd probably come across an emergency eject button that would catapult me through the roof. Mr Chatty, the chauffeur, didn't say a word to me throughout the drive. I didn't blame him really, he was probably still suffering from the humiliation at having to walk around in public looking like a right plonker. I pressed my face up against the tinted windows as we sped through the lattice of streets and flyovers, trying to lap up all the goings-on. There were thousands of expensive-looking cars everywhere. Tammy's Jag would've been quite plain out here, and I was aware that I'd just landed in Poser City.

As we drove south, out of the LA sprawl, I gaped open-mouthed at the huge luxurious houses with their exotic and dense gardens. The further out we drove, the more plush and immense they became, and each one was more isolated than the last.

Sometime later we pulled up by a huge iron gate. The chauffeur pressed his window down and muttered something into the security camera that was pointed right at the limo, and, as if he'd waved a magic wand, the gate swung open. By this point my stomach was in a right old twist. I wouldn't so much say I had butterflies; it was more like a stampede of elephants. I tried knocking on the bulletproof glass that divided me from the driver to get some idea of where I was being taken, but the old chap completely ignored me. Trying to remain calm I returned to gazing out of the window, where the driveway was lined with palm trees and exotic flowers in bloom. A rare short Californian shower had stopped and the petals looked like they dripped pearls.

I gasped out loud as we finally pulled up outside a magnificent mansion, which would have been the envy of Tammy's mother. The three-storey white stately residence – nothing humble about it whatsoever, I observed – with its six columns that soared halfway to heaven, was just overwhelming. My nerves were swallowed in a flash as I stared, gobsmacked, at what I saw.

The chauffeur stepped down from his seat, moved around the car, and opened the passenger door. As I climbed out I was suddenly acutely aware of my slobby attire. I'd flown over in a really unsexy and untrendy navy blue tracksuit, making comfort for the journey a priority. I now realised this had been a big mistake. I felt totally under-dressed and there was no hiding my muddy trainers that were so old and used that you could see my socks poking through.

As I came to grips with the fact that I looked like I'd just been picked up off the streets, I also became aware of the commotion coming from the house. There was music blaring, and a loud hum of voices floated over towards me picked up by the gentle evening breeze. I really can't face a crowd of people now, I thought in turmoil, just as Mr Guillem emerged on the veranda. Despite his bulky size, he was beside me in a flash. Gone was the smooth silk beige suit, replaced by blinding Bermuda shorts and a gaudy Hawaiian shirt. Cocktail glass in hand, he linked his arm through mine and guided me to the house.

The mansion was pleasantly cool on the inside, blinds down blotting out the glaring evening sun and stifling Californian heat. The booming music was just a distant murmur inside the *casa grande,* and as I took in the spacious hall and winding stairs leading to the second floor I thought I might actually get out of having to be presented to the mob of people I'd heard from the driveway. Alas, Mr Guillem gently urged me through to the back part of the house, restraining me as if I were a terror-stricken rabbit ready to bolt – which was, indeed, how I felt. We passed the pine-wooded kitchen with its marble worktop and through into a conservatory with floor-to-ceiling sliding glass doors. These gave me a perfect view of the back garden, which was more like a stately park. There was an immense swimming pool, with a built-in bar at one corner and bar stools that jutted out of the crystal clear water. What most captured my attention was the fact that there were at least fifty people milling around. I say people, but to be exact they were life-sized clones of Barbie and Action Man, and me, in my seriously unsexy tracksuit, was being forced to go out and meet them all.

In a desperate attempt to avoid being seen, I turned to Mr Guillem in my most pleading voice. "I'm really exhausted from the flight. What with this jet lag and all, I would really appreciate it if I could just escape to my room."

"Of course darling," he said in his smooth French-accented voice, and firmly took me by the elbow as he slid open one of the glass panels and guided me down the stone steps. The group at the bottom of the steps, who all looked as though they'd just come from a casting for *Baywatch*, fell silent as I approached.

I felt myself breaking out into a sweat. Quite apart from my unglamorous appearance, their stares just seemed to be burning holes in me.

Weakly I attempted to smile as I hunted for a friendly-looking face. My attention was turned to a huge-busted, blonde, blue-eyed bimbo. I would have left bimbo out, if she hadn't said in a real catty voice, "Your hair's real then? I thought that they'd put a wig on you."

To which I replied as sweetly as possible: "Yes my hair is natural. As is all of me – which is more I can say for your balloon knockers."

Before she was able to recover from the shock – I thought my reply pretty slick given my jet-lag – I felt a hand gently but firmly place itself on my arm. A rich feminine voice beside me said, "You must be exhausted from your flight over." Then, to Mr Guillem, "Fred, dearest, I'll take Chantelle down to the chalet. Get Sav to bring her cases down."

Still in her firm grip, I was led through the crowd as they all turned to gawp at me. I was taken past the pool and down the garden path towards a partially-hidden gate at the far end of the grounds. Once we were through the gate, my rescuer turned to me and, introduced herself.

"I'm Gabriella, but call me Gabby. The cow with the big tits is Vivien, but don't pay any attention to her. She's just jealous."

"Jealous?" I was amazed. "Of what? She's really pretty

and has got a great figure on her, even if it is all silicone."

"My dear girl," said Gabby, with obvious amusement in her voice. "You obviously aren't aware of your potential. Give me a week and you'll outshine Vivien and everyone else by far." Then, more to herself, "Boy am I going to have fun with you."

I looked at Gabby straight in the face, thinking she was just kidding around, but despite the amusement in her voice, I could see she was deadly serious. Up close, I placed her to be in her late thirties, with dark shiny red hair slicked back in a tight ponytail, which made her look deceptively young. Tanned skin with faint laughter lines etched around her sparkling green eyes, she was the same height as me (around five feet nine), and had an extremely fibre-fit, toned body.

In silence I followed Gabby down the track that led away from the secret gate. The garden was denser here; I rather felt that I was being led through a tropical forest. There was a clearing some way ahead, which, as I walked closer, I saw led to a snug wooden bungalow, built of select, authentic pine. There was a veranda that ran around the whole perimeter. It looked so cosy and welcoming that I had a sudden vision of Hansel and Gretel, and wondered if I was being led into some kind of trap.

Gabby led the way up to the front door and opened it letting me through first. I stepped straight into the living room which was very spacious, exquisitely decorated with a delicate peach three-seater sofa and a low oak rocking chair positioned in front of a 70" Plasma TV – fully equipped with internet connection, PlayStation and all the latest gizmos in entertainment. I sighed with relief. Well, if I was going to be held prisoner, at least I wouldn't be bored.

There was a sudden hustle behind us, and I could make out "Sav," obviously short for Savannah, struggle down the pathway with my hefty suitcase.

"*Su maleta, Señorita,*" she huffed, out of breath as she lugged my suitcase up the three wooden steps to the veranda. She was a young, very pretty Mexican girl, and I wondered if she'd come up to California hoping to make a break in the movie business and be the next Salma Hayek, or if she'd just been desperate for work and was willing to put up with the likes of Vivien.

"Gracias," I said. This was the only Spanish I could remember from three years of Spanish lessons at high school, which is a real disgrace, but I was rewarded with a generous smile. I realised that the likes of Vivien would probably never even look in the girl's direction, let alone acknowledge her presence by speaking to her. Gabby, however, let out a string of Spanish that flew way over my head, and in a wink Sav was gone up the garden path again. I was left with Gabby, who had effortlessly taken hold of my case and carried it through into the main bedroom of the bungalow. The bed was spread with gauzy silk. There was an en-suite bathroom and walk-in wardrobe that I could get lost in. I was aware that the clothes I'd brought over with me would occupy only one shelf. For once, I'd actually under-packed!

Before I knew it Gabby was ungraciously hauling all my belongings from my case. My leopard-skin g-string went flying, followed by my Union Jack bikini, and I just squirmed when I saw the box of fruit-flavoured condoms Tammy had given to me at the airport as a joke before I'd left. I remained rooted to the spot waiting patiently for Gabby to finish. I had no intention of confronting her, aware she could probably out-clout me in the blink of an eye. Finally satisfied at rummaging through all my stuff, she turned to me with an apologetic smile.

"Please excuse me, but I just had to make sure you weren't hiding a stash of drugs or any other dodgy shit."

What is it about me that causes this reaction in people? As if I could get away with getting anything remotely illegal past customs control. I mean, come on, they strip you down in a blink of an eye if the lip gloss in your bag is shinier than normal.

Gabby continued, "I refuse to work with anyone who is dependent on anything, and it's a relief to see you don't smoke tobacco either. It makes my job so much easier."

"What exactly is your job?" I asked, feeling at a

complete loss.

Gabby just smiled. "You'll find out tomorrow, but I advise you to get a good night's rest. There's food in the fridge, and if you need anything, whatever hour, just press this buzzer." She handed me a walkie-talkie. And for the first time in twenty-four hours I was left alone.

Starving, I made my way to the brightly-lit kitchen (despite the now sinking sun) and opened the fridge.

To my horror, it was filled with nothing but low-fat yoghurt and carrots.

Chapter Four

I was rudely awoken the following day at the crack of dawn by Gabby kitted out in running gear. Amazed at her energy at such a godforsaken time in the morning (5.30 am, to be precise), at first I thought she was just a night vision, a dark silhouette in the corner of the room. But all thoughts of hallucinations were swiftly cleared by the glare of the bedroom light and the glass of cold water she chucked over me as she yanked the bedclothes aside. A Nike sports bag landed with a thud on the bed beside me.

"You've got five minutes."

Whereupon she turned her back on me to step out of the room allowing me privacy to change. I stuck my tongue out at her and mock-saluted her as I said under my breath, "Yes, Sir!." I was knocked for six to hear her reply: "Ma'am. It's 'Yes, Ma'am'."

At least she's got taste, I thought, as I pulled some really stylish sportswear and a pair of hip Nike trainers out of the bag. Kitted out in less than three minutes I stepped out of the bedroom. Gabby was stretching by the front door. "Well that's a start," she exclaimed. "But honey, do us both a favour: trash your old sneakers."

Behind the bungalow was another gate which I hadn't seen the previous evening. Gabby unlocked it and let me through, and in an easy jog we both set off down the pathway. About 100 metres along the track we came to a clearing. There, before me, along an extensive stretch of virgin sand, the indigo Pacific glinted in the early light. The surf was calm, and peace radiated from its shimmering surface, which stretched far out to the horizon. I gasped in delight. I might just have to let Gabby get away with waking me up at this unearthly hour. The vista wins.

We jogged across the soft sand down to the Ocean, where the waves lapped lazily, and continued at a steady pace along the water's edge. My lungs, amazingly, held out, but my heart boomed and battled away and I wondered if I would be able to sue Mr Guillem if I was to have a heart attack on my first day. About a mile further down the shore we cut back up the soft sand and ran onto a green and very exclusive-looking golf course. Keeping to the verge and avoiding the sprinklers we headed up towards the clubhouse, which I could just make out in the distance. As we got nearer I heard the thud of tennis balls, and realised that we weren't the only maniacs to be up at this outrageous hour. Closing in on the plonking noise, and just when I thought my legs were on the verge of packing in, I heard a voice call out, "Hi Gabby, WOW!! Who's the new kid?"

I turned in the direction of the voice. Smiling at us, racquet in hand, and with the same tanned look everyone seemed to have, matched with brilliant white teeth, was a life-size copy of Barbie's boyfriend Ken. But my attention was drawn to his opponent: none other than big-busted Vivien, who looked like she was about to hurl her tennis racquet at me. She was clearly not impressed by the comment he had just made.

Gabby, who hadn't even broken out in a sweat, called back, "You'll find out this afternoon. She's got a two-hour tennis class booked with you."

Not once breaking her stride, Gabby continued up past the courts and out along the other side to the golf course. I've got to admit that if it hadn't been for the fact that I had Vivien burning holes in my back I would have stopped there and then. All my leg muscles were screaming, and it was slowly registering that the morning trot was just a warm-up.

Another couple of miles later we were finally back at the bungalow. As Gabby let me through the back gate I sped past her and flew up the front steps and into the chalet.

"You can stop," Gabby called after me. "You don't need to keep on running."

"It's not my desire to keep on running," I called back, "It's just that now I've got the 'runs' real bad after scoffing down at least a litre of low-fat yoghurt last night." The yoghurt dinner, mixed with the intestinal jiggle this morning, was more than my digestive system could handle.

With that, I dived into the bathroom. Gabby's muffled voice called out, "I'll be back for you at ten o'clock."

***

Three hours later, at ten on the dot, Gabby rapped on the door before turning the key to let herself in. And before I knew it, we were speeding along the highway into the city in her jet-black 4x4.

Our destination, or rather my destination, was Vidal Sassoon. The hair and beauty centre was huge; it was bigger than my local shopping centre back home. And a million times more exclusive. I was placed in the hands of one of the stylists as Gabby bluntly stated, "Get the hair sorted, then she's got fifteen minutes of rays."

To me she said, "So long, honey," and was gone.

I felt a bit sorry for the stylist left in charge of "sorting" my hair, knowing full well what a challenge that was. However, I've got to admit, three hours later a miracle had taken place. My hair cascaded down my back, smooth, silky and sleek, and I'd been given the added assurance that the style would hold out for at least eight weeks after having had it professionally straightened. Hair all under control, I was whipped off to the sun-ray department, told to strip off (underwear and all), and was funnelled into a Doctor Who cabin. With the fluorescent lighting, tinted goggles and being stark naked, I did feel like I was in some sort of time machine.

Gabby was waiting for me as I stepped out with my fifteen-minute tan and new hair, and although she didn't say anything there was something about the way she smiled to herself that made me realise she was thoroughly enjoying being my Fairy Godmother. Though I guessed that Mr

Guillem was really the brains behind it all.

The 4x4 was laden with shopping bags and I got all chatty and excited the whole drive back when I realised that the bags, brimming with new shoes and clothes, were all for me. We were similar in size, so I guessed she'd used herself as mannequin, though I wished she'd let me parade around the boutiques. Mind you, saying that, Gabby had probably correctly guessed that letting me loose in the stores was not a wise idea. Not so much for the bill I could run up, rather for the spectacle I would make of myself, oohing and aahing over the rich fabrics. She probably didn't want to be associated with a run-of-the-mill girl like me, and I didn't really blame her. But I was educated enough not to be ungracious and complain; instead I opted to hum away *Pretty Woman* until Gabby, at her wits end with my constant nattering and off-key droning, told me to "Shut the hell up."

After a well-earned catnap in the early afternoon, I found myself once again being driven by Gabby, who in the last twenty-four hours seemed to have become an extended part of my shadow, back to the exclusive golf course and tennis club. The tennis coach we'd come across first thing that morning was already waiting for me down on one of the practice courts. As I walked onto the court in my new tennis whites, looking like a real pro, a slight look of puzzlement came over his face as he looked at me intensely, trying to put his finger on what had altered in the meantime.

"It's the hair," I said, in answer to his befuddled expression. "And I'm Chantelle," I continued, holding out my hand.

"I'm Ken," he said, as he took it in a warm, firm handshake. I laughed, which just added to the look of perplexity on his face. I mean, I'd thought this morning that he looked like Barbie's boyfriend, so actually being called Ken was quite a coincidence. Or maybe not. Perhaps it was just a question of time before the Barbie Queen herself turned up, and then all I needed was someone to pinch me (preferably not on my backside) and I'd wake up.

As I moved to the base line, racquet in hand, memories

of my childhood and of not so long ago came flooding over me. It had been eighteen months since I'd last stood on a tennis court. My dad, who had been a semi-pro in his youth, had drilled me through hours and hours of tennis play. It was his way of dealing with my mother's death. It was the only time of day he was able to forget the pain he suffered, and I, in turn, strove to play the best I could, because every time I whammed the ball down the side line or cross court in a winning pass, I was rewarded with his proud smile. That was incentive enough for me.

Ken and I rallied for a while and I realised I hadn't lost my touch. Ken, in turn, after the first couple of comments he called out about footwork and ball spin, just hushed, comprehending that I was in no need of coaching tips.

After a fifteen-minute warm-up I called out, "Let's play a couple of sets?"

Obviously the excitement of the morning had got to me. Despite being pretty skilful, I'm not the competitive sort and always shrink from competition of any type and at any level. But here I was on the other side of the Atlantic, with new hair and new attitude. The surrounding courts were jam-packed. Most of the people on court had been at the mansion the day before when I'd arrived in my tacky clothes. They'd witnessed my clash with Vivien. Now I had the opportunity to prove that I was a tough cookie and better than the likes of Vivien in every sense, and I wasn't going to let that slip.

I won the toss and opted to serve. My first serve was an ace and I won the first game to love. Ken, who had started careless, confident and cocky, was jolted. Manly pride under threat, he was spurred on and took the following two games with relative ease. I could hear my dad's voice in my head just as if he was standing right beside me: *Don't rush your shots, Chantelle. Follow through properly and make your opponent run.*

And I did just that. One hour later, sweat literally pouring down my whole body and with Ken in just the same state, we reached tiebreak. By then, quite a crowd had gathered cheering us on – or rather, cheering me on. Ken only got a shout of encouragement now and again, from the local macho men whose worst nightmare would be losing face by losing to a woman. And of course there was Vivien. Her high-pitched screech could be heard above the rest, willing Ken on. I was vaguely aware that bets were being placed and it was Gabby who was acting as "bookie."

Some minutes later we were drawn at five points all, and I had visions of the match going on for ever.

As I moved back to the baseline for my serve I was aware of a dark-haired stranger staring intensely at me, and I suddenly felt week at the knees. I could have sworn that it was Robbie, though with his shades on, and the sun blaring and hazing my vision, I couldn't be sure. But just the thought that there was a remote chance that it could be him really got me inspired. With new-born energy I fired an ace down the centre of the court, not giving Ken time to react. I was buzzing, and one point away from victory. The crowd had hushed and I imagined that I was on Centre Court at Wimbledon playing for Championship point.

Ken's turn to serve. He sliced the ball down the sideline, but I was ready with my double-handed backhand and sent it whizzing back across the net and straight down the line like a bullet. A winning shot! The crowd cheered and Ken approached the net and clasped my hand in congratulations.

"Way to go, kid," he declared, full of respect. I just glowed.

The spectators called out their congratulations, the more generous comments coming from those who had earned quite a bit of dosh from betting on me. Thoroughly exhausted but elated I went in search of Gabby. I'd seen her talking animatedly with the dark-haired stranger, and I was just bursting to find out if he really was Robbie. But Gabby, much to my mystification, denied speaking to anyone.

What the hell was going on?

Nothing made sense. The luxurious living quarters I'd been allocated, the beauty treatments, the expensive new clothes... What was it all for? Gabby was obviously in charge of getting me in shape, but despite the hours she'd spent by my side she remained mute to my questioning about what I was really doing here. Mr Guillem was behind the whole project, but I doubted he was the key person. There was definitely a missing link somewhere, but the only way to discover who (or what) that missing link was would be for me to stick it out and brace myself for whatever was to come.

That night, after nearly two hours of intense tennis and a five-mile run at first light, I slept like a baby. My dreams whirled between Robbie, and attempting to escape from a battlefield of flying tennis balls. So, much to Gabby's despair as she attempted to wake me at 5.30 the following morning, she would have been more successful at resuscitating Tutankhamun. I refused to budge. Two mugs full of icy water were thrown over me. I finally started to stir thinking I'd peed in the bed. In a hoarse and broken voice, as if I'd been out on the booze all night, I turned to Gabby.

"Just tell me how long I have to put up with this military routine, and I promise to get up and change."

"Three weeks," came Gabby's quick reply, "and then you'll be flown out on location. So get your act together, sunshine, or else you won't be ready."

"Ready for what?" I probed, thinking I'd softened Gabby's conscience. But she was a tough old bird and totally ignored my question.

Despite the vigorous tennis match the afternoon before, my legs felt comfortable and I made it through the five-mile run with relative ease. The Pacific was running high and I spied surfers decked out in black wetsuits bobbing out on their boards, patiently waiting to catch the perfect wave.

"Can you swim, kid?" Gabby asked having detected my line of vision.

"Of course I can swim," I snapped back at her, I didn't mean to sound so sharp, but I was still feeling peeved at her for waking me up so roughly. I had a mind to tell her off, but I wasn't brave enough, at least not just yet.....

"We'll have some fun this afternoon then," she commented. Amusement lined her face, and I wondered what she had in store.

The morning took the same routine as the previous day. After the run Gabby disappeared for three hours, calling for me once again at ten o'clock on the dot. She sped me into town and I had an eyelash permanent dye done, lip liner tattooed on, eyebrows shaped, facial done, followed by a fifteen-minute whirl on the sun bed.

Back at the cottage, feeling refreshed and almost new (except for my lips, of course, which after the lip line tattoo now felt like I'd just snogged an Arizona Hedgehog), I spread a large towel down on the shaded grass area to the side of the wooden bungalow. I had a large fruit cocktail in one hand and an armful of glossy *Cosmo*, *Glamour* and *People* magazines I'd found on the kitchen table that morning and assumed that Gabby had left there. I tossed them down onto the fluffy towel as I positioned myself alongside. My gaze was drawn to one of the magazines that had fallen open, and staring back at me with his sexy smile was Lionel King. My heart started racing as I realised that he was the stranger who'd watched me so intensely the previous day at the tennis courts, and that in my obsession with Robbie I'd not recognised him. I looked closely at the image and realised how remarkably similar both men were: the same olive skin, dark hair, powerful build. Even their eyes looked similar, Lionel's being a shade greener that Robbie's bright blue.

I gasped out loud. I *knew* Robbie had reminded me of someone! But what a coincidence! Or perhaps my mind in a subconscious Freudian way was playing tricks on me, and any tall, dark, handsome stranger would cause me to get confused.

I turned to the accompanying article and started to read.

After a long-term but at times turbulent relationship, Hollywood's most sought-after bachelor is single once more, after putting to an end his romance with Queen of the Screen Vivien Francis…

My stomach suddenly felt queasy. No wonder the poor girl had her claws out. I even felt sorry for her. It was one thing to get dumped and lick your wounds in private, but to have it plastered all over the glossy magazines was quite another. It was enough to make anyone go crazy, even for a big star like Vivien Francis. I promised myself that I'd try and be friendly to her the next time we met.

There was a sudden commotion from the pathway on the other side of the fence that led to the main house. I heard Sav, as she dashed up, calling, "*Señorita, Señorita…*"

I let her through the dividing gate, though I could only make out her legs. The rest of her was hidden behind a huge bouquet of fresh flowers that wobbled in her arms as she let out a string of sneezes. Her eyes were watering by the time I'd taken the flowers from her.

"Are these for me?" I asked, perplexed, convinced that there must have been some mistake. Sav vigorously nodded her head and I thought her neck would snap in her excitement. "Who from?" I went on, madly hoping she would say "Robbie," although I knew that was wishful thinking.

Sav shrugged her petite shoulders. "*Admirador… Amante…?*"

"Admirer" or "lover"? Well, it was obvious that Sav hadn't the slightest idea either. Lover indeed; that will be day. Knowing my luck, they were probably from a real freak who would turn out to be some wacky stalker.

"*Gracias,*" I said to Sav before turning indoors to hunt for a vase large enough to fit the flowers in, though the bouquet was so huge that I imagined I'd end up having to put them in the bathtub. There was no note or card, and I thought cleverly that I would strategically place them in the middle of the dining room so that Gabby would see them when she called for me in the afternoon. She would know who they were from.

Gabby, however, was just as surprised as I was. In fact I think it was the first time I'd seen her at a loss, and I didn't know whether that was a good or bad sign. But the mystery of the flowers was left behind as we both strolled down to the beach. As we made our way across the soft sand I gasped out loud. The waves were massive.

"You've got to be nuts if you think I'm going in there?" I didn't give a toss if I offended Gabby.

"Don't be a sucker. They're baby waves. They're only about two metres high."

"Fuck that, I don't give a shit how tall they are. You're talking to a London lass. The highest I've ever seen water come up is when the toilets get blocked. But go ahead, I won't get in your way."

By this point we'd reached the shore, deserted but for the seagulls which cried out overhead. Before I knew it Gabby had dived into the surf and with powerful strokes was heading out into the ocean. She'd better not drown, I thought. I wasn't certain if I would be brave enough to go in to save her. Luckily Gabby was an exceptional swimmer, and it actually looked fun catching waves and body-surfing to the shore. On the fifth wave Gabby surfed I was madly contemplating going in and giving it a go, so when she shouted, "Come on you fairy, I thought you said you could swim," the new gutsy attitude that had overwhelmed me the previous day during the tennis match flowered once more. I dived in.

"Jesus, it's cold!" I cried out as the surprisingly freezing water lapped over me. This was followed by an ear-splitting scream as I felt something brush my leg in the dark depths of the murky blue water, visions of *Jaws* flashing through my mind. Gabby nearly choked with glee at my fear-stricken face. I, with a grin, had to admit what a baby I must have seemed as she fished out, and held up a small piece of plastic that had been floating just below the surface.

It had seemed fun, and was fun. After a while Gabby called out, "Make this your last one."

I positioned myself to set off with the booming wave, head down and between my arms, which were shaped like an arrow. I kicked off hard, maintaining myself at the crest of the wave as it rushed to the shoreline taking me with it. Not bad, old girl, I thought. Then the wave broke, crashed down on top of me and took me under.

I could feel myself tumbling all over the place and in a panic I opened my eyes under the gloomy depths. I desperately needed to breathe, but I was so disorientated I had no idea which way was up. *Stay calm…*! I let a few air bubbles escape in order to follow them, knowing that they would float in the direction of the surface, which, I quickly realised, was to my right. With one last effort, I thrashed out in that direction and came to the surface spluttering for air. Gabby was twenty metres further down the shore and I was relieved that she hadn't witnessed my close encounter with oblivion. I had, however, lost my bikini top somewhere along the way. I wondered how I was going to explain that one.

As casually as possible I made it over to where I'd left my towel and wrapped it around me as Gabby approached. She chortled as she neared, and as if it was the most natural event in the world, commented, "You'll probably find it washed up on the shore tomorrow morning. I know from experience." I was grateful for this, as it obviously meant that she, too, had at some point battled it out with the waves. The difference was, however, that I had no intention of ever getting back in the surf when the waves were up.

***

The following morning, five minutes before Gabby was due to appear jogging up the path from the main house, I was out in the garden area patiently waiting for her and carefully blended into the shadows so as not to be seen. On the dot she came into view. She stepped through the gate, as silently as a panther, and I wondered if she'd been a member of the secret service or a SWAT team, because she moved with stealth and there such was a military stance about her in general. Not wanting to miss out on my planned ambush, I quickly turned the switch for the sprinklers. Soon the silence of early dawn was broken by a loud hiss as the sprinklers spun around.

That will teach her for dowsing me with cold water in the mornings.

Gabby, who at this point was right in the middle of the

garden, dived on the grass and rolled to the safety of one of the hedges. I lost sight of her as I gurgled with the hilarity of the situation. But before I knew it, Gabby had me face down on the ground, arms twisted behind my back in a rock-solid grip.

This wasn't part of my plan!

Totally winded and struggling to get my face out of the turf, I could feel Gabby release her hold on me as she became aware that the ambush came from harmless me. I turned to face her spitting out tufts of green grass that I'd almost choked on. And Gabby, for the first time since I'd arrived, let out a cackle of laughter. I followed suit and we both sat there getting drenched to the bone, shaking with laughter until our bellies ached.

From that moment on, Gabby's attitude towards me changed. She became more chatty, and treated me as a human being instead of a mission.

***

The days turned into weeks, and in a spin of morning runs, tennis, beauty sessions and low-fat yoghurt, the time arrived for me to be flown to the location for the film I'd been contracted to do. I was in a state of pure nerves, as nothing about what was expected of me had been clearly explained. Despite Gabby's reassurance, I couldn't help but fret as to why I hadn't been given a script to study, or had anything explained with regard to my character's role. I was going into this venture headfirst, totally blind and at the rate of a steam train. There's no turning back now, I thought, as I sat on the private jet heading out to Nevada.

Chapter Five

I was met by Mr Guillem and driven out into the hot desert in an open-topped sand jeep. The dust swirled up around me as we sped along the bouncy desert track. Some time later, covered in sand and grit, I finally saw the film location. In the middle of No-Man's-Land a small town had sprung up. There were at least a hundred caravans of all sizes, whilst five huge army tents and several marquees had been set up, together with one immense barn. At least, that's what it looked like from a distance. There were two helicopters in a temporary hangar on the far side of the camp, together with several other sand jeeps and flashy-looking desert motorbikes. It was late evening, and people were milling around; the inhuman heat had finally cooled enough to allow the cast and crew to circulate.

As we sped at what seemed breakneck speed down into the valley where the camp had been put up, I spotted a posse of people all moving around one main figure. The tall powerful build was unmistakable even at that distance. The dark hair glinted in the evening sun. The bare chest was tanned dark brown, wiry and firm.

Lionel King moved with such grace that my heart skipped a beat, not because I was staring at one of the most famous actors around and that I was to work on his film, but because I could indeed confirm that *this* is who Robbie had reminded me of. There was no Freudian slip, Robbie and Lionel were *very* similar! Robbie who had conquered me, heart and soul, in one afternoon, and, however much I tried, I couldn't get him out of my thoughts. From the moment I'd felt his penetrating gaze (which felt like a lifetime ago), I knew I was lost. It didn't help that I was to be left on a desert location with Robbie's multi-millionaire film star double.

Mind you, thinking about it, I wasn't going to complain.

In a swirl of sand we came to a halt in the centre of the temporary town. I was helped down from the jeep by one of Lionel's assistants as Lionel himself moved towards me. My heart thumped, I was at a full-blown loss as to what I should say. But I needn't have bothered. I was left staring as Lionel walked straight past without the slightest acknowledgement of my existence. Even when Mr Guillem tried to introduce me, Lionel replied flatly, "Not now Freddy G, I haven't got time to waste."

I couldn't believe he'd been so obnoxious. Left gobsmacked as Lionel continued his way across to one of the huge marquees, with a trail of admirers in his wake, I hazily heard Freddy G (as everyone called Mr Guillem) call out, "Sandy, sweetheart, come over here will you? I want to introduce you to your roommate."

Aware that I must be the "roommate", I turned to eye Sandy as she approached. Dark silky brown hair cascaded down her back, her well-shaped legs seemed to go right up to her neck and as she approached I realised we were pretty much the same height and age. She gave me a friendly smile as she held out her hand to shake mine.

"You can't believe what a relief it is to finally have gotten a roommate. I hate having to sleep alone, especially here in the desert when any little noise in the night gives me the jumps, what with the coyotes an' all."

"That's enough, Sandy," interrupted Freddy G quickly. He must have guessed that after my degrading encounter with dickhead Lionel, Sandy's stories of night creatures might just make me turn on my heel and leave – even if I had to drive solo all the way back to LA.

"Help Chantelle take her stuff to your caravan and show her around, there's a good girl," he added as he gave her a pat on her behind. I didn't comment aloud, but much to my irritation I judged that in the eyes of many in the film business, the likes of Sandy and me were all just a lot of tottering mutton. Sandy seemed immune, however, as

50

without giving it a second thought she casually tossed one of my bags across her shoulder and led me towards the caravans.

Caravan Number Fifteen was to be my home for the next several weeks, and as I went inside I was surprised and immensely relieved to see how spacious and homely it was. The cooking/dining area was rigged out with a fully equipped kitchen, including mini-bar, whilst a large satellite television set took up part of the fully-furnished lounge area. There was a low deluxe sofa, a couple of bright pink beanbags, which I thought were a bit harsh on the eye but tolerable, and a colourful Mexican rug spread on the floor. You wouldn't want to stumble in here with a shocking hangover, but I liked it.

The bathroom was also spacious; brightly illuminated with a full-length mirror. As I stared at my reflection with Sandy next to me, it hit me that apart from our facial features, the two of us looked as if we'd been cloned. If Sandy thought the same she kept it to herself, and led me to the bedroom. The two beds were relatively close together, separated by an undersized bedside table. The main part of the bedroom was taken up by a huge closet and chest of drawers.

My attention turned to the bed that was obviously used by Sandy, as on the wall above the headrest and all along the bedside were photos of her: parachuting from planes, free-falling, hanging off cliff tops, riding speeding motorbikes, or diving through arrows of bursting flames. Slowly things stated to fall in place.

"I take it you're the stuntwoman."

"That obvious, is it?" Sandy giggled. I felt an instant admiration for her, though it also flashed through my mind that if she wanted to earn her living by trying to avoid getting herself killed, she must have lost her marbles somewhere along the way.

"And you," Sandy went on, "must be the body double for all the sex scenes."

Chapter Six

"SEX SCENES!! WHAT!!?" I exclaimed, my legs buckling under me in shock.

Sandy, aware that she'd not said quite what I expected – much less wanted – to hear, took firm hold of one of my elbows to steady me and made a quick attempt to remedy the situation.

"Just kidding," she grinned.

But I had a horrid feeling that it was no joke. My belongings unpacked, I sat there seriously shaken by what Sandy had let slip. In an attempt to take my mind off it, she took me back outside to give me a quick brief on the running of the camp.

Being a desert location, hair and make-up calls were often at 4.30 or 5 am, to enable work to start at first light and get scenes shot before the excruciating heat set in. Meals were served in Tent A. Tent B was laundry service. Marquee Number One was a converted recreational saloon. Marquee Number Two was props and wardrobe. Marquee Number Three was a first aid tent… Sandy's impromptu guided tour was suddenly cut short as a piercing screech shattered the calm of the serene desert evening. Some ten metres away, and heading in our direction like a sand storm, was Crystal Lee, currently the best-paid actress in Hollywood. The super cool and collected image the press always presented of her vanished in a flicker as I realised the ear-shattering shriek had come from her, and that there was nothing even remotely "cool" about her – at least on this first impression.

"You can tell Freddy G to go fuck himself. I told him yesterday that I refuse to do any more takes without my stylist here with me. If by tomorrow evening there's no change you can all kiss my ass goodbye as I'll be walking out of this godforsaken place and won't be coming back..." Crystal's tirade continued as she bulldozed past us.

Once out of earshot, Sandy confided, "That's Crystal Lee. And just in case you hadn't noticed, she's got a tongue on her like a whip. Lionel can't stand her; that's why he refuses to do the..." She hesitated in mid-sentence "... the... the proposed sequel to this film with her," she hastily added.

Yeah, right, you mean he refuses to do the sex scenes with her!!

So now I knew for certain. What Sandy had so innocently blurted out earlier on in the caravan was true: I was here to do the nude scenes.

It all made sense. The intense exercise for the final toning-up for close-ups of my naked body; the all-over sun-tan; the hair straightened to match Crystal's. When you analysed it, it was obvious. With careful lighting and camera angles, not too close-up on the face, Crystal looked a duplicated version of Sandy and me. Or rather, we looked like twin versions of Ms Hysterical Lee. That's it, I promised myself. The moment I get the chance to seek out Freddy G, I'll inform him that I have no intention of earning money by selling my body, on or off the screen.

Dinner over, Sandy and I moved out of Tent A. Over in the distance the sun was a deep orange fireball low on the horizon. I gazed at it sullenly, and it sunk in that I was, frankly speaking, seriously bloody homesick. The entire showbiz extravaganza was just a bit too much for me, and I'd gone and landed myself in the middle of a goddamn circus.

And, let's be honest about it, I was frightened. Sex scenes. Fuck!

Dinner had been like sitting through a casting for *The Comedy Club* mixed with *American Idol*; all and sundry battling it out to be noticed. It had left me with a splitting headache and heartache for home. I sighed as I glanced gloomily at the sinking sun.

"I'm just going to take a quiet stroll before I hit the sack," I said to Sandy as she moved off to get an early night, having a stunt scene to film the following day.

She gave me a warm smile as she advised, "Don't wander too far, honey," then sauntered off to home-sweet-caravan-home.

***

The sun had almost set by the time I'd scrambled my way up one of the sand dunes on the border of Flick City. I was on the side where the jeeps and helicopters were stationed, and I was half tempted to leg it down into one of the parked vehicles and pray to Lady Luck to get me out of this mayhem. But I wasn't that brave, so I turned my back on the village below and gaped at the wonders of the open space around me: ruby-red desert sand was visible for miles on end, and the air was silent apart from the whisper of the evening breeze. The relative silence was soon broken. Feeling the coke I had gulped down during my evening meal come up, I let escape a blaring burp, one that any monstrous five-year-old would have been proud of. I could even hear it echo across the Nevada night.

"That wasn't very genteel of you, was it?" said an amused, deep voice behind me. "And there was me thinking that British girls were all refined and well-mannered."

I turned, crimson-faced, towards the speaker. It was the last person on earth I expected to see. There, standing before me, his clear green eyes penetrating my own, was Lionel King. I forgot my embarrassment as I recalled the ungracious way he'd behaved that afternoon.

"I don't think you're quite the one to be tutoring me on good manners," I replied, in the most genteel voice I could muster, "when you're so evidently discourteous yourself." *Round one to me.* Lionel, however, just smiled alluringly. I was captivated by the fact that, up close, he reminded me of Robbie even more than ever.

Lionel was swiftly down on his knees, my hands tightly clasped in his (much to my embarrassment), as he looked at me apologetically.

54

"Please forgive me for my ignorance earlier this evening when you arrived. I didn't count on your enchanting presence until tomorrow. I didn't even glance in your direction. I didn't expect it to be you." His clasp tightened as I struggled to break free.

"Get up," I hissed. *God knows who was viewing the scene from below!* "Please let go of me," I implored, all in vain as he pulled harder on my hands until I came to rest on the ground beside him. His face was just inches from mine, his penetrating gaze leaving me dizzy. *He's going to kiss me.* As he was holding my hands I couldn't slap him across the face if he so much as dared to take advantage of me. As if reading my mind Lionel shifted slightly away from me, his smile lingered on his lips, clearly amused by my discomfort.

"I'd like you to join the crew on set tomorrow so that you can start getting a feel of how things work and familiarise yourself with the team. They're a great gang. I'm sure you've met some of the members already. Sandy's a great girl. If you have any snags, just ask her. And if you can avoid Crystal, you'll be doing yourself a favour. As for the rest, you'll sail through."

This is my chance, I thought. Aloud, I asked, "What exactly is my role in this film?"

Not losing his suave air, Lionel turned to me, jade eyes locking into mine in a gaze that sent a quiver down my back.

"My darling girl, all that's required of you is to be yourself and have a little fun."

Before I could insist further Lionel pressed on, tactfully changing topic. "So how do you like LA? Got any surfing in?" I wondered if Gabby had debriefed him about my close encounter with the dark Pacific depths.

"The tennis courts suit me better than the Californian waves," I admitted.

"Yes, quite a little ball slammer... Or so I've been told." He grinned, and I remembered the first time I'd seen Lionel down by the tennis courts watching me play when I'd mistaken him for Robbie. I now knew it was Lionel, despite Gabby's pretence otherwise.

"How about your accommodation back there? Bit more luxurious than your present combo, I should think."

"Well, I've got to admit," I answered, feeling more at ease in Lionel's presence than I would have thought possible, "I was becoming spoilt in Freddy G's spacious cottage, which is not good, because I'll have to return to the real world at some point. And his main house is just grand. But even the caravan here is bigger than my flat back in London, so I can't complain."

By this point we'd both settled back on the sandy terrain. As I gazed up into the night sky, now ablaze with shining stars, I heard Lionel's voice so very close beside me that I could almost feel his words caressing my face. With genuine interest in his voice, he asked, "So, given the opportunity to remain here, would you stay?"

I hesitated before answering. Robbie flashed into my mind, and I had an image of the two of us outside my dream home, that petite country cottage. A shooting star flashed across the night sky leaving a trail of twinkling stardust behind, and I momentarily closed my eyes and wished for that dream to come true.

To Lionel I replied, "Christ no! I don't know how you handle it, but it must be a goddamn nightmare having screaming fans faint right away if you so much as sneeze in their direction, and have paparazzi falling out of trees just to get a shot of you. It's way too wacky for me, thanks."

I hoped I hadn't sounded offensive, but you really did have to be half-whammy to put up with the never-ending Hollywood reality show.

"How did you get on with Gabby?" Lionel asked, changing the subject. He was propped up on one elbow, gazing at me with deep curiosity.

"I set the sprinkler on her." I confessed, holding back my glee at the memory.

"No kidding?" Lionel grinned at my amused look.

"Yep, she did the full-on body-dive to the ground thinking that the sprinklers were out to ambush her."

Lionel let out a loud boisterous laugh, presumably at the

image of Gabby taking cover. He had one of those contagious laughs, which started me off too, until I had tears of merriment running down my cheeks.

Yeah, Lionel is alright.

Chapter Seven

The following day, after being courteously escorted back to my caravan by Lionel, I was up with Sandy at the crack of dawn. As we walked passed Crystal's colossal caravan on our way to breakfast, we could already hear her shrill voice. Poor sod, I thought, to whoever was on the receiving end.

"Is she ever satisfied?" I asked Sandy.

"Beats me," Sandy shrugged as we moved into the breakfast queue. The smells of freshly-brewed coffee and newly-baked bread, cakes from the oven, sizzling sausages and bacon, fried tomatoes and onions did wonders for my taste buds. But I did feel a tinge of guilt as I realised that all Gabby's hard work was about to go to pot.

Breakfast over, I accompanied Sandy through hair and make-up. They toiled over her hair, getting it silky straight, but she didn't need much make-up on, as her scenes had no facial close-ups. Then we made our way to the sand jeeps and were taken on a twenty-minute white-knuckle drive through the desert dunes until we finally reached the location for the day's shoot. I glanced at Sandy as we alighted; her hair was all askew, and I wondered why anyone had bothered to style it.

The preparation for the first take got under way relatively quickly, just as the sun's rays gradually emerged from behind the rocky mountains that loomed over the valley, and caressed the sandy terrain into a red fireball. Lionel had arrived by helicopter together with the director – though it was obvious that Lionel played a critical role in the management of the movie. They whisked Sandy off up to the tops of a rocky cliff as I looked around for Lionel's stunt double. Gosh, I thought. With Lionel and his body doubles,

I'm going to have images of Robbie popping up all over the place.

I was soon aware that there was no one around who remotely matched Lionel's physique, and as I shielded my eyes against the bright morning light and glanced up to the mountain top, it dawned on me that Lionel, equipped with a safety harness, was about to do his own stunts. My heart suddenly started racing. As much as I hate to admit it, I found myself fretting over Lionel's safety, like a true *bona fide* teen fan. In a real state of nerves I watched as Lionel and Sandy sprinted together across the cliff edge and, in unison, did a death-defying lunge towards a helicopter undercarriage where they then swung precariously fifty metres feet off the ground. Even knowing that they were buckled into safety belts didn't ease the tension, and with each "take" I nervously started to bite my nails (much to my disgust, as I'd overcome that habit years ago). By mid-morning, my nails gnawed to the bone, the scene was finally wrapped.

"Thank God for that," I said to myself, relieved. My admiration for Sandy had grown with each "take." Lionel, I realised, was just a pure adrenaline junkie. It was also obvious how much he adored his job, as well as with being a perfectionist. Moreover, I realised that my dream lifestyle – living in the quiet English countryside having to fret only about the weeding – was poles apart from this pandemonium.

Lionel was on a complete high as he came down, and I seriously wondered if he'd danced with the white lady that morning to get him buzzing so. Having said that, Sandy was just as hyper. But I hadn't witnessed any substance taking while I was with her, so maybe it was just the thrill of defying gravity that did it for them.

"Hiya babe," Lionel called to me as he approached, with a real goofy grin stretched from ear to ear. "What did you think?"

"Honestly? I think you're mad! But I'll give it to you, both you and Sandy were just amazing, absolutely incredible."

"Have you ever flown in a helicopter?" Lionel asked.

Before I had a chance to answer and insist it was something that I didn't mind passing on, Lionel had grabbed hold of one of my hands and pulled me – well more like dragged me – over to where the helicopter was sitting.

"Come on" he said. "I'll fly you back."

"Can you fly this thing?" I questioned, rather alarmed, as he hauled me into the cockpit, panicking that I would never see my green homeland ever again or even touch firm ground under foot.

Before I knew it I was strapped into the passenger seat, big earmuffs on, and precariously swaying as Lionel shifted the helicopter for take-off. I was in such a state of nerves that I thought breakfast was on its way back up. But the lurching and swaying eased as we became airborne, and I was able to endure the take-off and watch the other members of the crew turn to miniature-sized figures.

I was suddenly reminded of Anneka Rice in *Challenge Anneka*. I can vaguely remember the episodes; my dad had been a huge fan. Whatever happened to her?

We flew out into the desert, and as I started to relax I was able to gaze at the spectacular views below. The red landscape had a life of its own; the steady breeze which picked up the dust particles and shifted them from one side to another as if caressing a lover was like gentle waves across an ocean surface. The seemingly smooth flat virgin terrain was broken here and there by formations of jutting rocky boulders similar to the one used by Lionel earlier that very day to perform his crazy stunt.

As Lionel did a U-turn in mid-flight to head back to our temporary set-up he yelled out to me and attempted some sign language that totally flummoxed me. I just prayed that he wasn't going to attempt any showy acrobatic tricks. At his insistent pointing to my right I finally turned – and there below, a long was off, was the city of Las Vegas. Even now, in pure daylight, bright neon lights were aglow in reds and greens. High-rise hotels jutted into the sky, as did the replicas of the Eiffel Tower and the Statue of Liberty. I clasped my hands together in delight. Lionel, who was probably aware of the impact Las Vegas had on me from this privileged bird's-eye view, hovered for a while before he shot us back across the desert valley.

***

Giddy from the helicopter journey, I stepped down weak at the knees but totally thrilled. I had a sudden urge to phone Tammy, she being the only one who would really appreciate the flabbergasting adventure I was having. In all truth she was the only one who would actually believe this wild fairytale. Anyone else would just think I'd become delirious.

"Is there anywhere I can phone from?" I asked Lionel, hardly able to contain my excitement as we crossed the car park towards the caravans. I had intended to sort myself out with a smartphone, but since my arrival I just hadn't been given the chance to sort anything out. Apart from my hair, of course.

"Call from my place," he offered and led me to his fantastic "home." It was five times the size of my shared combo, and came complete with bullet-proof panelling all along the outside, sturdy bodyguard, and vicious-looking guard dog. As we stepped inside, my already weak knees almost packed up on me.

In the middle of the lounge was a jacuzzi the size of my local swimming pool, spurting out frothy bubbles. Lionel even had D'Angelo humming out over the loudspeakers that were so well hidden it felt that the sexy-voiced soul singer was on the verge of leaping out of the tub. There was wood panelling all along the inside walls, and rich plush carpet lined the floor. Carpet! In a caravan! In the middle of a bloody desert! There were obviously no limits to his overindulgence.

There was more capital invested in this mobile home than I could possibly imagine. Any human activist in the world who could get their hands on this would have a field day selling it off in chunks to raise millions for those in need. Whereas little old me, well, I just moved through each section of that semi-palace in a daze. In the bedroom alone, you could put up a ping-pong table and it wouldn't get in the way. Having waltzed me through the walk-in-and-struggle-to-find-the-exit wardrobe (not that I quite understood his desire to show me his garments), the bathroom, the fully-equipped gym and the restaurant-sized kitchen, Lionel handed me a phone and tactfully moved away.

Tammy's voice down the line was sweet music to my ears. But I'm ashamed to admit that despite my excitement and earlier glee, I felt tears of homesickness well up.

"You'd love it over here," I said.

But Tammy wasn't listening to a word I was saying.

"Guess what? Great news!" She yelled down the line in what sounded like a state of pure ecstasy.

Tammy is that you? I'd never heard her so animated in my life.

"Do you remember when we went out to the country, the week before you left?" she shouted, not waiting for my reply. "And you remember that *really* sexy guy Robbie…?"

Oh shit! I closed my eyes, and collapsed into the swish armchair that was thankfully right behind me. Tammy was my best friend and I just knew that her next words were going to be like driving a dagger into my heart. It was going to be the first time since we'd become bosom buddies, all those years ago, that I would resent her and all her sodding great news with green-eyed envy.

The phone line began crackling, "Tammy, can you hear me?" I shouted. I could vaguely hear her over the interference, but it was impossible to make out what she was saying. Her voice suddenly came through clearer: "I'm dating him, I'm dating R…" as the connection ultimately broke and I was left staring at the phone, painfully repeating her final words in my head.

As I sat there stunned, it was some time before I realised that someone was tickling my back. I jumped and let out a scream. Foolishly I realised that there was no one behind the chair. Lionel, who must have thought I was being attacked, quickly emerged from the kitchen area with a huge Ninja sword. But the caravan soon shook with his boisterous laugh. I'd sat on the remote for the massage chair when I had flopped down and it seemed that he found this hilariously funny. In my state of heartache however, I didn't find the situation remotely amusing, and it wasn't long before Lionel twigged.

"Bad news from home, honey?"

He moved to take me into his strong arms, and I let him hold me, turning my head so it rested on one of his powerful shoulders. Tenderly he wiped the tears that slowly fell down my cheeks, and it was almost too much for me to bear.

I was in love with Robbie (well, probably not "in love" – I would at least have to have dated him a couple of time for that, but that was beside the point; the point was, not only was he on the other side of the world, but was now also dating my best friend), and there I was in the arms of his double, who just happened to be Hollywood's multimillionaire playboy.

I needed to get out and clear my head. I untangled myself from Lionel's embrace.

"Let me take you out to dinner tonight and cheer you up," he said, his eyes troubled as he held my gaze, voice soothing. But as I stared back, all I could see was Robbie.

"NO," I said forcefully, rudely in fact. This was quite the opposite of how I wanted to sound, but I was feeling rotten from what I'd just heard and not quite myself. I was crushed to see the look on Lionel's face. It was obviously a real kick in the teeth for him. I was probably the first girl ever to turn him down. He'd been a real sweetheart, too. If only he didn't remind me so much of Robbie. In an attempt to soften the blow, I added, "Believe me, it's nothing personal. I just need to be by myself," and without another word, I let myself out – dodging the guard-dog's sharp teeth as I went.

***

The next four days went by in a bit of a daze. Lionel, apart from giving me the occasional nod in recognition,

63

otherwise ignored my existence, and I was left rather crushed as I realised that if anyone was capable of cheering me up, he was the one. But he had obviously taken my words to heart, and was truly leaving me alone.

On the fourth day, whilst shooting another of the stunt scenes, Sandy badly twisted her ankle. She was supposed to do a free-fall from a hot air balloon, before pulling her parachute open. But the 'chute opened late, and she hit the ground at crunching speed. Amazingly she appeared to suffer nothing more serious than a sprained ankle, but was flown out to an intensive care unit to check for other, possible internal, injuries.

As a result, the director had no other choice but call for a two-day halt in the filming. Before I knew it Lionel had taken me hostage, not that I put up much of a struggle, and we were soon soaring across the desert in his throbbing helicopter.

Lionel totally ignored my probing about where he was taking me, a sassy grin playing on his lips. Giving up on trying to get an adult response, I settled back and immersed myself in the magnificent landscape below.

It wasn't long before I viewed the shimmering blue Pacific ahead of me. The white sandy coastline stretched for miles on end. As we hovered lower I realised we were coming in to land. Touchdown was smooth, thank God, and as the propellers slowed to a standstill Lionel jumped down from the cockpit and moved around to my side to help me get out. He put his hands on my waist and looked at me, then lifted me down with ease, and despite trying to act offended at being "abducted," I couldn't help but smile back at his goofy grin.

"Is that a smile I see?"

"That depends on what you have planned up your sleeve," I replied, attempting (unsuccessfully) to look serious. In reality I was so excited by the sudden adventure that I'd even managed to put aside, for a while anyway, the images of Tammy and Robbie that kept haunting me.

"Do you trust me?" Lionel asked. His tone became deadly serious as he moved towards me. Instinctively I stepped back, wondering what dodgy game he had in mind. He didn't allow me to answer, as swiftly he had me in his arms in a tight grasp. If he kisses me now, I thought, I won't slap him – but I might just swoon.

I closed my eyes in anticipation – and before I knew it I had a blindfold wrapped around my head, covering my eyes. Lionel got hold of my hands behind my back in a firm grip and whispered in my ear, "Relax, and trust me."

"Are you nuts?" But my struggle against him was in vain. Carefully he guided me forward. Except for the wind whistling slightly and the shuffle of my feet I couldn't hear any other noises around to orientate me. After what seemed like forever, but probably was just a few moments, I felt a change of surface underfoot. I swayed with each step and I didn't topple over only because Lionel still held me fast. I was soon aware of water lapping against wherever it was we were, and that there were gulls crying out overhead. Effortlessly Lionel picked me up in his arms and I held onto his neck with all my might. *Oh Christ, this guy's a weirdo… He's going to throw me into the water.* But a moment later he gently placed me down again. Whatever we were on swayed more and more, and when I was told to sit, I did so obediently. Cool metal was placed around my wrists and before I could land a punch and wipe out Lionel's smirk (which, though I couldn't see it, I was sure was there on his smug face), I'd been handcuffed. There was a sudden roaring noise all around me, and I soon had the ocean air caressing my hair as we raced along in what was obviously a speedboat.

As I sat there, salt spray grazing every pore, Lionel's words echoed in my mind: *Relax, and trust me*. He should have asked if I was prone to heart attacks or suffered from high blood pressure, because my heart was thumping away uncontrollably and wouldn't slow however much I tried to calm myself.

"Is this really necessary?" I yelled out over the deafening noise of the engine, tugging unsuccessfully to try and free my wrists. And what the hell did he have handcuffs for? I imagined, at least hoped, it was a prop he'd nicked from the set, but even so, it was a bit distorted and kinky for me. I yelled out again, but my words were swallowed up by the blustering wind, and Lionel, if he even heard me, didn't reply.

Finally the roaring motor was turned off, and the silence was almost overwhelming. The only noise was the soft lapping of the waves against the boat. I sensed Lionel sit down beside me, but he made no attempt to take off my blindfold, and I couldn't either because of those bloody handcuffs. Unable to see, my other senses were acutely tuned into any alteration in my surroundings. I was aware for the first time of the cologne Lionel wore: faintly musky, slightly spicy. There was also a new and unusual noise: a faint high-pitched squeak. Lionel, aware of the noise also, hushed me.

"Here she comes."

He slipped off the blindfold and released my hands. I glared at him, sending him one of those *if looks could kill* stares. But he was calmly gazing straight ahead whilst pointing with his finger into the blue ocean before us.

Before I had a chance to vent my fury at him for shipping me blindfolded out to sea, I saw a fin emerge from the dark depths below us.

"Oh Shiiiiit, Shark!!" I flapped in a panic. Paralysed I watched as, if in slow motion, the fin approached dangerously close, but just as I was about to let out an ear-splitting scream of horror, the fin jumped two metres high into the air. Dazzled, I watched the most beautiful dolphin tumble-turn in mid-flight before diving, with breathtaking grace, back into the sapphire depths.

I was left totally speechless. Suddenly aware that Lionel was observing me I turned to look at him. His intense gaze left me weak. The corners of his sensual lips were turned in a slight smile. His deep jade eyes held mine fast. Neither of us spoke for what felt like an eternity. Gone was my earlier anger at being carted off, handcuffed, blindfolded and all. My heart was still beating wildly. I was at a loss for words. Lionel remained watching me attentively, and though he moved as if to say something, appeared to hold back. I suddenly felt shy under his passionate gaze and was the first to break eye contact.

"Will it come back?" I asked, referring to the dolphin.

"For sure," Lionel replied. "You can even go swimming with her tomorrow if you like."

"Tomorrow?" I repeated, and as I turned slightly became aware that we were actually tied up against a large sparkling white yacht that in my earlier panic I hadn't noticed. Lionel helped me on deck. The yacht was just as the caravan had been, but a hundred times more so – spacious, very luxurious and tasteful. Below deck were six cabins, each fully kitted with beds or twin divans, wardrobes and private washrooms. At deck level was a fitted kitchen, fully stocked with provisions of every taste. There were two dining rooms – one indoors, the other half-shaded. There was a lounge with a TV and a reading room with a bar, plus a dance floor-cum-cocktail-reception area with another bar. On deck and above the wheelhouse were areas for lounging, sunbathing and fishing. Looking around I was in awe at how absolutely loaded Lionel must be. The insurance fees alone for this king-sized toy would trigger nightmares for most "ordinary" millionaires.

As I stood gawping at my surroundings Lionel moved into the kitchen area and said casually, "Honey why don't you go out on deck and make yourself comfortable whilst I rustle up some grub?" *Where was the crew?* This thing must have needed a small navy to run. I must have thrown him a distrusting look, as he was quick to add, "That's if you're happy to stay. I can take you back now if you like."

"No that's fine." I replied promptly. "I wouldn't miss the opportunity to swim with the dolphin for the world," I added hastily. I had to think of some excuse for virtually surrendering myself.

"Well I'm glad to know your only reason for remaining here with me is because you've fallen in love with Gigi the dolphin," he joked. "That does wonders for my ego."

Laughing back at him, I went outside.

It had darkened quickly, I realised. The evening stars

67

were already glimmering, having no city lights to outshine them. The ocean air was comfortingly balmy and warm. I lay down on one of the full-length deck chairs and let myself unwind after the hair-raising events of the day. The boat gently rocked with the motion of the tide.

"What bliss." I sighed, and promptly fell asleep.

Chapter Eight

The bright, warm morning rays were what woke me. It took me a while to get my bearings. I noticed that I was wrapped in a soft snug blanket and that a feathered pillow had been placed under my head. I could smell freshly brewed coffee. Suddenly aware of where I was, I cringed with shame. If Lionel had been slightly offended the previous night at the suggestion that my sole interest in remaining had lain with the dolphin rather than with him, I couldn't have proved the fact more blatantly than by falling asleep whilst he slaved away in the kitchen.

Sheepishly I glanced about me to apologise to him, but he was nowhere to be seen. I was gradually conscious of splashing noises coming from overboard. In a hurry I moved to the side and peered over. There in the water were Lionel and Gigi. Lionel, on seeing me, gave a friendly wave.

"Come on in," he yelled.

"I haven't got my swimsuit with me." I called back, suddenly disappointed that I wasn't going to be able to swim with Gigi after all.

"Nor have I," he called back. Needing no further encouragement I stripped to my underwear, thankful that I was wearing some sexy lingerie rather than my old grey cotton knickers, and dived into the turquoise ocean. It was invigoratingly fresh, and I shrieked from the cold, shock mixed with pure delight. Lionel, in several strong, firm strokes, was swiftly by my side.

"Good morning, my sleeping beauty."

"Sorry for falling asleep like that last night," I said, shamefaced. "And thanks for covering me with the blanket," I added, whilst treading water, looking around at the same time for Gigi. Her high-pitched squeak soon filled the air as she emerged some ten metres away in a high-flying leap. She dived back into the depths without causing a ripple. With electrifying speed she surfaced right by me, head and upper part of her body out of the water, flapping with her flippers as she let out a string of shrill cries in quick bursts.

Lionel held out his hand to her and she allowed him to caress her head, as she inched her way towards him. She flipped onto her back mischievously sending a spray of water all over him. Gigi then glided smoothly in the water towards me, and nudged me playfully with her nuzzle. I reached out a hand to touch her and felt her smooth soft face as she looked at me through clear intelligent eyes. She remained still by my side for some time allowing me to stroke her, as if aware of the impact she had on me.

"Hold onto her flippers." Lionel suggested, and I did so. Slowly at first she started to swim with me carefully clutching onto her, and then, with a powerful flip of her tail, we were charging through the ocean surface. I'd never felt so exhilarated in my life, despite choking down at least a gallon of salt ocean water. She led me in a large circle before guiding me back to the safety of the yacht. With a melon-sized smile across my face I arrived alongside Lionel. He chuckled fondly at my delight and patted Gigi tenderly. With a soaring leap into the blue sky she did one final showy flip and was gone.

Lazily I swam over to the wooden stepladder that hung overboard down the side of the boat. Just as I was about to clamber up I became aware that the name *Chantelle* was painted across the bow in bold letters, together with the figure of a dark-haired mermaid entwined around the inscription. I felt a shiver run down my spine that had nothing to do with the ocean water.

"That's a bit of a coincidence, isn't it?" I commented to Lionel as he approached.

"What is, babe?" He looked at me rather perplexed before he noticed I was staring at the inscription on the side of his boat.

"Couldn't have chosen a better name, hey!" he joked. "I guess you're just destined for me, honey."

So I have no say in this matter? To tell the truth, this sudden strange discovery had left me baffled and uneasy.

"Come on," Lionel urged as he got hold of the wooden rungs to pull himself up. "Let's go and have some breakfast."

As he hauled himself out of the water I gasped. Not only was he without swimming trunks, he was without anything. Stark naked he made his way aboard, flashing his bronzed behind in my face as if it was the most natural thing in the world.

I slowly climbed the ladder, hoping to give Lionel time to get some clothes on. If he's waiting for me nude, I just won't know where to look! Thankfully, by the time I reached the top of the ladder, he had a towel wrapped around his waist, but as I swung my legs over and stepped aboard Lionel just stared at me. I was tempted to dive back into the water where at least I would be saved from his steamy gaze that was sending my skin ablaze. I wasn't blind to the fact that my skimpy underwear had become totally see-through. I was also vividly aware that I found Lionel desperately attractive. I didn't know if it was because he reminded me so much of Robbie, or because Robbie was no longer an option for me. In any case, I didn't plan to analyse that right then.

"Has anyone ever told you that you have the most amazingly perfect body?" Lionel remained looking at me intensely.

"Oh, all the time" I joked. This was not what I wanted to say, as it made me sound so big-headed. But I was trying to keep things light, and it was the first flippant remark that came to mind.

"Well, we don't want you catching your death of cold," Lionel said flatly. "So wrap this towel around you."

He threw me a fluffy beach towel the colour of a sunflower. The acute look of ardour had gone from his eyes as he turned on his heel and moved indoors for breakfast.

Having gone without dinner the evening before and keenly aware of how hungry I was, I meekly followed, wondering what it was that had caused Lionel to go cold on me. Obviously my frivolous words had triggered a bad humour. But once inside the sunlit cabin, Lionel flashed me a warm smile as he handed me a mug of steaming coffee. The breakfast table was laid with a varied array of breakfast items. We both tucked in.

Food over, we stepped back out on deck. I moved over towards the side railing of the yacht, hopping to catch a glimpse of Gigi. Lionel shifted beside me.

"We don't have to be back on set until tomorrow night. We can either stay here until then or leave now. You decide."

I paused for an instant before answering. I wondered if it was a trick question. Was this for real? Or was I dreaming, and about to wake in my tiny bedsit flat back in London? I couldn't believe the mind-boggling situation I found myself in: that Lionel King, of all people, was proposing that I should spend the next twenty-four hours with him on his luxurious yacht in the middle of the Pacific Ocean, with only his pet dolphin Gigi as chaperone. Of course, I reckoned, it was probably the best therapy for getting over Robbie and the full-on infatuation I had for the guy, which was bizarre anyway considering I'd only met him a couple of times.

"Mr Lionel King," I semi-mocked as I turned to him with a shy smile, "it would be my pleasure to stay with you on this fine yacht of yours until tomorrow."

"Why thank you, My Lady," he teased back and took my hand in his, raised it to his lips and kissed it ever so tenderly.

Then, like a kid who had suddenly got his way, he burst out, "Ever gone fishing?"

"Oh yeah, all the time down the Thames."

He scuttled below deck and emerged laden with fishing rods, beer, sunhats, and a huge cheesy grin.

My, he's certainly irresistible when he wants to be. Though a touch juvenile. Mind you, living in that pipe-dream movie world, where everything seemed like a pleasurable game, it wasn't really surprising.

Lionel set up the fishing lines (for I had no clue which way round the bloody things went) whilst I carefully tied on my glam sun hat and placed over my eyes the large shades that Lionel had also given me. I felt like Jackie O in her prime on the *Christina*.

***

Fishing lines in position, we settled in the warm sun, ice-cold beers in hand. I had one of Lionel's shirts on, and my underwear was hanging out in the sun to dry. I was glad he hadn't fetched out someone else's bikini as I would have felt quite jealous. A bikini was a bit more intimate than just sunhats and shades, and I would have felt a bit put out wearing someone else's sexy two-piece, though I wasn't blind to the fact that the yacht was strategically anchored in the Pacific Ocean, where the blue sky harmoniously meets the turquoise water, and all that can be seen for miles on end is the soft glimmer of the sun's rays as they caress the ocean top… I mean, please, he couldn't have got a more smoochy setting if he tried, and it was obviously his love nest.

As if reading my mind, he said, "You know, you're the first person I've ever brought out here."

"I don't believe that." Oh come on, did he really think I was that naïve? He had female sunhats and shades to prove otherwise, for God sake! Unless, of course, he fancied wearing them himself, which was perhaps even more disturbing…

"Honestly," he insisted. "This has always been my secret getaway when things get too much and I just need to spend a couple of days alone, away from the crazy circus called stardom."

(And disconnect in female fineries?)

"I wouldn't have imagined," I said aloud, "that there was ever a time when things got too much for you."

"Believe me, there are times." He looked so desolate that my heart went out to him. Perhaps Lionel did have a sentimental side to him after all. Perhaps there was more to him than the playboy image the press portrayed. Possibly he wasn't as materialistic as I imagined him to be.

73

Curious to discover more, I asked him, "What on earth possessed you to become a movie star?"

It was something that bemused me; the reason why anyone in their right mind would willingly submit themselves to the persecution of sneaking paparazzi, stalking fans, living months on end away from home on some godforsaken location, getting up at inhuman hours to have kilos of make-up applied and to have hair pulled one way and another. Then there was the learning lines, the hanging about, the heat, the cold, the boredom, the tension, the petty hatreds and the freaked-out co-stars (Crystal to name but one)… Frankly, it was beyond me.

Lionel let out his boisterous laugh, which I was admittedly growing quite fond of. "Honey, why did you agree to fly out over here to the States to be a body-double in this film?"

He thought he had got me there, but I was ready for him. I had all my reasons neatly sussed in my head.

"It's all very simple," I replied, as if lecturing a five-year-old. "There's a quaint little cottage back home, south of London. It's built out of stone with an old thatched roof. Surrounding it is the most romantic little garden, where roses bloom in every shade of the rainbow." True, I was letting my imagination run away a touch, but Lionel would never know. "Towards the far side of the cottage grounds there's a stream that runs through the adjoining dense woods. And as soon as I've earned the million dollars I came out here for, I'm going to buy that house and live happily ever after."

"Well, I must say," replied Lionel casually. "That does sound all very sweet and simple. But who's the guy?"

"What do you mean, *who's the guy?*" I echoed back innocently. I couldn't believe that Lionel could be so intuitive.

"Come on, girl. How old are you? Twenty-three? Twenty-four?" I nodded on twenty-four. "You'd be bored out of your wits in the middle of the countryside by the end of your first week if you were all by yourself. OK if you were sixty or seventy and planning on retirement. But you've got to live a little before then. Take my word, I'd give you six months on your own in your dream cottage. Unless, of course, there is a guy and you plan to churn out babies on an annual basis." He was all mirth and merriment as he said all this. What a wretched sod! But in all truth he could be right. Put like that, it did sound a bit airy-fairy.

"Whatever!" I sighed with exasperation. I didn't want him psychoanalysing me, so to divert the topic away from me, I asked again, "So how about you, how did you get into the movie business?"

"Simple really. I was adopted when I was seven years old by a wealthy middle-aged couple whose family roots had always been entwined with Hollywood's fame and fortune. And by the age of ten I was starring in my first big screen movie." He paused, and I did vaguely remember reading about Lionel's past in one of Tammy's copies of *Vogue* or *Hello*.

"Ever since that first movie it's been a roller-coaster ride. Like everything, there's been good times, just as there's been bad, but all in all it's been worth it. Once you learn to deal with the constant press persecution, and learn to ignore the criticism, it's a cinch. I'll admit I've been lucky. I remember my earlier years being passed from one foster home to the next, getting beaten, going hungry, sleeping on cold floors. There were, of course, nice families who cared for me, but the moment I let myself get attached to them I was whisked off to another home. So the instant I was given my chance I grabbed it with both hands, and haven't looked back since. I haven't forgotten my roots, though, which is why I don't let the fame get to me. In any case, Gabby does a good job of bringing me down to earth anytime she feels it's necessary. Though that's more out of big-sisterly protection and full-on bossiness than anything else."

I gazed into his deep green eyes. He was either doing an Oscar-winning performance or there was sincere emotion in his voice as he talked of his past. Somehow, I doubted he was able to do that very often.

"I didn't know Gabby was your sister," I commented,

rather surprised. I actually felt quite honoured that Lionel's sister had taken the time to care for me – that is, if you can describe drumming me into shape in her rather rough way as "caring."

"Not blood sister," Lionel explained. "But sister in every other sense. She's my adoptive parents' biological daughter. They adopted me when she was fourteen, and instead of being jealous of the fact she had to learn to share her parents' attention with me, she was the one who most lavished affection on me. Sometimes I think they adopted me more for her than for themselves."

Together we fell silent for a while. Lionel, subconsciously or not, was letting me into his persona, and I, like it or not, realised I was falling for him.

Our moment of peace was suddenly interrupted as the fishing line bent dramatically. Lionel called out, "There's our dinner…" and jumped to his feet, beer flying, as he grabbed hold of the fishing rod and started to reel in the line in quick motions. The fish, at the other end of the line, put up an impressive fight, battling away as it tried to break free, and for a moment I thought Lionel would be pulled overboard. With one last mighty heave the fish was out of the water. As soon as it emerged Lionel called in a fraught voice, "Quick Chantelle, cut the line…"

Swiftly I was by his side, knife in hand, and as I took one last look at the massive porpoise as it flashed and thrashed, I slashed at the line and successfully cut it. Lionel fell backwards, knocking me down with him as the huge and beautiful blue and silver porpoise plummeted back into the ocean. Slightly winded from the fall I found myself sprawled on the deck floor, entwined with Lionel, both of us tangled in the fishing line. I could feel Lionel's heart thumping away under my touch as I tried to unravel us from the line. My hands trembled, and I knew it had nothing to do with the shock of falling backwards.

I could feel his penetrating gaze as he searched my face but I couldn't bring myself to make eye contact. Falling for Robbie had been one thing, but falling for Lionel was a whole different ball game.

"You OK?" he asked, his voice apprehensive. I nodded in reply and sat back, having finally untangled us from the line.

"I think we'll just make a little change to tonight's menu." Lionel managed to maintain the humour in his voice. "How about some good old spaghetti?"

"Sounds good to me," I replied, laughing.

I was relieved that he laughed, too.

***

The remainder of the day was spent lazing around the yacht deck. It was surprising really how much we had in common, considering we led totally different lifestyles. What was more surprising was how totally at ease I felt in his company, at least, when he was that one metre out of reach. Any closer and I felt myself plummet into turmoil by his powerful masculinity. Lionel, too, seemed to prefer keeping a slight distance, and was careful not to cross the imaginary boundary that had come up between us since we'd both been sent sprawling to the floor during our fishing escapade.

Dusk had long ago settled and dinner was well and truly digested as we both stood over the railings gazing at the shimmering dark Pacific water below as it lapped softly against the boat side. The moon, which cast a silver path across the dark ocean, was our only company.

"I dare you to jump in," I said recklessly. Despite the darkness it did look welcoming, and I rather fancied going in myself.

"Only if you come in with me," he challenged, and before I knew it he was stripped down and on the other side of the railings, but wearing shorts this time. He did a back-flip into the water. I followed suit, prudishly keeping on my improvised bikini-underwear.

The water was remarkably warm. I flipped onto my back and stretched my legs and arms out floating in the swaying salty water as I gazed up into the starlit sky. The view was just spectacular; there were sparkling stars all around and they seemed so close that I felt if I just reached out I could touch them. I sensed Lionel position himself near me in the bobbing surf and look, too, at the illuminated sky above. I wish I could always feel this peaceful and exultant, and as the thought crossed my mind, a shooting star flashed across the sky and I was aware that the last time I'd seen a shooting star Lionel had also been by my side.

"I hope it comes true." Lionel whispered softly beside me.

"You hope what comes true?" I asked, my own voice hushed in the stillness.

"Whatever it is you wished for." Lionel answered.

I wondered what he'd wished for.

We remained in the water until we had both grown cold. I was shivering as I climbed aboard and Lionel was quick to wrap a large towelling bathrobe around me.

"On warm summer nights like this I always sleep out on deck," Lionel said, as he rolled out a large mattress onto the floor and threw down some pillows and several blankets. "But feel free to use any of the cabins beds," he added, as he settled down on one side of the mattress.

Oh, just wonderful, I thought. He might as well have called out "Checkmate," because whichever move I made now, I was lost. If I settled down beside him he'd automatically think he'd sussed it for a one-night-stand, but if I disappeared into one of the cabins he'd think I was a right strait-laced cow.

I turned towards the ocean and paused for quite a while, gazing into the dark night around me, battling in my mind as to why it would be so bad for me to have a one-night fling with Lionel. As I stood undecided in the still night, breathing in the ocean spray, a very slight night breeze caressing my hair, I was suddenly aware of snorting noises coming from behind me. I turned, rather alarmed, and saw that Lionel had fallen fast asleep and was snoring away. I felt slightly guilty, and also humiliated, that Lionel had innocently fallen asleep whilst I dallied over his assumed indecent proposal.

Mind you, I had gone and done just the same thing the night before. I had to stifle a giggle: leave me alone with the hottest guy on the planet, and all we can come up with is a sleeping contest! I covered him with one of the blankets and sat beside him for a while. His snoring hushed as he rolled onto his side, his arm fell across my waist and I could feel my heart thump away at his touch. Was he really sleeping? Pushing all thoughts out of my mind I lay back on the mattress and arranged another of the blankets around me. This was pretty tricky, with Lionel's arm firmly holding me down.

Finally settled, I sighed deeply, smiled to myself and closed my eyes.

Chapter Nine

The following morning, as the sun's rays warmed the new day, I stirred awake, aware that Lionel's arm was still around me. I turned to face him and sleepily he opened his eyes. On seeing me at his side he smiled boyishly, captivatingly so, and with a slightly hoarse voice whispered, "Good morning, Princess," and placed a tender kiss on my forehead, before he sat up, as if it was the most natural thing in the world. So natural, and so chaste, that I didn't know what to make of it all.

We were soon back in the speedboat and shooting along the ocean's surface to return to the film location, though I would have much preferred to remain on the yacht. I sat without the blindfold this time and watched Gigi as she raced alongside the speedboat escorting us part of the way back.

Lionel and I remained silent. I was trying to get my thoughts and emotions under control and into some comparative order. Lionel, meanwhile, just seemed distracted. As we sailed into the bay there was something about it that looked familiar, though I couldn't put my finger on it. The pathway that led to the helicopter pad also seemed recognisable, but I didn't give it much thought. I was more concerned with the turmoil in my heart. There was something about Lionel that captivated me, and it had nothing to do with the fact that he reminded me so much of Robbie. Moreover, I had no intention of falling for a Hollywood playboy. It was too risky for me to fall head over heels for someone like Lionel, who wouldn't just be capable of breaking my heart in two, he would smash it to pieces. I had no intention of putting myself through that ordeal, so as I climbed into the helicopter I decided that as soon as I was given some days off

I would return to London to see if, away from Lionel and the manic movie mayhem, I could sort myself out.

It was late afternoon by the time I was finally alone and back inside my caravan. Sandy, I'd been told, would return the following day. Feeling exhausted and as if I hadn't slept for weeks, which was quite ironic considering all I'd done over the greater part of the last two days was just that, I went to bed early. Just as I'd closed my eyes, trying rather unsuccessfully to push from my mind all thoughts of Lionel, Robbie and Tammy, there was a loud rap on the main door. Carefully I picked my way through the dimmed caravan, stubbing my big toe into the kitchen table as I went. I cursed out loud as I cracked open the door to see who it was, half-expecting to find Lionel standing there. But to my surprise I found myself face-to-face with the director.

"How're you feeling?" he asked politely.

"Fine." I answered back warily.

"It's your big day tomorrow, sweetie, so go get your beauty sleep. I want you in for hair and makeup at 0600 hours and on set by 0800 hours. OK!" It was a statement rather than a question, and I nodded my head submissively.

"But don't you have to give me a script to follow or a scene to read or something?" I stuttered, not believing that this is how movie scenes were filmed, with absolutely no preparation whatsoever. I mean, come on, there was too much money involved.

"Not when Lionel's the lead guy," he said, as he turned and walked off. "Now get some sleep, there's a good girl!"

Left in a total fluster, I swore again. Christ knows how he thinks I'm going to sleep now!! Somehow, though, I did sleep, and the following day came around all too quickly.

***

I was too nervous to eat breakfast the following morning and turned up for hair and make-up right on the dot, the deep-seated roots of British punctuality not letting me down. I did wonder what they planned to do to me at the hair and make-up department that would take a whole two hours; they obviously thought I was in desperate need of assistance to be allocated so much of their time. The moment I walked through the doors into the powder and paint unit they were onto me like parasites. My hair was washed and re-washed, then blow-dried until it shone silky straight, with not one little kink remaining. Having bitten my nails off through pure nerves during the first stunt scene I'd witnessed, I was put through the torment of having false nails stuck on, bright red ones at that, and dead long. Not the slightest bit practical. How on earth will I be able to do my buttons up?

My toenails were painted the same blood-red colour. Paint was also plastered all over my face, though I've got to admit I liked the final result. Very natural. They'd done something wonderful with the eye-liner that made my honey eyes look like huge almonds, and I made a mental note to sweet-talk the lady who did my face make-up into revealing her tricks of the trade.

Hair, face and nails finally done, then came the moment I'd dreaded: the reason I was here.

I was told to strip and step into the tiniest skin-coloured g-string you could possible imagine.

"I don't think that's going to cover me very much." I said, trying to joke my way through the situation, but inside I was panicking like crazy. Christ, this is it.

I'd got my first nude sex scene coming up, and I felt a whole army of butterflies doing back-flips in my belly. I was thankful I hadn't had breakfast. I could feel the previous year's worth of food coming up in a monumental attack of nausea.

Starkers, except for the microscopic g-string, I stood in the middle of a brightly-lit cubicle and had fine body-paint sprayed all over me, leaving me evenly tanned and slightly glowing with golden star dust. I was left some ten minutes to fully dry and was then wrapped in a soft towelling bathrobe (very like the one I'd used on Lionel's yacht just two days earlier), and escorted to the set.

The day's shoot was to take place in the large barn I'd

seen from a distance on my first day on location. It was brightly lit and divided into several sections. I was guided to the far side of the barn amazed that my shaking legs hadn't packed up on me and that I'd actually made it, so far, on my own two feet. It was eight o'clock on the dot and Lionel was already there, together with the director, Freddy G and several camera crew. My guide, who was the lady who'd done wonders with the eye make-up, stayed with me. I couldn't bring myself to look at Lionel. I was furious with him for not having warned me, or prepared me for this moment.

It was, in addition, the first time ever that I was immensely relieved that both my parents had passed away. If Mum had been alive, the notion that her daughter was to earn money by doing naked sex scenes – semi-porn if you like – would have been enough to knock her off. And as for my dad, well, he would have just hit the roof!

And honestly, why on earth waste time and money on me to do these scenes, when there were thousands of body extras to choose from who had experience and training? I really did feel very sick and faint with the whole notion of what I had let myself in for. Was it worth it for a million dollars?

I could feel Lionel's piercing eyes on me as I approached, but still I refused to look at him. Evidently not blind to the fact I was inwardly fuming and utterly flustered at the same time, he called out in his clear confident voice, "Ladies, gentlemen, would you please leave us for a moment?"

The barn emptied and I was left alone with Lionel. We stood in silence for what seemed like an eternity before Lionel took my hand and gently guided me over towards a bed, which in my earlier state of panic I hadn't noticed but which I now took in with alarm. It was a huge king-sized bed covered in white silk, and a mosquito net hung amorously around it.

"I realise you're angry at me," he hushed smoothly.

That was a slight understatement. I was livid.

"And I'm aware I should have warned you yesterday, or the day before when we were together, that today we were starting the filming of these scenes," he continued. "But I didn't want to risk ruining the magic we had out there on the yacht. I've never felt that peaceful and happy in years, perhaps ever, so please don't be angry with me despite my selfishness at not wanting to break that harmony. And, believe me, shooting bedroom scenes isn't all that bad. But if you really can't bear the thought of going ahead with it, tell me now and I'll understand."

He tenderly reached out and lifted my chin in order to raise my eyes to meet his. I gazed into his deep emerald eyes at a loss for words. Lionel sweet-talking me didn't make things any easier. In fact his penetrating gaze and soft affectionate words left me in an even greater shambles.

"Do you trust me?"

I was aware that he'd asked this of me before, prior to leading me blindfolded into the Pacific, prior to spending the best two days I'd ever known, and was I aware that this was the main reason for my hesitation.

It wasn't that I didn't trust him. I just didn't fancy having my heart broken and stampeded over.

***

After I'd finally agreed to remain on set, Lionel disappeared, and I was left alone perched on the edge of the king-sized bed. The illumination dimmed slightly and the make-up lady who had escorted me over re-appeared.

"How're you feeling, honey?" she asked me as she moved over.

"Nervous," I replied honestly.

"You'll be fine. Lionel knows what he's doing. Just follow his lead, OK. Lionel's told the director that he wants this scene as natural as possible, so just follow your instinct."

I nodded meekly. Could that instinct include walking off the set?

"The sooner we start, the sooner we finish. So just step

out of your robe, sugar, and I'll position you on the bed."

Trying to keep my shaking hands under control I untied the bathrobe, and my ally, the make-up lady, slipped it from me. I then lay face down on the bed, under her instructions, and she pulled the silk sheet partly over me, leaving most of my behind uncovered. She then spread my hair out along the feathered pillow and positioned my arms, one alongside me, the other stretched out. By the time she'd finished I had, amazingly, stopped shaking, and just before she walked off she said comfortingly, "Just pretend you're fast asleep, honey. And if you need anything just call me. I'm Hannah, by the way."

The lights dimmed even more and I closed my eyes. I could hear slight shuffling coming from somewhere nearby, but, all in all, it was almost possible to imagine I was alone.

I remained motionless for some time before I was faintly aware that someone had sat on the bed, as the mattress gave slightly. I knew it was Lionel. I could smell his cologne just as I could the day he'd blindfolded me to take me out to sea. I sensed him lean towards me as he gently shifted his body weight. He paused slightly before he tenderly brushed my cheek with his hand. I remained still, eyes closed, acutely aware of Lionel who then ran his hand gently through my long hair and caressed my back in sensual butterfly strokes. By this point he was lying beside me and casually, almost as if without meaning to, he ran his hand down my side, which was closest to him. He repeated the caress but this time his hand lingered on the curve of my breast.

Blimey... A girl's got her limits, and at this rate I wasn't sure I could remain still for much longer. Hand still teasing my breast he leaned forward and kissed me gently at first on the lips. He playfully nipped my lower lip as he firmly turned me over. He continued to kiss me, passionately, his tongue teasing open my mouth, and I felt a wave of dizziness come over me. Instinctively, I ran my hands through his hair, holding him to me as he continued his exploration down my neck with quick teasing nips. Just as he got level with my breasts the director called:

"CUT!"

Lionel let out a faint groan of irritation. At least I imagined it was him; it could equally well have been me, having been brought down to earth with a bump on hearing the director interrupt us. In fact, he continued to call out instructions, and it was a while before I focused on what he was saying.

"OK," the director continued. "That's good. Lionel, this is when you hear an explosion from outside and you both dive to the ground. But Crystal can do that, we'll just wrap the sheet around her to hide her fat backside. Darling," (turning to me) "you were great. We'll just shoot some more angles of you lying face down on the bed and a couple of the two of you just before you turn her around, Lionel. OK?"

Hannah hustled over to re-position me as I tried to slow my thundering heart. But Lionel seemed as in control as ever, and I realised that he, used to doing this type of scene, wasn't affected in the slightest. I lay as still as I could on the soft feathered bed while the cameraman took close-ups of my behind from every angle possible. Firstly by myself, and then with Lionel lying by me gently fingering my hair and back. It was like undergoing torture, and it was music to my ears when the director finally called, "CUT! That's great folks. We'll call that a wrap."

Hannah was by my side in a shot, like a maiden chaperone, with my bathrobe. Just as I was safely into it, the director approached me with an approving smile.

"Wonderful. Same time tomorrow, kid."

With that he gave me a pert pat on my backside and I hurried off the set, Hannah at my heels. I wasn't going to allow Lionel the chance to detain me, even had it been his intention.

My mind was going a thousand to one as I hurried to the make-up department with Hannah shadowing me. Despite her reassuring words as to how good I'd been, I was in a turmoil. I found it quite perversely amusing that I was congratulated on how "natural" I'd acted. Of course I'd acted natural. It was natural. I couldn't have been more turned on in my life.

Inwardly though, I was fuming. I realised then that Lionel had had it all under control. The whole yacht number had been part of his plot to woo me, to captivate me so much that by the time it came around to do the nude bit I was gagging for it, whereas he, the trained and talented actor, just breezed through the scene as if he was going for a Sunday morning stroll. I realised that Lionel had no feelings for me whatsoever other than using me to get his film shot. What's more, I still had the following day to get through, and God knows how many more scenes after that, until I was free to return home.

Well, for the following day, and the other days, I'd be ready for him. We'll see who out-performs whom!

***

The next morning I was on the set at eight o'clock on the dot, head held high as I walked over to where Lionel and the director were standing. I looked Lionel straight in the eye and flashed him a curt smile before turning to the director for the basic instructions on the breakdown of the scene. Directions understood, I positioned myself and waited for the magic words.

"ACTION!" the director called. I was ready.

With my back to the camera I seductively let slip to the floor the towel I had around me and with a slight sway of my hips moved to a shower and let the water run, bending over slightly as I tested its warmth. As I stepped into the shower cubicle I pulled the see-through shower curtain across and let the water cascade over me in warm rivulets. I lifted my face towards the showerhead and lifted my arms to push my damp hair back from my moist forehead. I remained poised, facing upwards, for some time before I sensed rather than heard Lionel step into the shower with me.

His arms came around my waist as he tenderly kissed my neck. I closed my eyes and leaned my head back against him. His hands slowly wandered down and I felt him playfully tug at the virtually non-existent panties I'd been given to put on (not that you would wear panties in the shower, transparent as they were to the camera lens, they were used as a sort of optional prop for decency which Lionel wasn't respecting). If he pulls any harder, I thought, he'll snap the delicate material. I also thought that if his hand wandered any lower I was quite within my rights to turn around and slap him. Or knee him in the balls, which would have been my preferred option.

As if reading my mind, he let go of my insubstantial slip and slowly trailed a line upwards until he cupped both of my breasts in his hands. Tantalizingly he traced his fingers in light circles around my nipples until they hardened, whilst he continued to playfully tease my earlobe with his soft tongue. Battling to keep my emotions in check, I was aware that I was tingling all over. Not even the barely lukewarm water was doing any good at cooling me off. He ran a trail of quivering butterfly kisses across my cheek until he lingered on my lips, gently at first he pressed his lips to mine and then as if unable to hold back any longer he turned me roughly so that we faced each other under the tumbling water and he kissed me passionately as if his life depended on it.

I returned his desire. I leaned against the shower wall and hooked my leg around him, clasping him close. One of his hands remained pinching my inflamed nipple whilst his other hand moved down the hollow of my back. Lionel lingered on the delicate slip I had on before he slipped his hand below, down between my two firm, rounded bum cheeks. I continued to kiss him back passionately, not wanting him to stop, aware, under a surge of giddiness, that I was not the only one fully aroused. I could feel his member hard against my thigh as he pressed himself to me.

I could faintly hear someone calling out, but under the falling water and my intense fervour, it was some time before I realised that the director was yelling:

"CUT!!"

Glad that I was the one to hear the order first, I firmly

pushed Lionel away. As if totally under control, I said, "Sunshine, cut's been called." And, with that, I casually stepped out of the shower and into the bathrobe loyal Hannah had ready for me.

"That was great, guys," continued the director. "There's no need for a re-take."

I was inwardly disappointed at this, as, surprisingly, I was getting quite into the swing of doing these steamy sex scenes. More importantly, I felt I'd got even with Lionel this time around. I left him to cool off in the shower whilst I nonchalantly walked off.

"Honey, you're a star," continued the director, taking me to one side. "You've got a couple more scenes next week, and then it'll all be done and dusted. You're a natural, babe," he added, with his familiar pat on my bum. So I've been told, I thought, quick to move off the set, well aware that I wasn't ready to face Lionel so soon after so much ardour. The passion was still playing havoc with my insides and I didn't want to give myself away. I might be told I'm a natural actress, but I knew that Lionel could read between the lines.

When I arrived back at the caravan later I gave strict instructions to Sandy not to let anyone in to disturb me, unless, of course, it was the director. I had a feeling Lionel would pop over, and I had no intention of letting him smooth-talk me, especially as he did it so well. My intuition was spot on as later that evening there was a firm rap on the entrance to the caravan. I quickly moved into the bedroom as Sandy turned to open the door. I could hear Lionel's familiar tone and my heart starting pounding nervously. It didn't matter how hard I tried to check my emotions, Lionel had an uncontrollable pull on me, which seemed to get stronger with each passing day.

His voice faded, and the caravan door shut once again. A moment later Sandy peeped into the bedroom, where I was sitting on my bed casually trying to skim through a copy of *Vogue*.

"I told him you were out," she said, as she sat beside me. She gently patted my knee as if I was a small child in need of comfort. Which, in a way, was how I felt.

"He looked kinda concerned," Sandy added. "I know it's none of my business, but I've worked with Lionel before and I've known him for years. And, well, he's OK you know. He's a genuine guy who doesn't fool around, and I think he really cares for you."

I remained silent, surprised at her observation and also privately thrilled by it. Sandy paused a while longer before adding, "Anyway, as I said, it's none of my business, but I just thought you'd feel a bit better if I told you."

A weak smile curved my lips and Sandy playfully knocked me with her shoulder. "That's it girl, you're so much prettier when you smile."

"Thanks Sandy," I said back. "You know, you're OK too." I rolled my shoulder and bumped her back.

***

The following days passed in a whirl. Each morning I joined the crew on the daily location and enjoyed watching the proceedings of each take. The shooting of the movie was coming to an end, and the cast seemed to pick up somewhat knowing that soon they would be back in California.

Lionel, meanwhile, kept his distance and avoided being alone with me at all costs. I realised it was what I'd wanted, but was conscious, too, how much I missed his company. The abrupt cooling between Lionel and me was for the best, I convinced myself, and as soon as I returned to LA I planned to take some time off before the next project Freddy G had lined up for me, and recover from all the movie mayhem by going back home to London. I really missed Tammy, and the idea that she was dating Robbie was no longer a concern.

Towards the end of the following week I waltzed through my last two scenes, shooting them both on the same day. They were solo scenes and much easier to pull off than those shot with Lionel, especially as they were less of a strain on my emotions. The scenes were sequential; in the course of the first I had to strip slowly in the half-light of the bedroom.

My character's lover (or rather, Crystal's character's lover – I was only her body double, after all) had abandoned her in his attempt to save the world, as only occurs in typical Hollywood action films. And so, sadly, she/I undressed whilst silently pining for him.

"Great, sugar," was all the director could say as I seductively took and re-took off my clothes in several takes. I was thankful that we weren't filming in the middle of winter, as my tits would have frozen off by the second take. I also pondered whether or not the director actually knew my name; what with "sugar," "honey," "sweetie" etc, I sounded like I belonged on the Pick & Mix range.

During the second scene I had to remain poised on the bed for several seconds as if asleep, then slowly stir and stretch out my arm across the mattress. Realising I was alone, I silently sat up and then moved over to the moonlit window and pensively gazed out – whilst the cameraman took every feasible angle of my lower body.

Remarkably, by the end of this lot of filming, I felt relatively comfortable standing nude in front of so many people. What got me through the scenes was my belief that my face wouldn't be exposed on the film. No one would actually know it was me, so I acted with total freedom, letting go of all inhibitions.

The day following my final shoot, Freddy G said that he would be returning to LA that very afternoon and would be taking me back with him. I felt rather reluctant to leave, though I was aware that the others would be following shortly after. So, with Sandy's words of "See you at the cast party," I was whipped into one of the sand jeeps and rocketed across the desert terrain in a mighty scary ride with Freddy G at the wheel.

Never again will I step into the passenger seat with Freddy G, I declared to myself, as I shakily got down from the jeep forty minutes later feeling I'd just been on a two-hour roller coaster ride. Hair all askew I climbed aboard the private jet and tried to relax on the brief flight despite the continuous turbulence. What with Freddy G's maniac driving and the rocky flight, I felt awful, and was sick in Gabby's 4x4 as she drove us back to the cottage, much to her distain and to my mortification. I left a nasty, sickly pong inside the vehicle, and I was sure she'd have me up at three in the morning to get her own back for this.

But Gabby didn't have me up at three in the morning the following day. Amazingly, she actually let me have a lie-in, which was obviously what I desperately needed as I didn't stir until 2 pm. She had, as of habit, let herself in, and sat waiting patiently for me in the lounge, a large salad lunch prepared for me. Gone were the freshly-baked rolls and pizzas, I realised. I sighed. Some things never change.

Chapter Ten

The next couple of weeks passed in a paradise of serenity –
that is, if you overlooked the compulsory morning runs and
low-fat diet. I spent the first few days lazing around the
garden flicking leisurely through glossy fashion magazines,
or amiably strolling along the beach at dusk. I felt like I was
on holiday. But this soon changed when Gabby announced
that the whole movie crew had "elected" me to organise the
cast party – with her help, of course. Finally, the great day
arrived, and I was buzzing. I even managed to out-sprint
Gabby up the garden path, much to her surprise. Gabby and I
had done a lot of work for the party and I think we both
proudly felt that it was our personal creation.

The party was to be held at the main house. I had the
swimming pool decorated with floating candles, and there
was a huge flower arrangement right in the middle on a
buoyant pad tied to the sides by invisible cord. The lawn was
decked with tables and chairs for the buffet dinner, and I had
used a colour scheme of blue, peach, pink and yellow to
harmonize the outdoor furniture with balloons of the same
shades, which hung from every tree. Large candleholders
were spiked into the soft ground to illuminate the night when
the sun had set.

I'd personally spoken with the catering team to organize
the menu. I deliberately didn't let Gabby near the food list, as
she would've swiped off at least three-quarters of the menu in
horror, but I did request a generous amount of salad varieties,
stir-fry vegetables and low-fat desserts to keep her happy. I
selected Mexican tortillas, risotto dishes such as almond and
lemon pilaf and sesame millet with pan-fried courgettes,
asparagus and avocado cream. I organised veggie dishes of

couscous with spiced tofu and mixed pepper sauce, red bean and lentil chilli, griddled courgette quiche with pine nuts, leek and feta parcels, and artichoke and red pepper *gougère*. For the non-vegetarians I chose sushi, together with dark-red mottled lobsters, pale pink poached salmon and seafood salads of squid and octopus. As a surprise for the American crew I ordered up good old English shepherd's pie as well as fine roast beef to be served cold, a wide selection of cheeses and generous amount of cold hams.

I really let myself go on the desert selection too, which was a real treat after Gabby's constant calorie-counting. I ordered apple cake with maple syrup and lemon, raisin and almond flapjack, apricot lattice, ricotta cheesecake, fruit pavlova, lemon wedges and my all-time favourite: chocolate mousse.

To keep Gabby happy I put her in charge of organising the drinks. I think she was quite bemused at finding herself being bossed around by me, but I loved it – not just bossing her around, though I admit that was fun after all she'd put me through, rather the whole organisation of the affair. It was as if I'd been dormant and had ultimately revived with the thrill of getting everything coordinated to perfection.

I got to know the musicians, a four-piece band who would entertain us with a little light jazz throughout the meal, then subtly swing things up a touch to get people up and dancing. I had that allocated off to the right of the lawn beside the private terrace and Italian garden. I just prayed the weather would hold, because I had no Plan B except to have everyone leg it into the stately home. And, civilised as we all were, I just knew that the house would get trashed if the crew were turned loose in there.

The day passed agonizingly slowly. I toiled over painting my fingernails and toenails in an attempt to kill time, though all I managed was to get the varnish smudged on my fingertips. But I was too excited to care. I wanted to dash up to the main house to supervise the final preparations, but Gabby had strictly forbidden me to do so. Finally there came a point, however, when I didn't care anymore about her

94

instructions – I just had to see for myself that all was operating efficiently.

I skipped up the path that led to the main house and pushed hard on the dividing gate, which, to my disbelief, didn't budge. It was locked. What a cow, I thought. Gabby was obviously behind my imprisonment. She'd evidently sussed that I'd get so excited that I wouldn't pay any attention to her orders. Not intending to be thwarted by the locked gate, however, I looked for a possible way to climb over, and as I did so I came across a slip of paper that was pinned to the side of the dividing fence. It was addressed to *Chantelle.*

I tore the scroll open. The handwriting wasn't familiar and I instantly knew that it wasn't from Gabby.

My Dearest Chantelle;

If I know you like I think I do, you'll be reading these words, as you would have attempted to cross the gate to supervise the final preparations. I've been told that you've done a magnificent job in the organisation of the whole affair and from what I've witnessed during the course of the day, tonight will be the best planned fiesta ever held at the main house. Believe me when I say RELAX, everything is under control.

I cannot wait to see you later tonight, please reserve a dance for your loyal servant;

Lionel.

P.S: Look under the switch for the sprinklers.

The paper fluttered in my shaking hands. As much as I tried to pretend otherwise, I was thrilled at the thought of seeing Lionel again, and this letter from him sent me into a state of jittering nerves. I'd originally intended to try to avoid Lionel that evening, and during future events, in order to protect my heart. Now, however, I was rapidly changing my mind.

I dashed across the cottage garden toward the sprinkler switch and rummaged around. There, partially hidden and wrapped in delicate silver foil, was a rather large gift box.

95

Unable to stop my heart thumping, I tore the wrapping off and opened it.

Inside, on a red velvet cushion, was a pair of blazing diamond chandelier earrings. I almost keeled over on the spot.

I was aware that the gift was far too expensive to accept without losing my dignity. I mean, my mother had taught me that nice girls didn't take jewellery from men just like that. But after mooning my backside to a movie camera crew for days, plus knowing that images of me naked would shortly be exposed to the whole wide world, I figured I didn't have much dignity left over to fuss about. So, titanic chandeliers in hand, I zipped back into my wooden château (as I liked to call my flashy accommodation) and proceeded to try on the earrings in front of the bedroom's full-length mirror. Earrings in place, I swished my hair from side to side admiring how the diamonds sparkled in the light. They'd be as good as torches on a dark night.

I removed the precious stones from my ear lobes and placed them safely on the dressing table for later that evening and re-read Lionel's note, which I then hid safely under my pillow in a daft bout of romanticism.

The magnificent gift had sidetracked me, somewhat, and it was after reading the note a second time that I twigged that Lionel was not only back in LA but had also been at the main house that morning. That he'd stood right outside the cottage not so long ago and I would be seeing him later on that evening. Where did he live? What was his house like? Would he ever take me there?

I also realised that I felt truly, madly, deeply for the guy and that not even wild horses could curb my emotions. Finally admitting to myself what had probably been obvious and inevitable from the start was a real weight off my shoulders. I wasn't going to play any juvenile games this evening and if he offered to take me back to his place for the night, I would ignore all my parents' (God bless them) good upbringing and words of wisdom.

***

It was nine o'clock. Gabby would arrive at any moment to escort me up to the main house. I glanced at myself one more time in the full-length mirror. Gabby's military routine and the beauty sessions had done wonders. I almost didn't recognise the girl in the mirror. My long dark hair cascaded down my back in a cloud of silky waves, I wore it swept back from my oval face, which had lost the slight puppy roundness I'd always had, and I realised I actually had high, slanting cheekbones. My honey-coloured eyes against my golden tan shone bright like huge liquid almonds, thickly lashed (thanks to my Max Factor mascara, and, of course, Hannah's tips). I had generous lips that had always been Tammy's envy. The look was completed by the shining diamonds, which I admired and tenderly reached to caress with my hands, as they glinted from my ears. I half-turned in front of the mirror and craned my head around to view myself from that angle. I wore a cream-coloured lace dress that hugged my figure showing off my curved breasts and, of course, what I got paid to flaunt: my high, petite, rounded rear. My million-dollar asset.

But despite the sexy image that was reflected back at me, I was in a state of nerves. At the end of the day, behind the make-up and expensive clothing and diamonds, I was still just simple Chantelle Rose from South London. I felt way out of my league, and deep down, I also felt that Lionel King was way out of my range.

Gabby finally called for me some twenty minutes late, which for her was totally out of character. So, of course, I'd started panicking that the catering staff hadn't shown up or that the musicians had copped out.

"Everything is under control," Gabby was quick to say, on seeing my alarm- stricken face. She was clothed in a softly flowing emerald dress that exposed the whole of her back. It was the first time I'd actually seen Gabby out of sports gear, and she looked remarkable. Indeed, she looked more human in her elegant attire than in her daily sportswear

97

when she often looked intimidating and slightly scary. I wondered for the first time if she was married or had kids. She'd literally thrown herself into becoming my shadow since I'd arrived, so that I'd just assumed she was single and desperately bored.

We crossed through the dividing gate together. Already the garden was milling with guests.

"Looking as amazing as you do," Gabby whispered to me as we moved together up the path, "it would be a sin not to make a late entry. You are going to be the Belle of the Ball, despite Crystal Lee being here, and all the other rich and famous. Mark my words, kid, tonight is gonna be your night."

There was genuine pride in Gabby's voice, which wasn't really surprising considering she'd played such an important role into moulding me into the figure at her side.

There was a hush as Gabby and I approached the main circle of guests who were standing close to the pool. Everyone turned to stare at me. That, and the silence that enveloped the group, was almost enough to send me scampering back down the pathway. I was rescued, thankfully, by my tennis partner Ken as he took me by the arm and led me towards the bar area.

"You rock, Miss Chantelle," he declared.

"Why, thank you, Ken," I sweetly replied. "You're not so bad yourself," and leaned heavily on his arm for support. Despite the mass of people around I'd caught sight of Vivien Francis glaring at me, her face a mask of pure loathing. Her eyes looked slightly glazed, too, I noticed, as I moved past her, and I was also aware that she swayed somewhat and wondered how much she'd drunk. I'd a horrible feeling she was going to scream abuse at me and cause a scene. She remained silent, but her look of hatred intensified as it seemed she'd become aware of the diamond earrings which flashed in the evening sunshine. With her knife-like glare stabbing my back I escaped to the bar and ordered a double martini.

Martini in hand, I did the rounds checking all was top-notch. I felt like the lady of the manor as I glided from one select group of guests to the next. Those who knew I was behind the "wonderful" organisation congratulated me and I just glowed with pride. Others congratulated me on how "fantastic" I looked, which made me blush with embarrassment, especially as the majority of the comments were directed to my bosom rather than my face. Having swept over the party area checking it all out, I was acutely aware that Lionel was nowhere to be seen. Close to an hour had passed since I'd made my appearance, and if mine had been a late entry, then Lionel was on the verge of being a much-lamented "no show."

Refusing to let him spoil the evening, I downed my second double martini and, chocolate mousse in hand, made my way over to the dance area where several members of the cast, including Sandy, had gathered. Gabby soon joined us and we got a bit of boogying going to Eurhythmics' *Sisters are doin' it for themselves*. I was really warming up, thanks to the generous helpings of martini, when the lights on the dance floor suddenly dimmed and a low murmur came from the musicians' corner.

Silence came over the guests like a blanket, and a totally different melody started from the darkened stage. I had the name of the song on the tip of my tongue. So concerned was I with placing the tune that I was unaware that a spotlight had been focused on me and that the voice that sung was familiar. Blinded by the light I could just make out a silhouetted figure move in my direction. I remained rooted to the spot as the crowd around opened up to let the figure approach. My pulse quickened. It was Lionel.

For some reason I was surprised to find that he could actually sing really well. I identified the melody, *My Girl,* as he embraced me with one arm, the other holding the microphone. He gazed deep into my eyes as he held me tight and swung me around. I followed his lead, oblivious of those around, so much so that as the tune slowed to a finish, I was caught unawares by the clapping that followed.

Someone whisked the microphone away from Lionel's

hand and he held me close for the next slow song.

"Sorry for arriving so late, I was dealing with an uninvited guest," he whispered to me as we swung around on the dance floor. I wondered if he meant Vivien, as I hadn't come across her again during the course of the evening, and I doubted she would have witnessed Lionel's romantic performance in polite silence.

"You are by far the most beautiful lady here tonight," Lionel continued, murmuring softly into my ear as he then tenderly kissed my ear lobe right beside the flashing diamond.

"These earrings belonged to my mother, and her grandmother before her, and now I want you to have them."

I stepped back a pace bewildered, and looked him straight in the eyes. I might have lost my principles in filming nude scenes, but I still had my tact and discretion. I couldn't possibly accept a family heirloom that was worth a small fortune. The earrings belonged to Gabby, or to Lionel's future wife. And it was far too ridiculous to even imagine that he might be considering marrying me.

But before I was able to reply, I heard a horrific commotion coming from the house veranda.

"*THAT FUCKING HUSSY…*" screeched out over the music, which, giving credit where credit is due, was quite an achievement.

Everyone around, including the band, paused in silence. Then, before I knew it, red-faced, big-busted Vivien hove into sight. Black mascara ran down her face, which was turning blotchy pink and white, and I wasn't sure if it was a reaction to the alcohol she'd consumed or from the fact that she'd obviously been crying. I actually felt sorry for her and remembered my vow to be kind to her, but my good intentions disappeared in an instant as she charged towards me like a maddened bull.

"*THOSE DIAMONDS ARE MINE YOU BITCH!*" she screamed.

Vivien was just a scary couple of metres away from me and I found myself transfixed. I could see her neck veins bulge in rage. Then swiftly, but as if in slow motion, I saw Gabby step into the firing line and slap Vivien sharply across the face as, at the same time, Vivien hurtled her handbag through the air. It knocked me smack on my forehead and sent me sprawling backwards onto the lawn.

I lay flat on the grass for what seemed an eternity, more from the shock of being smacked across the head with a curiously heavy handbag than by the actual injury. She must have put a rock or something in that bag before hurling it at me.

In a flash, Lionel was down on his knees by me.

"Honey, are you alright?"

I meekly nodded my head.

"Just get that lunatic out of here." I wasn't too sure if I said it aloud or not, but Gabby took firm hold of Vivien and roughly marched her out.

Slowly, with Lionel supporting me, I got to my feet and hobbled down the pathway that led to the cottage. When Lionel and I reached the dividing gate, I turned to him and looked him straight in the eye. His intense green eyes were deep with concern. I felt so confused. At one moment I'd been happily dancing in his arms, the next I was under attack from his ex. Vivien had declared that the earrings I'd proudly worn throughout the evening were, in fact, hers. For all I knew (and for all I cared), she might have been telling the truth. Who was to know if Lionel had whispered the same words to her as he'd done to me, offering the family heirloom to Vivien in a moment of passion as he had offered them to me tonight? Was this a final attempt to win me over and woo me into his bed?

I inwardly laughed at Lionel's possible foolishness, for he'd won me over the first evening we'd sat together in the Nevada desert. He'd made me laugh when I was down. He'd won me then, I realised, despite my infatuation at the time with Robbie. I'd fallen for him weeks ago, and not even all the diamonds in the world could have made me desire him more. Money and riches didn't mean anything to me. But at this moment, head throbbing, party trashed, I just wanted to be alone.

"Lionel," I said and I knew my voice sounded sad, "I'm not going to be good company right this minute. I would really appreciate it if you just joined your other guests and got the party going again so that this evening doesn't turn into a complete shambles. We can meet tomorrow if you like, but right now I've just got to be by myself."

Without saying a word, Lionel leaned forward and tenderly kissed me on the forehead, right where Vivien's handbag had landed, and moved off towards the main house.

I was left alone and I felt totally depressed. I'd been looking forward to this evening for so long, and with so much expectation, that the blow, in more ways than one, was a real let-down. I was, to say the least, totally pissed off. I unfastened the lace dress and slipped into bed and before I knew it I must have passed out. What with the martinis I'd drunk and the bash on the head, it wasn't really surprising.

Chapter Eleven

At 5.30 am on the dot, I was wide awake. I wondered if Gabby's influence would haunt me for the rest of my life as I found myself stepping out of bed and rummaging around for my running gear. My head felt truly sore and I rebuked myself for having drunk so much alcohol the night before, totally forgetting for an instant Vivien's little showdown, until I paused in front of the dressing table mirror and gasped out loud. My forehead looked like it had grown a lemon overnight. No wonder it was hammering away. I also gazed at the diamond chandeliers which still hung from my earlobes, having forgotten to remove them the previous night before clambering into bed. Every time I look at these earrings I'll be reminded of one of the most wretched nights of my life, I reflected as I removed them carefully and placed them safely into my knickers drawer, making a mental note to return them to Lionel, or even directly to Gabby, as soon as possible.

Maybe one day I'll be able to laugh about last night's unfortunate incident, I thought, as I raised my hand to my forehead and felt the bump. Or perhaps not. Even my optimism has its limits.

Head still thumping away I did an easy jog down to the ocean shore. It was probably not the brightest idea to go for a run with a splitting headache, but the fresh ocean breeze helped to revive me, and I paused for an instant taking in the glimmering indigo surf. Huge waves were crashing down on the shore, reflecting, it seemed, my own personal turbulence. I paused for a moment longer, and just as I was about to kick off again into my steady jog I became aware of a slight high-pitched scream. I looked around me trying to pinpoint where the cry had come from. Apart from the crashing waves the morning was silent. I turned to gaze once more into the ocean's swell, and it was then that I caught a glimpse of something bobbing in the water before being sucked under by the strong currents.

I stood motionless, eyes fixed on the dipping surf. There it was again, and this time I could clearly make out an arm that was thrashing out in an attempt to remain afloat. A head was half out of the water, too, and dark blonde hair was floating around. Without thinking of the possible risks I kicked off my trainers and stripped off my T- shirt before diving into the stormy water. My heart was hammering away and the adrenaline that charged through my entire body made breathing difficult.

As the first booming wave approached I let myself float to the crest, from where I was able to get a clearer view of the bobbing head. I wondered if there was a shark in the water that was taking the body down instead of the strong currents. I could deal with the waves, but the thought that there might be a great white lurking under the murky depths almost knocked me out cold. Pushing all panicky thoughts from my mind I concentrated on swimming with powerful strokes in the direction of the drowning figure. As I crested the next roll of menacing waves I was aware that the figure was no longer floating. I turned in the water hunting for any signs of movement. At least ten seconds passed in eerie stillness before the blonde head emerged once more, thankfully just a few metres away.

I approached in solid stokes and had an inkling that I recognised the struggling figure before me. Then it clicked; of course I knew the half-drowned blonde, though, I swear to God, what confirmed that it was, indeed, Vivien, were her huge boobs which seemed to act as lifebuoys. How could she possibly sink with those two balloons holding her up?

And down she went again.

I plunged under after her. Eyes open, I could just about make out her dark silhouette in the murky depths, and reached out for her hair, which sprayed upwards. I firmly caught hold and pulled upwards whilst I simultaneously kicked downwards.

Getting our bodies level, I put my arm around her waist locking her to me. She was, at this point, either totally unconscious from her struggle or too weak to move as she remained limp at my side, but to my despair we sank downwards together instead of returning to the surface. It was then that I became aware that the daft cow had tied a diver's weight belt around her waist, and this was what was dragging us down. I struggled to unclasp the belt, desperate to breathe and get some oxygen pumping into my lungs, but I knew if I was to let go of Vivien then there was no chance of saving her.

Somehow, after much fumbling, the clasp came undone and the heavy belt sank with shocking speed downwards to the ocean's bed. With one last effort I kicked hard and we both started ascending towards the surface. The water lightened with each approaching kick, and just as I was about to erupt from lack of oxygen we broke the surface and I gulped for fresh air.

I turned onto my back in an attempt to recover somewhat, floating Vivien face-upwards, half beside and half on top of me. *What a stupid fucking cow!* I wanted to scream. Her attempt to commit suicide had almost worked. Although she'd obviously regretted her action on finding herself half-drowned, she was obviously still too pissed from the previous evening's load of alcohol to unfasten her diver's belt and, what with the huge waves, had almost accomplished what she'd so crazily set out to do – and had nearly taken me with her.

I should have felt sorry for her, and I guess I did, but right now all I wanted was to reach firm ground.

I took my time, not out of personal desire but because my poor legs just wouldn't go any faster against the strong current. Agonisingly, it seemed to be five kicks towards land, three paces back. A bit like country dancing, actually, but without all the fun. There were a couple of close calls when several huge waves crashed down around us, but eventually, miraculously, I felt the soft sand underfoot. Stumbling as I went, I clasped Vivien under her armpits and heaved her a couple of metres onto the beach. I laid her down and felt for her pulse; thankfully, though feeble, it was there. Her breathing, however, had stopped. I checked that there was nothing obstructing the inside of her mouth and positioned her for mouth-to-mouth. The one and only time I'd done artificial resuscitation was when I'd tested for my life-saving Bronze Medallion down at Morden swimming baths, and I'd practised on a plastic life-sized doll. As I looked down at Vivien, with her big silicone lips and huge breast implants, there didn't actually seem to be much difference. It was such a callous thought, especially at such a delicate time, but deep down I knew the motive. I was just as jealous of Vivien as she was of me. The difference was that I didn't go hurtling my handbag around in an attempt to vent my feelings.

After several bouts of blowing down her open mouth I sat back exhausted and checked if she was breathing unaided. My answer came as she threw up all over me, despite my quick attempt to turn her to one side. Leaving her in the recovery position I scanned the horizon. I didn't want to leave Vivien alone in case she had a relapse.

"Come on, Gabby," I said to myself. "It's not like you to be late."

As if on cue, I could just make out Gabby's gleaming red head bobbing as she jogged steadily down the path that led to the sand and Ocean. I was up on my feet and started jumping, flapping my arms about as I shouted, "*GABBY, GABBY, GABBY.*"

I called out over and over until I was sure that she'd spotted me. She was by my side in a flash. On seeing Vivien unconscious she extracted her minuscule mobile phone, dialled 911 and asked for an ambulance. Totally bushed, I collapsed on the sand beside Vivien.

When the rescue team arrived I heard them ask Gabby, "Which is the bimbo that half-drowned?"

***

Despite the medical team's urging that I go to hospital for a check–up, I refused. I was fine; slightly shaken up, but all right. Gabby agreed to escort Vivien to the hospital, and promised to check on me the moment she returned.

It was early afternoon when she knocked on the front door to the bungalow. I'd left the door open and was sprawled out on the sofa, with the shades down to keep out the blinding sunshine. My head was still thumping.

"How're you feeling?" Gabby asked concerned.

"Okay," I replied, though in all truth, despite my life-saving adventure, I felt thoroughly crestfallen. Firstly (and most importantly), because I'd anticipated a visit from Lionel during the course of the morning, as I was sure that he would've heard about my heroic activities. Secondly, because I'd had time to think about Vivien's action. It had sunk in that she loved Lionel so much that she'd been willing to end it all on the realisation that he, Lionel, didn't love her as much as she loved him. It was such a poignant notion that I couldn't stop fretting over it.

"I'd like to go and visit Vivien," I said to Gabby in a sudden gesture of compassion. Gabby looked at me rather surprised and remained silent, perhaps to give me time to change my mind. But my mind was made up.

"Also," I added, as I got to my feet and made my way to the bedroom and pulled out the diamond earrings from their hiding place, "I think these are rightfully yours." Gabby looked intently at the precious stones, and for a moment she seemed lost in thought. As she turned back to me she shook her head slowly.

"Those belong to whoever Lionel wishes them to go to. They were left to him by his biological mother, who died two months after he was born. I assume these are the diamonds Vivien was screaming about when she attacked you last night. She may well have seen them before, but I can guarantee you that they were not hers, nor, as she claimed, ever destined to be hers. Lionel would never, and had never, offered them to Vivien."

Gabby's revelation left me somewhat perplexed. Firstly,

because Lionel, who'd only known me for a few weeks, had offered me jewellery that would have held great sentimental value to him. And secondly, because of Gabby's firm conviction that Vivien would never, ever, have been offered the stones.

That afternoon Gabby dropped me off at the hospital so that I could visit Vivien. I'd insisted on going, though Gabby, for some unknown reason, had strongly argued against it. She parked the car inside the reserved grounds of the private hospital and told me she would wait. I had the suspicion that Gabby, deep down, really disliked Vivien, which wasn't really surprising.

I made my way to the room where I'd been told I would find her. The hospital seemed quiet. It was comparatively small, and looked extremely exclusive. I imagined it was where all the rich and famous got treated, not just for health but also undoubtedly for surgery of a more cosmetic nature. What also got me was that there were no stalking paparazzi around. Obviously the story hadn't leaked to the press yet.

Up on the second floor all was silent, eerily so; there was of no sign of patients' family members or friends. Every one of the doors was either shut or just slightly ajar. When I reached Vivien's room I knocked softly before pushing the door open.

I stepped through quietly and stopped dead in my tracks.

Vivien lay on the bed, fast asleep, hair spread around her pretty face like a golden halo. She looked so serene and peaceful, it was a shame she didn't always look that way. But what jolted me was that, sitting in a chair beside the bed, with his arm reaching out to clasp Vivien's hand, was Lionel. He, too, was fast asleep. Viewing them together, holding hands, I felt as if my heart had been pierced by a shard of ice.

No wonder she looks so mighty happy and peaceful, I thought. In sudden anger I turned on my heel before either of them woke and hastened out to the safety of Gabby's 4x4. Gabby looked at me sheepishly. She obviously knew that there was a chance I would see Lionel there, but hadn't had the guts to be honest with me. I refused to comment either way. She was his sister, after all, and I didn't think it was wise to openly confess how cheated I felt.

My mind was made up: I was flying back to London as soon as possible. Freddy G had informed me during the party the night before that I was to have a six-week break before having to join the crew on the next film in which I was to body-double.

I needed to get away. And pronto!

Chapter Twelve

Freddy G had worked a miracle. Less than thirty-six hours after I'd saved Vivien from the murky depths of the Pacific Ocean, I was sitting First Class on a British Airways flight back to London.

I'd had just enough time to pack some of my stuff, tidy up the cottage, say a stilted goodbye to Gabby (though I knew she was the last one to blame for my heavy heart), and phone Tammy to get her to meet me at the airport. Lionel hadn't bothered to visit me, and I felt totally let down. I'd given the diamonds to Gabby for her safekeeping and placed the slip of paper with the details of the significant bank transfer that Freddy G had issued into my account into my bra top for the journey across the Atlantic.

I'd decided to go ahead with the purchase of the country cottage down in Kent. I planned to spend much of the following six weeks doing all the repair work needed on the house, and bringing myself back to reality after the last crazy few weeks of living in Never-Never-Land.

The flight over was relatively smooth and I spent most of it asleep. This was a shame; all the special First Class treats were wasted on me.

I went through passport control and customs in a flash. I think it was the first time ever I wasn't given the total body search, and put it down to the fact that I still had silky-straight hair. My heart went out to a poor kid in his late teens with big Afro hair who was halted right in front of me and told to open his case. I should really write a complaint about hair discrimination, I thought, as I went through the automatic doors and out into the arrivals lounge.

"CHANTELLE!" Tammy flung herself into my arms. She

was more excitable than a young puppy. It was heart-rending, really. I was glad that someone genuinely missed me.

"You remember Ray, don't you?" Tammy went on. I turned to stare at Robbie's friend, the Good Samaritan tractor-driver who'd rescued Tammy and me from the mud bath. That now felt like a lifetime ago. My brain was thrown into fast-forward as I attempted to bring myself up to speed with the situation. After that fragmented phone conversation, I'd been blindly convinced that Tammy had been dating Robbie. But there, before me, looking like two infatuated adolescents shyly holding hands, were Tammy and Ray. And as Ray moved off to fetch the parked car Tammy gleefully blurted out, "You owe me fifty quid."

"Obviously not gay, then."

I didn't even want to contemplate the prospect of seeing Robbie again. The idea of it was far too complex to mull over in my state of jet laggardness.

***

The arrival back at my bedsit off Streatham High Road was excruciating. I'd forgotten how tiny it actually was.

It was so dark and gloomy, too. I hadn't quite noticed before the extent to which the sun's rays failed to reach my windows. Or maybe I had, and had automatically blanked it out in a reflex action of survival. As I looked around it also struck me that not only was the flat diminutive, dim and dismal, but that all of a sudden it seemed to vibrate. That was when I remembered that the railway line passed right behind the block of flats, and that I actually knew the train times to the minute, without ever having to consult a timetable. I left my luggage in the bed-cum-sitting room and went out on to the balcony that overlooked the main road. There was pigeon crap all over the railings, and I wondered if perhaps I ought to hold up a brolly, just in case.

I do recall what I'd loved so much about this flat when I first moved in. My father had just passed away, and for the first time in my life I'd found myself totally alone – family-

111

wise that is, as Tammy has always been by my side when needed. The flat, the whole area, had seemed so alive. I found it comforting that there were people milling about at all hours of the day and night, though the word I'd probably use now is lurking. Though I didn't know those people in the street below, it somehow reassured me that they were there. I used to fall asleep with my head up against the bedroom windowsill, in the comfortable knowledge that there were people close at hand that could hear me if I shouted for them. They would probably have totally ignored me, but that's beside the point.

As I stood on the crap-covered balcony, a police car screeched past, followed by another one, and another one and a further two, and then an ambulance, followed by two huge law enforcement vans. The street was a continuous string of flashing blue lights and screaming sirens.

I appreciate that most would think, considering some recent and not-so-recent terrorist attacks on the city, and the yobs out on the streets causing havoc, that it was best to be cautious. But those blues & twos passed more frequently than I changed my socks.

It was an impossibility to get to sleep that night, lying in my rickety old bed in the half-light, as the street lamps reflected an eerie glow through the drawn curtains. Moreover, I felt that if I slept I would wake and find that the whole American adventure had just been a sweet dream, and that the reality was that I was an hour late for work down at the café.

The only thing I had that proved otherwise was the letter Lionel had left me the day of the cast party – and, of course, Freddy G's international bank transfer that was now ready and waiting in my account. This I planned to put to good use the following day, for I intended to drive (well, at least, endeavour to drive in my clapped-out Mini) down to Kent and negotiate the purchase of the country cottage, which Ray had told me was still on the market.

At some point during the night I must have fallen into a profound sleep. I had one of those erotic dreams where I was running through fields of dandelions, butt-naked, with both Lionel and Robbie running after me...

I awoke with a start – and a gasp – and put the memories of the dream straight out of my mind as I threw off the covers and glanced at my watch. 6.45 am. I didn't know if it was the jet lag or if Gabby had successfully made it into my subconscious, but finding myself wide awake, there was nothing to do but go for my daily run.

It was towards the end of summer, early September already, but it was already light at that early hour. I'd never gone for a run along the streets of London, so it was quite an experience, though not one I'd be keen to repeat too often. The concrete pavements were hard on the feet, not like the sandy beaches I'd been used to.

I passed a homeless person slumped in a shop doorway. A tatty-looking mongrel, snuggled up with the sleeping figure, looked at me through sad brown eyes. I flitted by several businessmen on their way to the office; sleep still lined their cheerless faces. I took a short cut that headed down to Tooting Bec Common, which was just a mile from my flat; at least there I could get some soft grass underfoot. But overall it was a thoroughly intimidating experience, what with the cars that slowed down and men that yelled out vulgar comments as I jogged along, together with the underlying sense that someone would pounce on me from the bushes. I made it around the common in a flash, desperate to get back into my flat without any mishaps.

All in all, it had been a truly dismal and daunting start to the day.

I had a quick shower and dressed with added care, as before I drove down to Kent I had one little score to settle. In a white halter-neck top, cut very low, showing off some cleavage and emphasising my bronzed skin, together with a flowing, turquoise skirt that fell just below my knees, I set off down the road.

I was aware of the amount of looks that came my way. "I didn't realise angels existed," one man called out. I was conscious of several wolf-whistles, too. It did wonders for my confidence, although I wasn't sure that what I'd set out on was the most grown-up idea I'd ever had.

I paused just outside Café Cappuccino where I used to work. The little old lady was there patiently waiting for her breakfast, and I was so relieved to see she was well. I'd been haunted by images of her choking to death on her muffin the day I'd had my little outburst with my then boss. I pushed open the café door and stepped inside. Even from here, at the entrance to the coffee shop, I could quite clearly hear my ex-boss yelling obscenities at whoever had made the mistake of offering to work under his slave-labour conditions. I turned to the little old lady and gave her a conspiratorial wink (though I didn't think she recognised me), and patiently waited for someone to appear from the kitchen. Some time elapsed before the boss appeared, red-faced as always. He looked at me trying to place me. When at last he did, he let out a sarcastic snigger.

"My, my, look what the cat's brought in. Come grovelling back for your job, sweetheart?"

I nearly gasped in disbelief. Was he really that dim-witted? Did he really think I'd walk in, dressed to the nines, to ask for that crappy job back? I guess there are no limits to personal delusion.

"*Please*," I drooled out slowly in my most exasperated tone. "Do I look like I need a job?"

His jaw just dropped as he took me in, top to bottom, for the first time. And that alone made the revenge visit – petty and small though it was – well worth it.

"I just came to pay for Mrs Harrison's breakfast."

It was the least I could offer the old darling after having her choke on her false teeth and muffin the day I left. With that, I put a fiver down and turned to leave. As I reached the door I turned to Mrs Harrison as she called to me, "Chantelle my dear, you look just sparkling."

"So do you, Mrs Harrison. Enjoy your breakfast." And with that I pulled open the café door and with a swish of my hips, I walked out into the sunny street.

Chapter Thirteen

The drive down to Kent took me somewhat longer than I expected. Driving my battered Mini down the motorway wasn't quite the same as Tammy's speedy Jag. I even got overtaken by a double-decker bus whilst trying to fight my way out of the city. No out-sprinting macho men at the lights this time around; I was lucky if I could drive off without choking the engine.

I drove straight to the country cottage. The big *For Sale* sign was still up, and I was half tempted to hack it down, but there was no chainsaw handy. Which was hardly surprising, really; unlike a lucky penny, it's not something you tend to find lying around, and just as well. The possible damage in the wrong hands (because my hands were perfectly safe, of course) could be vast. I parked my car as close to the driveway as possible and made my way around to the front gate. But however hard I pushed on the rusty iron, it wouldn't budge. Obviously no one had visited the house for quite a while, but then I realised that this was actually to my advantage as it meant I was probably the only one interested in buying it.

Hitching my skirt into my knickers, I climbed over the gate and jumped down into the garden, seriously excited at the prospect of owning the cottage at last. But to my dismay, what I saw as I glanced around had no resemblance to the picture I'd held in my mind throughout the past few months. The garden, which not so long ago had looked so dainty, now looked more like bushland. The grass was almost knee-high, and all the beautiful flowers were strangled by weeds. I could hear frogs croaking, I was aware it wasn't frog breeding season. I'd actually been quite good at biology during A-levels. I'd paid acute attention to the mating habits and seasons for all species, or rather I'd paid acute attention to the rather good-looking biology teacher I'd had. Still, I'd got an A, and the stimulus used is irrelevant. With this mild weather, the frogs were probably popping their heads up to practise their croak, and I wondered if the river had flooded the back garden and turned it into a vast pond.

There was a sudden movement in the tall grass around me. I tried unsuccessfully to stifle a shriek as I scampered up the steps by the main door in an attempt to escape the grass snake, or rat, or whatever creepy-crawly it was.

"My, we'll make a fine country lass, won't we Chantelle?" called a voice shaking with mirth. I didn't have to turn round to know it was Robbie, and I swore under my breath. Why was it that attractive men always caught me off-guard when I found myself in stupid situations?

Apart from my un-cool scamper through the grass in an attempt to escape what was probably just a harmless bug, I was also aware that my skirt was still hitched into my very slight and rather flimsy panties. So now, instead of openly flashing my behind for the world to see, which was actually becoming my speciality, the skirt I wore puffed out all around making it look like I was wearing a huge nappy.

I tugged at the turquoise fabric, untangling the skirt from my silk knickers, as I turned to face Robbie. I moved slowly in an attempt to remain serene. I couldn't afford to let my emotions run away with me again. I didn't think my heart could handle much more disarray.

I remained silent for a while just staring at Robbie. The hair, the chiselled jaw- line, the slight cow's lick on the right-side of the high, proud, forehead. The height, the powerfully-built shoulders, the well-muscled, hair-free torso. It was uncanny how much he resembled Lionel. How on earth am I going to get by without mixing their names up?

"You look like you've just seen a ghost," Robbie called out, as I remained motionless on the doorstep.

"Have you ever been told you look like Lionel King?"

"All the time," Robbie answered flippantly. "I've even

signed an autograph or two on his behalf." Changing the subject, he then asked, "How did you get in? Obviously not through the gate. Nobody's opened it in ages."

I nodded with my head to the top part of the gate.

"Ah, so you climbed over," he said. "Trespassing, are we, then?"

"You can't trespass on your own land," I said acidly. It was only half a lie. And, anyway, who was he to dictate behaviour to me?

"I hope you've come prepared to do some work, then," he replied quickly, a slight smirk on his lips.

"What do you mean by that?" I shot back. For some reason it didn't feel like our re-encounter was going very well for either of us. I knew I was sounding all defensive, and Robbie seemed set on making me apprehensive about staying.

"You'll soon find out for yourself." With that he turned on his heel and left me stumped on the doorstep. Trying not to give his words much importance, I concentrated on making my way around the house to the back garden. As I caught my foot in a bramble bush that seemed to have sprouted out of nowhere, I could hear the roar of a motorbike down the country lane, and assumed Robbie had left me to carry on alone. He must have had his bike well hidden, because I hadn't seen it on my arrival. Nor had I heard him approach as I was scampering around the undergrowth.

I finally managed to fight my way past the brambles and stumbled into the back garden of my future ideal home. The grass back there wasn't just knee-high, it was almost head-high, and I could hardly make out where the garden actually ended. I realised that at the very least I would have to add a lawn mower to my shopping list. And maybe several goats and donkeys to bring this grass maze under control. It's got potential, I said to myself, desperately trying to believe it.

I decided against venturing any further down the overrun garden path. Instead, I approached the back door to the cottage and peered in. Through the spiders' webs and the dust I could just make out a large kitchen area. Sheets were draped over all the furniture, and I was starting to give credence to Robbie's words that I would have my work cut out. But I relished the challenge.

First thing the following morning I was going to the Estate Agents.

***

I planned to spend several nights in the same Rural Inn where I'd stayed the first time I'd visited with Tammy, though I hadn't booked in advance. As I walked into the reception area I was received by the same girl who'd attended Tammy and me on that previous occasion. But gone was her cheery face; to be honest she was downright rude. She huffed and puffed over the fact that I hadn't pre-booked, and practically chucked my room key at me. I put it down to a severe case of PMT, and promptly filled out the guest card, picked up the key and made a nippy escape to my room out of her firing range. I was still feeling jet-lagged, and was fast asleep by 7.30 in the evening, despite having *EastEnders* blaring out on the TV. Thankfully I'd figured out how to activate the automatic timer to turn the TV off before sleeping, otherwise I'd have probably scared myself silly if I'd woken to some dodgy late-night film.

I awakened with a start nonetheless. I looked around the room with its orange wallpaper and dragonfly curtains, and, for an awful moment, worried that maybe I was responsible for the appalling decoration. Then I realised where I was, and that the room was not some multi-coloured hallucination. My stomach rumbled. I hadn't ever felt so hungry, not even under Gabby's carrot diet. Quickly I got dressed and headed down into the dining area. The Inn was still and spooky as I trod along the soft carpet and made my way down the stairs. I could hear a grandfather clock chime somewhere towards the back of the little hotel. Subconsciously I counted with each chime. 1... 2... 3... 4... 5... as I continued down the stairs. *Five*, I echoed in my head. *5 am!* No wonder it was so spookily silent. And where in hell's name was I going to find food at this godforsaken hour?

Without giving it a second thought I made my way to the kitchen. Feeling rather guilty about what I proposed to do, but not letting it affect my conscience too much, I slipped into the food larder as silently as a fox in a chicken run – and with the same intention.

There was so much to choose from I didn't know where to pounce first. There were slabs of York ham, mutton, cheeses, pork pie, veggie quiche. I zoned in on a huge wedge of apple pie, stuffed it into my mouth and wolfed it down. Okay, from a sneaky fox I'd become a hungry wolf. I then turned to creep back to my room, but suddenly, with a rare feeling of guilt, dug out four quid from my jeans pocket and placed it on the then empty apple pie plate. Leaving a trail of crumbs behind me, I hastened back the way I'd come.

I paused by the stairway. There was a noise coming from one of the upper landings.

Someone was moving around above me. The wooden floorboards squeaked, and whoever was lurking around swore faintly under their breath. The tone was masculine, and I wondered if a burglar had broken in. Not that there was much to steal up there; the food larder was by far the best bet. Trying not to let my imagination run away with me I tried to convince myself that it must be another of the guests, suffering from insomnia or sleepwalking. Or, like me, hungry.

I remained rooted to the spot attempting to decide on the best course of action. There were several options. One: confront whoever it was – though this option didn't quite appeal to me. Two: try to leg it to my room without being seen. This option was highly unlikely to succeed, as my room was right in the line of vision of where the noises were coming from. Three: dash outside and try to fetch help, though I doubted I'd find anyone around at this unearthly hour. A final option was to phone the police. But if it turned out to be just the Inn owner – perhaps he had heard ME and was investigating – I would risk causing a hubbub over nothing and come across as a complete and utter loony. Not to mention a sneak thief and larder lout.

I was still trying to work it all out when a horrified scream came from above, followed by a crash and scattering of broken glass. There was a scamper of feet and then a masked figure appeared at the top of the stairs and slid down the banisters in full flight – straight towards me. Terrified, I glanced around. The only thing that was handy that I could use to protect myself was a rather hefty umbrella stand. I struggled to lift it and then sent it hurtling through the air. I was actually quite chuffed with my effort as it whammed right into the intruder and sent him sprawling to the floor. He lay absolutely motionless, and I wondered, for a dreadful moment, if I'd actually done him in.

The owner of the Inn, kitted-out in a *Spiderman* onesie despite being well over fifty, clumped down the stairs and imperiously sat on the burglar.

"Mary, call the Constable will you?" he called up the stairs, then turned to me with a wide grin. "Not bad for a City lass!"

The police arrived shortly afterwards, and the crook was unmasked, handcuffed and taken away. I didn't recognise his face, but then that wasn't surprising considering I wasn't from those parts. But the owner and his wife, judging from the string of abuse they hurled at him as he was hauled away, were obviously already acquainted with him.

The mystery was, how on earth had the burglar entered the Inn when the door had been locked and there were no signs of a forced entry anywhere?

"George, we'll just have to look at the security cameras to see what actually happened," Mary said to her husband as they climbed back up the stairs. I, who was a step behind them, asked as casually as possible, "Do you have cameras in the kitchen area?"

"In the kitchen, larder, garden, hallway…"

I didn't pay attention to the other zones mentioned. Shit, shit, shit! I'm going to get caught red-handed too!

I scuttled to my room and tidied everything up expecting to get chucked out the moment they saw the images of me lurking around the food larder. I ventured out of my room again the moment I'd plucked up enough courage to admit that I'd also stolen from them during the early hours, and headed to the reception area to ease my conscience.

Both Mary and George were intently watching the images recorded by the cameras. I peered over Mary's shoulder just in time to see images of me zipping through to the larder and rummaging around. The image of me ramming the apple wedge into my mouth didn't come across well at all – professionally speaking as an actress, that is – but, at least my four quid gesture was also in shot. All the same, I cringed in shame and couldn't even stutter out a "sorry" when both Mary and George turned to stare at me.

"Thank goodness you decided to have a midnight feast when you did, lass, or we would never have caught the bleeder." George grinned, and I was flooded with relief.

"Did you find out how he got in?" I asked, tactically directing the topic away from my little escapade.

"There's a recording of Catty, our receptionist, letting him in," Mary said sadly. "After all we've done for the lass. But she and that fellow of hers, him what you clouted to the floor earlier, are just a pair of good-for-nothing rascals." Mary sighed and shook her head. I then realised the reason behind Catty's ungracious behaviour the previous evening. She was obviously in a total state of jitters over the planned robbery of her employers.

"What gets me," George continued, "is that if they are first-time offenders they'll both walk away from this with just a fine. Which is less than I can say for the hammering my artificial heart valve has been under. And it's just as well that Catty's not as bright as she makes out, silly lass, she'd completely forgotten about all the video cameras we have installed."

Personally, my shoulders and back weren't faring too well either after that early morning exertion, and after breakfast I half-hobbled out of the Inn to carry on with my plans to buy the cottage. After several minutes of letting my Mini's engine warm up, spitting out puffs of black smoke as it did so, I slowly chugged into town and headed for the Estate Agents.

The local village was one of those quaint hamlets where all the main shops and commercial buildings were on the one main high street. The Estate Agent was three-quarters of the way down. A bell chimed as I pushed the door open.

"Hello," I called out into the subdued and gloomy interior. There was no reply.

"Hello," I called out a second time. "Is anyone there?"

Whilst I waited patiently for a response I glanced around the room. Several pin boards were hanging up, with photos of property for sale. I scanned the pictures seeing if any showed the cottage I'd so set my heart on. There was a comfy-looking sofa settled against the left wall and on the far side of the office was a wooden burgundy desk and leather office chair. Papers littered the bureau. As I moved over to the desk, wondering if I might find details of the cottage amongst the stack of papers, a door opened in the far wall and a middle-aged lady appeared. The business was obviously run from the family home, the front room being set up as the office.

"May I help you?" enquired the kindly-voiced lady.

"I'm interested in the cottage for sale that's located about ten miles from here. If you could give me some more details about the property and the selling price. It's the one that you come across just before the nature reserve and the—"

"River," the lady finished for me. "Yes, I know which one you mean. You're the lass that helped George and Mary out this morning, aren't you? My, you are brave," she added in awe, whilst I thought, Gosh doesn't word fly fast in this neighbourhood? And how on earth did she know it had been me? Surely I wasn't the only new face in town.

Well, at least she didn't say, "You're the one that stole their apple pie," or (just as shameful) "You're the lass that got stuck in the mud some months back…"

"My son isn't here right now," she went on, "and he's the one who visits the property with each interested client. But as you know where it is I can give you the key and you can go and take a look for yourself. It needs a touch of work done, but nothing dramatic. And the asking price is very reasonable: only two hundred and twenty thousand."

That is quite cheap, I thought. I was tempted to write a cheque out straightaway and not even bother with the preliminary visit, but not wanting to seem too keen I accepted her offer of a key and an unhurried look around the cottage.

As the lady bent forward to the desk drawers to search for the key, a necklace she'd kept tucked into her blouse fell forward – and I had to lean heavily on the desk to stop from falling over in surprise. Glinting before me, hanging from a delicate silver chain, was a diamond stone, cut to exactly the same unique design as those in the diamond chandelier earrings Lionel had offered me. That, I realised with a jolt, had been just four days ago, though it felt more like four decades. I remained gazing at the precious stone and as the lady handed me the key, my eyes still fixed on her necklace, I murmured, "What an unusual diamond. Where did you get it from, if you don't mind me asking?"

"Not at all," the woman replied. "I'm very proud of this jewellery. I never take it off. But it's not actually mine, I'm just safeguarding it until the rightful owner, my adopted son, claims it back from me. I think he will probably want to give it to his wife – when he finds Miss Right, that is. And she'll be a lucky girl, too. He's a wonderful boy – well, man – even if I do say so myself. I'll be heartbroken to give back the necklace. But it's his, after all. And I know he'll make the right choice. I adopted him when he was just one year old. My husband was from Oregon, and we lived there for a while before we moved back to England. The US government gave us a really hard time about taking the boy out of the country, but that's another story. My son's biological mother sadly passed away when he was barely two months old and she left him this precious stone."

She paused for a minute, a sad smile played on her lips as she seemed to reminisce about something. I started to feel a bit faint as the pieces started to fall into place. But it was too much of a coincidence, surely. I leaned heavily on the desk to stop myself from swaying.

"It's a reminder to me," she went on, "that you have to treasure life, like this jewel, and that life can be as fleeting as the rays that dance through it." I'd noticed that she had used the past tense when talking about her husband, and I imagined that she was thinking of him. She went on, "You may have met my son already. He's called—"

"Robbie?" I whispered, overwhelmed by the realisation that it had to be. They were so similar, but *that* similar? They had the same early childhood story; they both had the same unique diamonds. Their looks, their build. It was such a coincidence, but there could be no other explanation.

Lionel and Robbie were twin brothers.

***

Robbie's mum held out the key and I shakily reached out to take it. I looked into her kind brown eyes and promised to return the key that afternoon. She must have thought I was slightly peculiar, as I remained some moments longer, positively hypnotised by her necklace, before turning to leave. Somehow, in a complete daze, I lumbered out of the agency.

Zombie-like, I returned to my parked car and sat motionless, trying to gather my wits about me. I wasn't sure if it was my duty or not to inform each brother of the other's existence. Maybe things would probably be best left as they were. Morally though, they had a right to be told. I found it incredible that they had been split up when their mother died; obviously something crucial must have happened for this to have occurred. The mother had precious jewellery, but no family members to keep the boys together? I was sure that the authorities wouldn't – or shouldn't – have let this happen, but, incredibly, it had.

In a stupor I drove out to the cottage. This was not a wise move, as, in my trancelike state, I almost managed to hit a fully-grown cow and her calf. By the time I pulled up outside the cottage gate I'd decided that, at least for the moment, I would leave things be and try to ignore the fact that Lionel and Robbie were twins.

No wonder I fancied the pants off both of them...

Chapter Fourteen

Kitted out in jeans rather than a flimsy skirt, my clamber over the garden gate was a piece of cake this time. Excitedly I skittered up the pathway to the front door and placed the key in the lock. Surprisingly the key turned with ease and the door opened with just a minimal squeak. It was dark and gloomy inside, and I went to the windows to draw the curtains open. A cloud of dust swirled up around the first set, and the second lot just disintegrated in my hands. I comforted myself that I wasn't too keen on the strawberry-patterned cloth anyway, and turned to view the living room.

There was a huge stone fireplace built into the far wall, wooden floorboards covered the floor, and the low ceiling still had the original timber beams. The furniture was sparse: just one rather large oak bookstand, complete with several mammoth cobwebs. I'd calculated that everything would have to be replaced in any case, and by the looks of things I wasn't only going to have to get a good bonfire going, but would also have to fumigate the whole house to boot. The sight of so many cobwebs was starting to make me itch all over.

The living room led, through a large archway, to the kitchen. This was what I'd been able to glimpse the previous day as I'd peered through the glass doors from the garden. It was spacious, and despite the grime-covered windows it was a lovely bright room, though sadly lacking all kitchen appliances. There were the tell-tale gaps under the kitchen sink where I imagined that the washing machine, dryer, dishwasher had been. There was a built-in larder that smelled really dire, and I didn't dare venture past the doorway. I had visions of dead rats or rotting cheese. I held my breath and slammed the door closed.

I made my way back to the living room. Beside the archway was a hallway that led to a flight of stairs and, in front, a wooden door. I turned the key that was in the lock and with a squeak pushed it open. I was charmed to see a quaint little bathroom. Surprise surprise, it was in need of some repair, but the tiling was exquisite: rustic cream with a frieze of blue flowers. Leaving the door ajar I made my way up the winding stairway. I just prayed that nothing would give under my weight, and it was a relief I wasn't allergic to dust. With each trudge upwards, a pall of powdery filth filled the air.

Up on the first landing there were three doors. I felt like Alice in Wonderland, trying to decide which of the doors to open first. Which would lead to the least dire room? I ventured to open the door to the right of the stairway. This appeared to be the master bedroom, with a huge double bed, another item to add to the bonfire. Judging from the state of the rest of the house, I imagined the bed was probably filled with lice and God knows what else. A window overlooked the garden. From this raised view I could see what looked like a garage below. I tried to open the window to get a better peek, but it seemed wedged closed. I could also make out a greenhouse at the far side of the grounds. This would be ideal to convert into a garden room for reading during those sunny autumn afternoons.

Room number two overlooked the undergrowth that had sprouted up in the front garden. The third door led to another charming bathroom, the same tiling as the one below.

As I wandered through each room, my mind went into overdrive, imagining the changes I would make to rejuvenate the place. Despite the dust and grime and the peeling wallpaper, all I could see was the potential behind each room. I made my way to the second floor I was already colour co-ordinating everything in my mind: shades of peach and soft rose; fairy-light curtains to frame each window; fresh varnish along each wooden rail to bring out the coppice gleam.

Despite Robbie's warnings, I was going to make a

winner out of this cottage.

The rooms on the second landing were very much a copy of the ones below. The roof, however, slanted lower, and natural sunlight shone through skylights and filled each room.

I carefully made my way down the stairs, mentally running through each and every item, idea, change, that would be necessary. I was going to give the cottage a facelift that any Hollywood Queen would be proud of.

By the time I clambered once more over the garden gate to the safety of my Mini I was happily humming away to myself *My Girl*. Of all the melodies in the world to choose from…

My loyal though totally ancient Mini was another of the items that was going to be added to my "must replace" list. Just as I was about to hop into the driver's seat I noticed a slip of paper tucked under the right windscreen wiper. I tugged the paper free and unfolded it.

My elation over the cottage vanished in a flash as I read and re-read the note. It was just seven words long, but each made me shiver. Cut-out newspaper letters had been strung together to form the message:

HOLLYWOOD BITCH, YOU ARE NOT WANTED HERE.

My legs wobbled slightly as I glanced around me, wondering if the sender was watching me from the dense woods. Despite my thumping heart, I had to pretend I was calm. Despite tears of fright welling up inside, I had to pretend that I wasn't on the verge of breaking down and crying. Pulling myself together, I opened the car door, which I'd left unlocked, and before I got in I held my right arm high and stuck-up my middle finger, swinging it around in a clear gesture of *FUCK YOU*. I hoped that if the crazed stalker was still lurking around, he or she would get a clear view of my cool, unimpressed and bravo attitude.

Boy, was I scared. I whammed the door of my Mini shut

so forcefully that the whole vehicle vibrated. I punched down the lock on the door and mumbled over and over as I fumbled for the car keys.

"Please, please, please God, let the car start first time... Mum, I know you've probably gone and disowned me from up above, but I promise not to do any more nude scenes if you just help me get out of here!!"

Then it dawned on me, with a wave of pure and utter dread, that I'd left the car keys on the windowsill in the master bedroom on the first floor as I'd tried, unsuccessfully, to open the window.

"Thanks Mum!!" I wryly muttered under my breath.

I peered through the car window at the surrounding woods. I really didn't fancy going back into the house, or even getting out of the car. I'd a good chance of getting attacked by the lunatic who'd followed me out here.

Where was my showy spunk now? So much for sticking my finger up in the air in a bravado pretence that I didn't care.

I took several deep breaths and braced myself. This is when I see what I'm made of! With that I swung the car door open and pelted up the driveway towards the house, practically hurdled the gate and took the doorsteps in one flying leap. My hands shook uncontrollably as I let myself into what I now began to think of as a dark and sinister house. I shot across the living room like a bullet and took the stairs two at a time. I swerved into the master bedroom and drew a deep sigh of relief on seeing my car keys glinting in the sunlight. I pounced on them and as I was about to turn to leave I heard a distinct noise from down below. At least I thought I did, but my heart was pounding so hard that I could hardly hear anything except the thump-thump, thump-thump as blood pulsed through my veins.

Then I heard a voice.

"Chantelle? Where are you?"

Christ! I had indeed been followed inside. In reflex motion, I sped back to the windowsill and pushed hard on the pane. It didn't budge. In a panic, I picked up the mouldy pillow from the bed, placed it against the window and punched my fist right through the glass. The noise would have alerted whoever was below that I was making my escape from above, so without a second to lose I clambered through the now shattered window, amazingly without ripping my jeans or injuring my bare arms. I lowered myself onto the flat garage roof below, free-falling the last two metres like Sandy at her best. I slipped and stumbled to my knees. As I did so I glanced up to the broken window above just as a dark head leaned out and looked down at me.

"Robbie!!" I exclaimed, half in shock and half in relief. I wouldn't have put it past anyone at this point, but I doubted Robbie was behind the hateful, scary note that had been left on my car.

"Girl," he said, totally baffled (and I didn't blame him), "what on earth are you doing?!"

And with that there was a large moan below me as the garage roof gave way, and I fell through.

Lady Luck was on my side, which was about time considering all the persecution and trauma I'd suffered that day. The garage I'd plummeted into was, in fact, a hayloft, and my landing was cushioned by stacks of straw. I remained motionless, sprawled out on the yielding but itchy surface, until Robbie poked his head through the entrance.

"Are you alright?" he enquired, obviously concerned. I just nodded my head in response. I was so exhausted by my attempt to escape, and so utterly relieved that my body was still intact, that I didn't even feel the slightest bit embarrassed, though I was aware that Robbie was looking at me in astonishment.

"I was under the impression," continued Robbie slowly, as if conversing with a simple-minded child, "that you were planning to buy this place, not wreck it to bits."

"I am planning to buy it," I answered. And I was. The stalker could go to hell. "I was just testing the fire escape possibilities!"

Chapter Fifteen

That evening I met up with Robbie down at the local for a couple of pints to celebrate my house purchase. I'd signed the paperwork and had handed over the deposit in exchange for the keys. The deeds would be signed on my return, but in my books I was officially the owner of a rather run-down rural cottage in the middle of nowhere, but even said like that I was thrilled. Everyone seemed in high spirits at the *Head in Arms*. All and sundry seemed to be crowded into the place, and, being the small hamlet that it was, where word flies around faster than a nuclear missile, everyone congratulated me on my act of bravery that morning which had felled the burglar.

As it turned out, Robbie, among his many accomplishments, was the town's handyman, so I arranged to leave him a list the following day of what I wanted done first, regarding bringing the cottage back to life. In the meantime I planned to return to London for a day or two, to sort out bank transfers and buy a new car.

By the end of the evening I was rather pissed, and Robbie had to escort me back to the Inn.

Not surprisingly, I awoke the following day with a stinking headache. I faintly recalled Robbie shepherding me to my room the night before, gently settling me on the bed and easing my shoes off before tucking me in. I then quite clearly recalled that he kissed me on the lips and I, disgracefully, had put up no resistance whatsoever.

Well, I wasn't going to worry my little head over that now. What did concern me was that I wasn't too sure if I'd actually received a phone call from Lionel at some point during the night, or had just dreamed it. But even more worrying was that I could recall saying in my dream-like and drunken state, "Hi Robbie honey…"

To which Lionel shot back down the line and into my dazed head, "Who the fuck's Robbie?"

Everything from there on seemed rather fuzzy, so I assumed I must have dreamt the whole phone call scenario. The only way to verify was to check my mobile's log of received calls. To my horror a call from the States had indeed come through at 1 am, and, what was more amazing, I'd had a forty-minute conversation with Lionel. I'd obviously come up with a jolly good excuse for calling him Robbie for him not to have slammed his end of the line down. I hoped I hadn't been stupid enough to tell him that I'd discovered he had a twin brother over in rural England. He probably wouldn't have believed me in any case. He must have been aware that I was sloshed and would have doubtlessly found it quite amusing to listen to me rabbit on in an uncontrollable slur.

Trying not to make any sudden movements that would worsen my hammering head, I tiptoed into the bathroom, stepped under the power shower, and doused myself with cold water until my thumping skull began to ease. Not bothering to dry my hair, I quickly dressed and made my way to the dining room, pen and paper in hand, and ordered a pot of steaming coffee and a full English breakfast.

Feeling refreshed and somewhat human again, I started my list to Robbie of where to begin the work on the cottage.

Dear Robbie,

As you're aware I shall be in London for the next three days. Meanwhile I would be very grateful if you could start work on the house, concentrating on the following:

Mow the grass (front and back garden, that is if you can find a mower tough enough to chomp through the bush land. If not, just plough a tractor through there!)

Sell all the hay in the garage. (Actually, if you can use it for your horse, it's yours.)

Fix the garage roof and bedroom window. (I promise not to run through any more escape routes.)

Burn all detachable furniture. (Beds, mattresses... etc etc)

Fumigate the whole house.

I'm sure this will keep you busy. As soon as I get back I'll help you out. If you feel it's necessary, get some hired help in, though I'll leave that decision in your capable hands. We'll fix the bills when I get back.

See you very soon.

Yours,

Chantelle.

P.S. Thanks for escorting me home last night. I hope I didn't say anything offensive to anyone along the way!

I re-read the letter/work plan. It sounded rather aloof, but I was pretending that I couldn't remember he'd kissed me. I thought it was the best course of action as I didn't want the scene to be repeated, and ahead of us we had several weeks of working together. I was determined to get the house fully fixed in the following six weeks, before I went back to the States.

Then I would just take things step by step.

If I felt that Lionel was just bent on using me and breaking my heart, I'd simply return and become a hermit. Not that anyone was going to believe that, of course, but I was firmly trying to convince myself that it was true.

Breakfast over, I hastily dumped all my gear in the boot of my soon-to-be-retired Mini, left the note for Robbie in Reception, and trailed back to London as fast as my little Chitty Chitty Bang Bang could take me. Stored in the glove compartment was the menacing letter I'd found the previous day. I had no intention of reading it again, but I thought it best to safeguard in case I had to take matters further. I'd decided not to mention the incident to anyone, for various reasons. If I told Tammy, she would waste all her time fretting over me. I couldn't tell Robbie, or anyone else from the hamlet, because I had my suspicions, but I couldn't be sure. If I were to receive another menacing note then I would investigate it myself, if I could (and had the guts), or tell the local boys in blue. I imagined that the girl Catty, who'd been the receptionist at the Inn, was behind it. It made sense considering I'd half-killed her boyfriend. I wasn't sure how she knew I had flown in from Hollywood, but the way gossip flew around the town, it was definitely possible.

I drove round to Tammy's that evening, having really missed our girly chats whilst I'd been away in the States. I was relishing the detailed gossip on how things were going with Ray. Tammy, however, looked stricken as she greeted me. She was ashy pale.

"Tammy babe," I said as I gave her a quick, strong hug. "Are you alright?"

Tammy nodded her head but I could see tears well up in her big blue eyes.

"It's Lionel King."

"Lionel King?" I repeated, perplexed.

"You can't kid me," Tammy persisted, and without further explanation she handed me her latest issue of *Glamour*. There, splashed across the cover, were the words:

"Lionel King and Vivien Francis together again!"

I let the magazine slip to the floor. Tammy had been right, I couldn't kid her. Though I would've liked to be able to kid myself – and to kick Mr King in the balls! The inevitable had happened. I hadn't even been away for a week before Vivien had successfully pounced. *Fuck, she's a sly cow...* I then went ahead and tortured myself by picking up the magazine and turning to the article. There was the hard evidence: pictures of Vivien and Lionel leaving the hospital together, Lionel with his arm protectively around Vivien's shoulders as he guided her towards his car.

"She sure didn't waste time faffing around, did she?" I spat under my breath.

And Lionel? Well, he surpassed Oscar-winning acting by far, the bastard! He sure had me fooled into believing I was something special to him.

Tammy, meanwhile, said in unexpected surprise, "Gosh, come to think of it, doesn't Robbie look awfully like Lionel King!"

134

Chapter Sixteen

The following day, after a really restless night, I found myself prancing around my miniscule living room to *Tina Shore's Salsacise* exercise video. It's sexy salsa dance and aerobics rolled into one. I'd found it covered in dust on my living room bookshelf. I'd been given it a few years back by an ex of mine who was a complete fitness freak, and I'd forgotten all about it.

So there I was, at 6.30 in the morning – bored to tears, unable to stop my head spinning around in circles, Lionel at the forefront of my thoughts. I tried desperately to give him the benefit of the doubt, to believe that the images of him and Vivien looking so lovey-dovey together were just a bogus piece of paparazzi work. But I had a horrid, underlying feeling that it probably wasn't. In which case, what on earth had the forty-minute conversation I'd held with Lionel actually been about?

It was because of all these doubts and worries causing mayhem in my tired mind that I'd found myself out of bed and aimlessly wandering around my flat. That's when I'd stumbled across that long-forgotten exercise DVD. There had been another one alongside: *Learning to Line Dance*. I don't have a clue how that got onto my book shelf, what with its *Electric Slide* and *Boot-Scootin' Boogie*. I thought it much too severe to try to get to grips with at such an early hour, and, anyway, I didn't want the neighbours calling the police with a complaint about noise as a result of my *Achey Breaky Heart*.

After a rather dicey start, I soon got into the swing of dodging my bedsitting room furniture as I *Cha-Cha-Cha'd* around. Midway through the salsacise session I was startled by my mobile phone's piercing tone. It's not actually a ring; it's a donkey *EEH-HAA* bray. I work on the theory that no one in their right mind would use a donkey tone, thus I always know when it's my phone sounding, avoiding those rather embarrassing moments on public transport of rummaging around one's handbag in a mad attempt to answer the phone as everyone else does the same. Of course, I do get some odd looks, but so what?

On hearing the donkey braying out in true Old MacDonald style, I halted in mid-shimmy, just as I was sussing out the Mambo arm-leg coordination, and searched for my mobile.

"Don't hang up," I called out, blindly convinced that at that early hour the only person who would phone would be Lionel.

"Hello," I answered, breathless from the aerobics and added exertion of whooshing around the flat hunting for my phone despite the ear-shattering donkey call. The caller ID came up as "unknown number," but that was normal; Lionel was a huge star and his personal number was probably permanently hidden, and he'd just forgotten to undo the option on calling me.

"Hello…" I called out again. The line was silent but not dead. Whoever was at the other end hadn't hung up, though apparently couldn't hear me.

"Lionel, is that you?" I said, my heart in my mouth at the thought that it had to be him. I was convinced that he would declare his love for me. He couldn't possibly love Vivien; she was so bloody hysterical.

"Hellooo… Lionel, can you hear me?" I attempted a further time, straining my ears in the hope of hearing something at the other end. The straining worked. I was suddenly aware of someone breathing down the line. It wasn't an exaggerated "huff" and "puff" but there was definitely someone gasping down the line. For an instant I thought it was my own wheezing I could hear echoing back, but suddenly the line went dead and I was left in total silence.

I slumped to the sofa, attempting to not to go overboard

with the notion that it had been the nutty letter-cutter-outer that had made the call. If it had been, then I'd have to admit that Catty couldn't possibly be behind the intimidating note, as she had no idea of my number. Then again, I quickly realised, I'd written my number on the guest card I'd filled out the first night of my stay at the hotel. Who's to say, maybe she had a good memory. The idea that Catty could be the one behind the call was actually a relief for me. For some reason, she didn't seem such a menace, and it also made sense, as I had, after all, thwarted her boyfriend's plans. In any case, I tried to reassure myself, the dodgy call had probably just been nothing more than pure coincidence.

***

Later that same morning, still buzzing from the salsa caper, I zipped in and out of Barclays Bank to cash part of Freddy G's bank transfer. I'd also been given a large sum in US Dollars, which I changed into Sterling. Hard currency in hand, strapped to me in a bum bag which I'd hidden under my summer blouse, I actually looked about six months pregnant. Either that, or that I'd really pigged out on ice cream all summer.

I headed off to the car dealers. I was half-tempted to pop into the Mercedes showroom and get myself decked out with a real flashy coupé. However, as I was still in semi-control of my wits, I bypassed this idea and walked into a Renault garage.

As soon as I was through the sliding glass doors at the Renault showroom my eyes homed in on a sleek metallic grey van. Perfect, I thought, as I made a beeline towards it. I was intercepted by a toffee-nosed trainee – obviously the son of the branch manager, as he was way too stuck-up to be an average employee.

"Can I help you?" he asked, voice flat, showing total indifference as to what I might say.

"I'm interested in the new Renault Trafic."

The information seemed to fly over his head. Son of the

boss or not, he'd obviously not done his homework. He just stared at me.

"The grey van over there!" I politely simplified for his benefit. He smiled at me in a thin sour way. I'd evidently offended him. I also towered over him, which I don't think thrilled him either. And so our personal battle began.

"Don't you think you would be better off with something a little smaller?" he smirked, looking me up and down, head slightly cocked to one side.

Supercilious git!

"If I'd wanted something smaller, I would have asked for something smaller."

He'd already started to get on my nerves, and in my mental state, what with jet lag, dodgy phone calls, menacing letters, and lover-boy Lionel back with Vivien, I felt at the end of a very short and very explosive fuse. In other words, this bum, who was just too superior to do his job properly, was approaching ground zero.

"So you think you could drive this van?"

It was obviously beyond him that I could be capable of co-ordinating a large vehicle through city traffic, when, in fact, my dexterity was pretty slick. I'd proved this to myself that very morning as I'd sashayed around my tiny flat, successfully dodging furniture whilst synchronizing leg and arm movements to the Salsa beat.

"Whether or not I'm capable of driving the van is my problem, not yours. Now if you don't want to sell it to me, and don't want to earn your commission, that's fine. I'm sure another garage will be willing to serve me. Despite being female." And with that, I turned on my heel to leave.

The manager came rushing towards me as I made my way towards the exit.

"Please excuse my son," he pleaded, just as I had my head out of the main door. (S*o I was right!)* "He's new. Now I believe you are interested in the new Renault Trafic?"

I nodded in agreement.

"May I say what a wonderful choice that is, the automatic direction makes manoeuvring extraordinarily easy…"

"Please," I interrupted. I didn't know what was worse, the son's blasé attitude or the dad's total sucking up. "You don't have to give me all the sales patter. I just want to buy the van."

It was such a simple operation, which for some reason or another was turning out to be a long, drawn-out and somewhat painful undertaking. Following my hint, the manager shut up, all the paperwork was done and dusted, and an hour later I was sitting, very high-up I might add, in my sparkling new van and zipping around outer London. I drove through Fulham, into Putney across Putney Bridge and then all around Richmond Park. I almost ran down a deer, but the brakes worked spot-on, thank goodness.

It was a totally different perspective riding in the van; it felt so much more secure. Driving the Mini had always been quite daunting, not just because I was never sure if I would make it down the street without stalling, but being such a small car, I always felt I was driving around in a tin can, constantly being bullied by the surrounding vehicles. In my spacious new van, however, I noticed that the other drivers kept a respectable distance. They were obviously aware that a collision with my giant motor would probably mean just a little dent for me and a whole new bonnet for them. Reverse parking and three-point-turns, I decided, were a bit too ambitious for my first day. I resolved to leave these manoeuvres for the quiet country lanes.

By early evening I was pretty shattered. I had one more errand to do: load my spacious van with IKEA furniture, but I decided to leave that to the following day before I headed back down to Kent.

Suddenly the desire to speak to Lionel overwhelmed me, so I fished out my mobile and dialled his number. I calculated that it must have been around nine in the morning his time; not too early to ring. The tone "burred" in that funny American way several times before the call was answered. I had no idea what I planned to say, I simply just wanted to hear his voice. The voice that came down the line, however, was the exact opposite of Lionel's deep robust tone. It was Vivien's unmistakeable screechy squawk.

I was so startled to hear it down Lionel's personal phone line that I almost flung my mobile phone out the window in a sudden panic attack. Luckily for the pedestrians below, I simply hung up. I started to shake and I wondered if Vivien's hysterical behaviour was actually contagious. Lionel was evidently the link. The more time spent in his company, the more liable to hysteria one became.

I predicted that I was in for another restless night, as I settled on my single bed mattress. And indeed I was. I was up at 4 am. Not giving a toss what the neighbours thought, promptly got the line-dancing DVD on. I found it quite easy, and did the beginners tape from start to finish. I ran through it three times before I actually felt exhausted enough to sleep again, and thankfully I did fall into a deep, dreamless doze that took me right through to 11 am.

***

My next stop was IKEA. IKEA is always a fun experience. There's so much to contemplate that other mental torments and worries are always momentarily blocked out.

I zoomed in on the *Opportunities* section and stamped my name on a dining- room table that had been reduced to half its selling price due to a tiny dent in one corner. I also earmarked a round kitchen table that had a fine, almost invisible, scratch on one of the wooden legs, together with two tall, slightly lop-sided lamp stands. These would go wonderfully well in the sitting room.

Considering the money I'd earned – and deservedly, too! – selling my naked butt, I could have probably kitted out my entire cottage at Harrods. So why was I buying *slightly marked/damaged in transit* stuff in IKEA? *Always look for a bargain… A thrifty girl is a treasure indeed…* my mum had taught me. And despite my Hollywood tan – which I still had, though it was fading fast in grimy London – I was still my mum's obedient, careful little girl. Well, almost…

Feeling chuffed with my purchases so far, I was all enthusiastic as I set off to the first floor to continue my furniture-buying spree.

Just as the doors of the lift were closing, a fellow in his mid-forties hurriedly stepped in with me. He didn't say anything to me, just stared. I wondered if I had bird crap or something in my hair, and he, being a polite Brit, was just going to keep quiet instead of speaking up.

As I stepped out of the lift on the first floor I pushed the matter to one side as I started to ply through the different departments. I'd made a mental note of my priorities and so whooshed through to the bedroom department and purchased an exquisitely designed king-sized bed with matching headrest carved out of oak wood. I then bought two much more simple single beds with iron headrests and legs, plus corresponding mattresses, bed linen and pillows.

I paused in front of a mirror as I skittled around just to double check I had no dubious "thing" sticking out of my hair. To my relief my tresses were all in order, though slightly frizzy now; the professional straightening was slowly losing its magic as the days passed. Nonetheless, there, reflected in the mirror, was the same guy who'd started my paranoia in the lift. He was half-turned away from me, intently peering at a picture frame as if it contained an original Van Gogh. Trying not to let my imagination run riot, I pushed my trolley along, having got a friendly-looking staff member to take the chunkier items I'd bought down to the purchase section.

What with the tables and matching chairs that I'd also stumbled across, beds and mattresses, my van was going to have its work cut out on just its second day. Confident that there would still be a little room left over, I bought a lovely wooden TV cupboard with petite drawers and swinging doors, plus several brightly-coloured curtains, fluffy peach towels, and all sorts of kitchen utensils.

Feeling the need for a break I headed to the cafeteria, parked my trolley to one side and queued up for some desperately-needed strong coffee. The early morning *Toosh push* and *Slappin' leather* session was finally taking its toll.

As I sipped from my coffee mug I spied, once again, the same guy that seemed to be shadowing me around IKEA. This time I caught him looking straight at me and it was obvious that he was trailing me.

I'd spent the last two hours piling my trolley high with items, one after another, and the dodgy bloke didn't have a trolley near him – or even one of those huge IKEA sacks, which are great to use for storing laundry. Not that I'd know, of course, as it's strictly forbidden to remove them from the store (unless, of course, you're willing to pay a quid for one – and frankly I'm not). I was tired, sore, and generally pissed off with the world. So I decided that I'd brace myself and confront the fellow head-on. I gulped down the last of my coffee, scalding my tongue in the process, and strode across the cafeteria using my trolley like a battering ram. Days of pent-up anger and frustration were about to be vented on my IKEA stalker.

"Do you have a problem with me?" I shouted, "Or do you plan to keep leaving notes on my car until I return to the States?"

The poor bloke jumped back a step and blinked at me. I quickly bit my tongue, scorched as it was. That last bit about threatening notes had totally slipped out unintentionally.

"I'm chief of store security," he answered hurriedly, producing his pass from his inner pocket and flashing it under my nose. I turned puce. Long gone were my tact, discretion and self-control. I could sense everyone in the cafeteria, staff and customers alike, turn as if in slow-motion and stare at me.

I'd let my paranoia run wild, and as a result found myself in a most awkward and terribly embarrassing situation. I wondered if they had security camera images of me sneaking out that sacred IKEA sack I'd so blatantly stolen the last time I'd been to the store almost a year ago, when I'd purchased a wardrobe for my flat and a few other bits and bobs. (OK – I'll admit now that I nicked it, but it does make a jolly good laundry holder.)

On the defensive I stared back at the security guard. "I

don't think I've done anything wrong to deserve being shadowed around the store," I said. "But if you believe otherwise, then please enlighten me."

"If you would please follow me," he growled.

"And if I refuse?"

I sounded so aggressive. It wasn't like me at all to cause trouble or to be so hostile. I was obviously in dire need of a good night's sleep. Or, as I'm sure Tammy would have psychoanalysed, *You're in need of a good shag, my girl.* She would have been right, too, but that option seemed highly unlikely. With my current love life in such a shambles, a good night's sleep was probably all I would get.

"If you don't behave and follow me," the security guard hissed, bringing me back to the present, "I could just strip-search you here."

I almost slapped him in the face for that, but not wanting to be the cause of any more scandal I meekly followed him. My trolley ever so accidentally bumped in to his heels a couple times on the way. He couldn't be set on strip-searching me, surely; I didn't think that was legal. And even if it was, at the very least he'd have to call for a female colleague to do it.

"Why don't we be civil about this?" I implored as I found myself guided to the private staff quarters. "I do plan to buy the furniture I've selected." In any case, I didn't think that a queen-sized bed together with mattress and headrest could be subtly taken out of the store unobserved, even if someone was ludicrous enough to try.

I wondered if my frizzy hair, which was now making a comeback, had something to do with it all.

"I would like to know," the security guard said, as we finally found ourselves out of hearing range of the store's other customers, "what it is that you are hiding under your blouse."

Was this some sort of come-on? The only thing I had under my blouse was my 36B bust, but I wasn't going to let him have a peek at that! Then my gasp of indignation turned to a silly giggle as I realised he was referring to my bulky

143

bum bag, which did bulge out rather suspiciously.

"You mean this?" I blithely sighed, relieved that it was only going to be a minor misunderstanding. I lifted my blouse just far enough for him to see the bum bag, and I observed that it was his turn to glow crimson.

"Please forgive me." he stuttered.

He obviously thought he was going to find some IKEA article under there, and I wondered if there was an IKEA item actually small enough to fit around my waist, or anyone's waist for that matter. Bar the vases, candles tea-towels and things, most IKEA kit is packaged into huge cardboard boxes. And who would go all the way to IKEA and face the queues for just a couple of candles? Clearly, I wasn't the only one in dire need of a good night's sleep.

Apologies accepted, I made my way to the tills and wheeled through all my goods, paid with my wad of cash, and pounced on a couple of junior staff to help me lug my new purchases into my spanking new spacious van.

Van finally choc-a-bloc with my precious goods, I revved the engine and started my journey south out of the city and into the quieter country lanes.

It was almost dusk by the time I pulled up outside my soon-to-be rural abode. The garden had been transformed back to the neat little pasture I'd first seen with Tammy, apart from the fact that there was a little spot of horse-manure on the grass. I realised that Robbie had obviously taken me at my word and got some four-legged friends in to chomp away at the overgrown lawn.

It was hard to believe that only ten weeks had passed since Tammy and I had accidentally stumbled into this cottage's grounds. What had happened since then had been a whirlwind action-packed adventure, but one which I wouldn't change for the world. Despite my achey-breaky heart, I felt suddenly strong and positive. My mind was made up. Vivien might have thwarted me once, but I had five weeks ahead of me to prepare my crusade against her. As John Dryden once said: *For they conquer who believe they can.*

144

Chapter Seventeen

Robbie met me for lunch the following day at the Rural Inn café. I'd gone to the solicitor first thing in the morning and had signed all the official documents. I have to admit I struggled to pay attention as the deeds were read out. I sat there and tried to look as if I understood all the clauses and legal terminology, and was quite proud of myself as I'd only had to stifle a couple of yawns throughout.

Robbie looked rather solemn during lunch. I wondered what was wrong, but decided to overlook his mood thinking maybe it was just the weather. I'd woken that morning to dark thunderous clouds, which threatened to chuck down with rain.

We drove to the cottage in my van. I was just as chatty as ever, but I don't think Robbie paid attention to anything I said. It was a total one-way conversation and I actually felt quite breathless by the time I pulled up at the front drive to *my* new property. The main gate opened without even a minimal squeak. The front garden looked even more fabulous as the sun suddenly broke though and the clouds moved aside. I jumped down from the van and sprinted up the cottage steps to the front door, which also opened with ease. As I pushed the door wide I gasped with delight. Cobwebs, dust and all that iffy furniture had gone, and the cottage looked almost brand new. The floorboards still needed some varnish, but the living room looked so bright and spacious, much more so than I originally imagined.

I could pull off my line dancing in the front room without a snag.

I went through to the kitchen. The tiles were mushroom beige, which I hadn't been able to see before due to the accumulation of dust and grit that had lain on the floor. The kitchen sink and the worktop sparkled.

"You're an angel, Robbie." I cried out in glee, throwing my arms round him.

I stepped out into the back garden. The tall, wild grass had gone. I was enchanted to see that a beautiful garden path, of decorated stonework, ran all the way down to the far end of the large garden. To the right of the house, running all the way down to the far end where the grounds met the woods, were rambling roses, delicate urns, and pots of garden flowers. On the other side was a vegetable patch, though I doubted anything grew there at present in its neglected state. But the potential was there to cultivate potatoes and sweetcorn, strawberries and tomatoes. Suddenly I was starting to feel all domesticated and homely. I didn't know if this was a good thing or not.

The glass windows of the greenhouse glinted in the sunshine. The structure was octagonal, with a pointed roof. It was really rather large, much bigger than a normal garden greenhouse. I would deck it out, I dreamed, with garden chairs and a *chaise longue*, to laze on during those pleasing sunny afternoons when the only company needed is a good book and a glass of fine wine.

I turned back to Robbie. He was gazing at me, a solemn expression still etched across his face. Considering that the stormy clouds had shifted, he was obviously affected by something else apart from the earlier threat of rain.

"Are you going to tell me what's wrong?" I asked. "Or am I going to have to play guessing games to try and figure out what's troubling you?"

"I didn't want to worry you," he began, as he rifled through the pockets of his jeans, "but considering that I've stumbled across two of these letters in the last two days, I think you should read them yourself and then consider the possible danger you're in."

I didn't have to look at the slips of paper to know that they would contain cut-out newspaper letters, strung together in menacing phrases. Nevertheless, I took them from

146

Robbie's hands and opened each.

The first read:

"HOLLEYWOOD STARLET FOUND STRANGLED IN COUNTRY COTTAGE..."

With shaking hands I fumbled with the second scroll. The brash, intimidating letters jarred up at me:

"CHANTELLE ROSE, YOU CAN RUN BUT YOU CANNOT HIDE."

I remained silent for a while. I doubted now that the eerie phone call I'd received was a coincidence. I also doubted that Catty was behind the threat.

"Do you remember the day you came looking for me and caught me when I jumped onto the garage roof?"

Robbie nodded at the memory. Everything considered, it was probably quite hard to forget.

"Did you come across anyone along the lane or nearby when you approached?" Robbie shook his head slowly.

"Well," I continued, "these aren't the first of these letters. I got the first one that day, and when I heard you I assumed it was the person behind the threats. That's why I jumped out the window, to escape. Do you think Catty could be behind it? It makes sense, considering that I stuffed her boyfriend's getaway."

Robbie continued to shake his head.

"It can't be Catty," he said softly. "Her parents packed her off to a distant relative up in Aberdeen the very day the police hauled her boyfriend in."

A shiver ran down my back on hearing his words. I'd blindly assumed that the letters were just the simple result of Catty's spiteful anger because I'd frustrated her and her lover-boy's plans.

But if Catty wasn't behind the letters, I was in more trouble that I imagined.

"I'm going to the police." I said. And with that, shoulders squared, I turned on my heel and headed back out to the parked van.

***

Robbie insisted on coming with me, and we arrived together at the local police station, which was smaller than the garage at the cottage. It hit me that crime was doubtless pretty rare in this tiny village. Indeed, the officer who attended me looked like he should have retired years ago. I couldn't see him doing a full-out sprint down the country lane decked out in his Bobby's uniform, especially wearing one of those towering helmets.

I did wonder if he had a spare truncheon that I could borrow and hide under my pillow, just in case someone broke into the house whilst I slept.

I was given the full run-down of policing principles, which was of no relevance to me whatsoever. Finally, I was told that without some evidence of who the letter sender might be, there was little or nothing that they could do, except patrol the area from time to time.

After wasting much of the afternoon dawdling at the constabulary and getting nowhere, I left with Robbie and privately wondered if it would be easier to get a hunter's licence so that I could blow the brains out of anyone who so much as sneezed on my land. Inwardly, however, I knew I was in such a state that buying a gun was not a good idea. If I heard anything in the garden I'd probably wipe out the entire rabbit population in one day.

At the same time, I was determined not to let the threatening notes get on top of me. There had to be some sort of reasonable explanation behind it all, I was sure, and I was adamant to find out. I was beginning to understand why my dad used to always say I was as stubborn as a donkey! I'd knocked Catty off my suspect list, unless she could astral-project, and my imagination hadn't yet reached that extreme. Without Catty heading my file of possible felons, and her lover boy behind bars, there was actually no one else I could think of who could be behind such threats. Unless, of course, I suddenly realised, there was someone in the village who'd been keen on buying the cottage, and I'd innocently gone and ruined it for them. With this idea fresh in my mind, I turned to Robbie.

"Robbie, your family runs the estate agents. Was there anyone else interested in purchasing the cottage who could now feel angry enough to threaten me?"

Robbie shook his head. "The only person who was interested in that cottage, and who had always dreamt of owning it one day, was me."

He smiled at me sadly, his bright blue eyes glistened slightly and for an apprehensive split second I thought he might just break down and cry. I suddenly felt thoroughly guilty. I'd bought the house on a whim. I hadn't really even thought about the consequences. My mind wasn't even properly focused on the house refurbishments. It was just something to occupy my time until I flew back out to the States. And to think of all the work Robbie had put in on the cottage. Just for me. I cringed.

"What were your plans for the house?" I asked with genuine curiosity. Had he planned to use it as a personal residence? Or to set it up as a rural getaway for tourists? This actually had been my underlying idea – a nice little earner for me when I wasn't living in the place myself – though of course, I hadn't really thought that through either. With another cringe of shame I realised I'd been treating the cottage like a toy, whereas to Robbie it was almost a living, breathing thing.

He gazed into the distance, lost in his thoughts. I'd crushed his dream in less than a week.

"I planned to convert the garage into private lodgings. Then some distance behind the greenhouse, which I don't think you've actually seen yet, is a derelict stable which I planned to reform, together with the main house, and then offer an all-in-one vocational horse-riding camp to holidaymakers."

A derelict stable? I inwardly winced yet again. I hadn't even bothered seeing the whole of the property.

He remained gazing out into the distance. He may have been Lionel's twin, but he was so much more solemn and aloof. Well, I guess it wasn't really surprising, considering his life-long dream had suddenly been wiped out. And by me, of all people, who had just stumbled across the house by chance a couple of months earlier.

As I took in his sombre profile it suddenly occurred to me that Robbie could well be the one behind the notes. But as soon as the thought crossed my mind, I scolded myself for being so distrustful. Nevertheless, as much as I tried to drive the thought from my mind, the more I started to have doubts. It made sense. He knew I'd been working in the States. Ray, who'd become an extended version of Tammy's shadow, would've informed him. Furthermore, I, myself, had innocently left Robbie my own phone number several days previously, before I'd driven to London to sort out my finances. On top of it all, wasn't it true that Robbie was the only person I ever came across down that country lane? And he always seemed to appear out of nowhere.

I couldn't stop the awful suspicion that it had to be him. And worst of all, I was driving us both back to the lonely country cottage because we'd planned together to unload the IKEA stuff from my van. My imagination began to run hot and my blood began to run cold. Driving to the secluded house with Robbie was the last thing that appealed to me now. I was vividly aware that he'd probably have me out for the count before I stepped through the front door. On the other hand, I couldn't back out of our plan either, as I needed him to think that I didn't suspect him. If I alerted him to my thoughts I felt that I risked finding myself face down in the river.

I could feel his intense gaze on me as I drove down to the house. In an attempt to ignore his penetrating stare and get my mind as far as possible off the threatening letters, and the creepy feelings that were beginning to engulf me, I chattered non-stop about the most irrelevant thing that came to mind: Cricket. I don't know why I chose it as my topic of conversation, or what on earth I said to maintain a one-way rabbit which lasted the entire fifteen-minute drive to the cottage.

As I parked the van up the front drive, I braced myself for Robbie's pounce. What I wasn't prepared for were his words.

"I think you're the most beautiful woman I've ever seen."

I had to do a quick double-take. For a split second I was convinced that Lionel was standing before me and I almost threw myself into his arms, which considering my new-found fears about Robbie would have been a bit like putting a gun to my own head. I laughed nervously at his remark. He clearly planned to woo me before going in for the kill. I couldn't stop shaking. And I'd run out of cricket commentary, too.

"Don't be a tease," I replied, my nervous laugh suddenly sounding hysterically loud as I attempted – somewhat in vain – to make light of the situation. "I look an exhausted wreck and I haven't slept for days. You, on the other hand, are a true gentleman, and I don't know what I would have done without all your help and support."

At least, I thought, if it were on his mind to tackle me when my back was turned, I'd make him feel as guilty as possible.

Thankfully I was saved by the distinctive donkey call of my mobile. It was Tammy. She was arriving early the following day with Ray to help out. It was the best news I'd been given all day. I was soon to have my boon companion back with me. And I doubted Robbie would try anything in the meantime. Well, I prayed he wouldn't. After all, it didn't give him much time to dispose of me.

We unloaded the goods from the van and into the living room. I didn't know how on earth we were going to get the huge beds up the narrow staircase, but Robbie assured me that, as Ray was arriving the following day, the task could be left until then. This was a relief. I didn't fancy hanging around the isolated house with number one suspect Robbie as my only companion, or, for that matter, risk straining my back by lumbering the beds up the stairs. I had to keep myself in rock-solid shape in case I had to land a highflying karate kick into someone's face. Saying that, with the exceedingly tight jeans I was wearing – they seemed to have shrunk several sizes in the wash – the only thing that was likely to have happened was for them to rip right across my bum if I so much as bent my knee up.

I was desperate to get back to the safety of the Rural Inn, where I planned to lock myself securely into my room and attempt to get a decent night's sleep. Perhaps then my overheated imagination and taut nerves would be restored to some sort of normality.

We drove back in relative silence. Robbie remained rather broody, but as he reminded me so much of Lionel that I actually found myself feeling sorry for him. Could it be that I had, perhaps, jumped the gun in casting him as the next Jack the Ripper?

I pulled up outside his home and just as he was about to clamber down from the van I leaned over and gave him a quick peck on the cheek. It was such an impulsive, innocent, gesture that he actually blushed. I think I did, too. Not allowing him to speak, however, not wanting to risk my heart been softened by his melancholy azure eyes, I quickly called out, "I'll see you tomorrow Robbie, and thanks for everything."

With that I pegged it, as fast as the van and winding lanes would take me, back to the Rural Inn.

Chapter Eighteen

I hadn't been kidding when I'd said to Robbie that I was exhausted. Indeed, I was so bushed I slept for ten hours straight. It was six o'clock in the morning when I woke, so you can figure out at what ridiculous hour I went to bed. Moreover, as I could no longer blame jet lag on my early morning waking habits, I was starting to contemplate that Gabby had indeed brainwashed me for life with her craze to be up before the cock crows.

Feeling rather spunky and alive and not half as pent-up as the previous evening, I decided to make an early start and head down to the cottage and attempt some wardrobe construction before Tammy arrived.

In the bright first light it was hard to believe that I could possibly come to harm, and if it hadn't been for the accumulation of letters now stored in my new van's glove compartment, I could have almost convinced myself that I'd dreamt up the whole episode.

I parked in the front drive, let myself into the house and set about unpacking the cardboard box which contained the wooden TV cabinet.

The cardboard container had seemed relatively small, but out came slab after slab of wooden wedges, as well as a whole sack of nuts and bolts which went flying loose from the carton. I've always underestimated what an utter nightmare it is trying to piece furniture together. Unless one is a real fan, DIY furniture construction can be like doing one of those never-ending thousand-piece puzzles where all the pieces look identical.

Four hours later I proudly stood before my TV cabinet. I had to admit it was first-rate, and almost instantly forgot that

I'd had to dismantle half of it halfway through the construction when I realised I had the doors back to front. I also had to readjust some of the bolts, as the drawers didn't slide properly. The added fact that I had at least a quarter of the screws still unused was a bit unsettling. I'd have to be careful that the whole thing didn't collapse to the floor as soon as I placed the TV on top of it. Nevertheless, putting pessimism aside, I stood proudly before my work of art. By the time I came round to purchasing more DIY furniture I would have forgotten all about how much I'd sweated to get the bloody cabinet up and standing.

I took all the empty cardboard boxes out into the garden thinking I could get a bonfire going in the afternoon. As I ambled down the stonework garden path I remembered Robbie telling me of the derelict stables located behind the greenhouse and decided to check them out for myself.

Just as I drew level with the greenhouse, my mobile went off. The *Hee-Haw* sounded so loud in the quiet outdoors, where all that could be heard was a slight rustle of leaves in the breeze and the distant tweet of birds, that I literally jumped. Somewhere far off I could hear a donkey braying back, and I had images of herds of animals stampeding across my nicely-cut lawn, drawn by the sound of my mobile. Must change the tone, I thought, as I fumbled to withdraw the phone from my back pocket. Once again, the caller ID wasn't shown.

"Hello," I answered. The line remained eerily silent, and with each passing second I could feel my heart hammering away more and more rapidly.

"Hellooo..." I strained down the line, trying to keep my voice level, although I could hear it waver in fear. I wondered if the stalker was watching me from some hiding place, and was getting off on seeing me quaking in my shoes. At the same time, the thought that my life was being made intolerable was enough to fire me up and push to one side all other considerations.

"Look you bastard," I yelled down the phone, "I've had enough. You're not even man enough to seek me out face to face. You're pathetic, and you can go kiss my arse!"

I paused to catch my breath, frantically thinking of more abuse that I could yell down the line. I heard a biting intake of breath at the other end.

"Hi honey. Having a bad day?"

It was my turn to gasp – but in total dismay. It was Lionel. I hadn't even imagined it could be him calling me, as it must have been at least two in the morning over in LA.

"Lionel!" I exclaimed. "I didn't know it was you," I blurted out in a rapid attempt to unravel the awkward mix-up; doubly awkward as it was the second time in our last two phone calls that I'd managed to get him muddled. In our previous call I'd called him "Robbie," and now I'd gone and called him "a bastard." In all honesty, I wasn't sure which would have offended him the most.

"Well I sure feel sorry for whoever has got you all riled up," he continued as I felt myself slowly cool off. "Apart from sounding like you're about to kick some shit, at least this time around you sound sober. So how are you?"

Very funny, I mused inwardly. Out loud, and not attempting to be subtle, I said, "I'm fine. How's Vivien?"

"I wouldn't know. I haven't seen her since I escorted her home from the hospital."

What a bloody liar.

"Lionel, don't lie. I phoned you three days ago and she answered the phone. And it's all over the gossip magazines that the two of you are back together."

He let out his boisterous laugh and I could almost feel his body shake with merriment down the line.

"My dear," he said, "I do believe you're jealous."

He was dead right. I was wildly jealous, though I wasn't going to give him the satisfaction of hearing me admit it.

"Rule number one," he continued, still laughing. "Never believe what you read in the gossip columns. Rule number two: believe me. When I say I haven't seen Vivien since she was discharged from the hospital, it's the truth. If she answered my phone, she shouldn't have. But if it's as you say, you probably called when I was down on the tennis courts

155

and had left my phone, by accident, at the bar. Satisfied?"

I let out a half grunt. It was my way of saying, "I believe you," but without clearly letting on how totally relieved I was. Lionel then continued with a ten-minute run-down of Hollywood goings-on, and said something about the Oscars. I recalled that the Oscars had been postponed this year by a good seven months, due to an earth tremor that had rocked the Kodak Theatre. But I was no longer paying any real attention, as I had suddenly caught sight of a shady silhouette moving about down by the stables where I'd approached whilst conversing with Lionel. Could it be Robbie? I stood dead in my tracks trying to pick out and identify who, or what, it was as I heard Lionel's insistent voice down the line.

"Chantelle, are you alright? You sound really distracted."

"Just a little problems with one of the neighbours," I said. "I'll call you back later." With that I hung up and slid behind one of the garden trees in the hope that, despite my bright pink vest top and washed-out denim jeans, I would be successfully camouflaged by the green surroundings.

So intent was I in trying to single out the apparition in the stables that I was caught thoroughly unawares by the approaching footsteps behind me. Hands went around my eyes and I was blinded. Fear shook my whole body before pure survival instinct kicked in. I drove my elbow with all my might into the body behind me as I stamped down hard with my heel onto the toes of my attacker.

"Jesus, Chantelle!" Tammy's voice called out in pain. "My, are you in need of a good spliff, or a decent shag!"

I hugged and kissed her in relief and linked my arm through hers as I apologised for my violent behaviour – although I didn't explain it. It wasn't that I didn't want to confide in my best friend, but I still needed to think things through calmly. And Tammy, love her as I do, isn't the most level-headed person around, startling as that may sound coming from me. As I turned towards the cottage I observed Robbie, standing at the far end of the garden path right by the kitchen door, and I wondered how on earth he'd managed to get there so swiftly and silently. Hadn't I just seen him by the stables?

I let Tammy lean on me as we hobbled down the garden path together. Tammy was limping theatrically – well, maybe she was in genuine pain after I'd stamped on her toes. I, in turn, laboured under her hefty weight. As we approached Robbie, Ray came in from the front drive and held out a white envelope.

"Hi Chantelle," he said. "I found this on your doorstep."

With shaking hands I took the envelope from Ray's outstretched hand and turned to look at Robbie. I was convinced that I would see some guilty look on his face. Instead, he held my eyes in an unwavering gaze.

"Thanks Ray." I said and slipped the envelope into the pocket of my jeans. I had no intention of opening it in front of Tammy. Being as panic-stricken as she usually is over the slightest thing, the only thing I would've achieved by showing Tammy any sinister letter would have been to have her install a whole army of private detectives and bodyguards in and around the cottage grounds. Although my nerves were strung as tight as a violin wire, I thought it best that one of us should keep matters in perspective as much as possible and avoid a whole drama queen scenario.

As Robbie and Ray set about getting the beds up the narrow stairs, which required some serious abracadabra wand-waving, Tammy and I drove into the village to stock up with provisions.

***

"Isn't it exciting!" exclaimed Tammy as soon as we set off in the new Renault Trafic and headed towards the shops. "What will you wear?"

I was so preoccupied by the still unread letter in my jeans that I had no idea what Tammy was referring to.

"Tammy, what the hell are you going on about?"

"The Oscars, of course. What else?" She let out an exasperated sigh. "They're in less than two weeks' time and your Lionel has been nominated for Best Actor. And I read

157

that he's going to appear with a 'mystery lady'. That's you isn't it?"

I didn't know which piece of information to absorb first: the fact that I was thrilled by Lionel's nomination, or the fact that he, himself, might have given me the same information over the phone that very morning and I'd totally ignored it.

I scolded myself for not paying more attention to what Lionel had said. I pulled up on the fringe of the village and parked the van. I didn't fancy manoeuvring it through the narrow streets that led to the shops, and I certainly didn't envy the local bus driver, who at that very moment had only just managed to scrape around the bend that led to the village centre.

As we stepped down from the van and made our way along the high street, to the local supermarket, I was stopped and greeted by quite a few people. Some were familiar faces from the evening spent down at the local pub. Others, however, were total strangers.

"Gosh, you're popular!" exclaimed Tammy. "They obviously love you here."

Not everyone, my dear.

The rain that had been threatening all morning started to pelt down, so Tammy (her limp miraculously cured) and I had to do a full-out sprint to get into the safety of the supermarket. As I dived through the doorway I crashed head-on into a middle-aged man who was on his way out, and managed to smack him with a mighty head-butt. He reeled back, and his shopping bag clattered to the floor. Tins of baked beans rolled out into the street and into the gutter. Muttering apologies, I scampered after them thinking it was the least I could do. I hadn't caught sight of the man's face properly as it had been half-hidden by a yellow anorak (the type of anorak I'd only ever seen before when channel-hopping and BBC 2 was showing one of its fishing documentaries), but what I had glimpsed looked strangely familiar, though I couldn't place it. Once I'd collected up all the tins I turned back to the supermarket entrance to return them, with more apologies. But the only person there, eyeing me rather suspiciously, was Tammy.

"What on earth are you doing? You'll get soaked!"

"Where is he?" I asked, puzzled. These tins hadn't sprouted from nowhere. But the road was empty, except for the pouring rain.

I stepped into what was probably the smallest Tesco in the whole of the UK, and approached the girl at the checkout till with my armful of baked beans.

"The fellow in the yellow anorak who just bought these tins of beans. He left without them. Maybe you could hold onto them until he comes back."

The girl, who really needed to get her hair roots sorted out, just nodded. "He's not from these parts, though," she drawled, "so he may not be back." Maybe that explained why he took off so fast, I thought. He probably thought I was out to mug him. I really had to get my hair straightened again, and the loss of a few tins was obviously of little importance to him. I put the whole thing out of my mind.

I'd planned to do a barbecue out in the garden that afternoon, but in view of the weather I didn't think it would be a success.

"Look, Tammy," I cried out in delight as I picked up a fondue set that was on sale. "We could have fondue tonight!" I plopped it into my trolley together with a whole load of bread and cheese. We got some white wine, a crate of beer, some emergency provisions in case we found ourselves washed in for the remainder of the week, and a whole load of munchies: crisps, Pringles, dried fruit and nut assortments, biscuits, cakes, and anything else edible that didn't require microwave or oven cooking. At the moment, I had neither. Why on earth hadn't I thought about buying a microwave at IKEA? I'd managed to buy bargain bits, but what happened to practical purchases?

Almost two hours had passed by the time we got back to the cottage, where had found Ray and Robbie sitting sheepishly on the front doorstep. They were both soaked to the skin.

"Is there any rational reason why you are both sitting

there like a pair of drowned rats?" Tammy asked. The very same question had also crossed my mind.

"The door closed on us as we were taking the plastic bedcovers out to dump," began Ray in explanation. "And..."

"And you left the key on the inside," I finished for him. "Together with the one and only spare set of keys."

I put my hands on my hips and glared at them both, as I realised that I would have to break one of the windows to get in.

"We thought we'd leave it up to you to decide which window to break." Robbie said, as if reading my mind. I looked at him. If it wasn't for the fact that he was soaking wet, I would've thought he'd planned it, so that he could get in and get me later when Tammy and Ray had left.

"Very generous of you both," I shot back, feeling rather peed-off. I moved around the house to the back garden to see if I could spy one of the cottage windows slightly ajar, which would save me from smashing one open. It was still raining cats and dogs and I didn't fancy having a gaping hole until the glass was replaced.

I glanced up to the second floor windows and it seemed to me that the bathroom window was partly open. I calculated that if I stood on someone's shoulders I could almost get level with it. I wasn't sure if I could squeeze my bum through, but it was worth a shot.

"Who's going to lend me their shoulders?" I called out as the others moved close. Robbie, who had also spotted the semi-open window and understood my intentions, volunteered. Under any other circumstances I would have had my qualms about heaving myself onto someone's poor shoulders. Slim as I am, I'm a trim five-foot-niner, enough to put anyone off playing piggyback rides with me. Robbie, however, was a different case, especially taking into account my private suspicions about his motives. If I had to step on his head, I wouldn't think twice about it.

We settled a wooden bench up against the wall to help give us some added height, and following a somewhat unsteady start I was soon sitting on Robbie's shoulders. The tricky part was trying to get myself to a standing position. Robbie took hold of my hands to guide me, Ray steadied Robbie from behind, and Tammy had her mobile ready at hand in case she had to do a hasty 999 call. I slowly shifted from my precarious sitting position. First, I brought my right foot up and placed it on Robbie's broad right shoulder. I then slowly shifted my left foot. They say that girls don't sweat, we just glow. Well, sweat, and buckets of it broke-out on my forehead as I flustered about trying to maintain my balance. I was on the brink of breaking my neck by toppling backwards. Why was it that the same procedure was so much easier to accomplish at the age of nine? Fifteen years on, it all seemed so much more difficult.

Both feet finally on Robbie's shoulders, I braced myself against the stone wall of the cottage and stretched upwards. I could just about reach the window ledge. To my immense relief, the window swung inwards as I pushed. I'd made it to half-time one goal up, but I still had to haul myself up and climb through the gap. This was going to be a totally different and much more challenging exercise.

Without any compunction I stood on Robbie's' head; I don't know how his neck didn't snap. I was conscious that as I'd taken my trainers off he was probably getting a good whiff of my cheesy feet. I finally got my arm inside the window and gripped hard on the under-ledge. I then pressed down on Robbie's head a couple of times to use it as a springboard and vault myself all the way through and into the bathroom. After a couple more test bounces I took off and scrambled through the window. I was aware of a clatter below me and I sensed, rather than saw, Robbie fall to the ground as the bench and Ray gave way as I took wing. There was an acute tearing sound, but I didn't give it much thought as I quickly clambered to my feet and stuck my head out of the window. Robbie was half-hidden under the broken bench, but moving, and I have to admit I was relieved. I didn't fancy having half the town turn on me in revenge at having knocked off their favourite handyman.

It was still pelting down with rain so I ran down the

stairs to let the others in. I somehow managed to trip on the second to last step, slammed into the bathroom door at the base of the stairs and shuddered to a halt in agony, convinced that I'd dislocated my shoulder.

Body parts in place, but bruised and sore all over, I hobbled to the kitchen door, which was the door nearest to the back garden where the others still stood, and let them in. They were all soaked to the bone. Obviously the best solution was to try to get the living room fire going. As if reading my thoughts, Robbie left and returned, his arms piled with wooden logs that he'd fetched from the garage. Before I knew what was happening, he had a true Boy Scout fire blazing. It was just as well I hadn't done him any permanent damage, as I didn't think my Girl Guide attempts to start a fire would have been such a success. But I put that down to being kicked out of the Girl Guides at the tender age of thirteen, when, in all truth, making camp fires hadn't yet been covered in depth. Don't ask me why I was thrown out. I didn't think it was such a crime to pass around my whiskey-filled billy-can during campfire song time…

It was not until after the fire was blazing away that I was aware Tammy had positioned herself right up behind me and was trying to shift me out of the room.

"What are you doing?" I hissed as she nudged me forwards.

"You've got a huge rip in your jeans," she hissed, as she continued to shuffle me out of the living room, "and all that's covering your behind is your virtually non-existent g-string." Which probably explained why my bum cheeks felt so hot. I'd obviously roasted them as I'd stood with my back to the flames.

With the relentless downpour outside, there was little or no chance of escaping to the Rural Inn to get another pair of jeans. Tammy, thankfully, had a suitcase full of clothes with her, despite being here only for a couple of days. And everything she owned was dead stylish, even her hankies. So, though I fished out only some tracksuit bottoms to slip into, they were from the trendy *Adidas* range and exceedingly comfy. Before joining the others down by the fire I dug out the envelope I'd put in the front pocket of my now-ruined jeans earlier that morning. I felt remarkably calm as I tore it open to read the contents. In the customary, bold, cut-out newspaper letters it read:

ROSES ARE RED
VIOLETS ARE BLUE
LIFE'S A BITCH
AND SO ARE YOU!

Well, at least it rhymes.

For some reason I didn't fell as threatened by this latest letter. There was something quite childish about the adapted verse. Indeed, I concluded, perhaps the menace wouldn't go further than the letters, and that at the end of the day, I wasn't under any major threat after all. That's optimism for you on a rainy afternoon! This surge of buoyancy was doubtless due to the fact that I had my house full of people, even if one of them was my number one suspect. I wasn't too sure if I'd have felt as light-hearted about the matter in the dead of night, with only my ice-pick for company.

As I skipped down the stairs to join the others, I realised there was something strange about the cottage that I hadn't noticed when Tammy and I went shopping. There was furniture dotted about that I hadn't seen before, and which I certainly hadn't bought. Was the climbing up walls, through windows and the pain of slamming into doors giving me hallucinations? There were two low wooden rocking chairs, a stool and a sweet little patchwork sofa, and I hadn't a clue where they'd come from.

Tammy, Ray and Robbie were all enthusiastically toasting marshmallows around the fire as I entered the living room. Robbie looked at me as I approached and noticed my confusion.

"Oh, the furniture. I hope you aren't offended. My mum had it all locked in a storeroom we have. She planned to give it the chuck, but I thought it would come in handy here."

163

"Oh!" I replied weakly. "Thanks, Robbie." This got me truly befuddled. Somehow, making gifts of furniture didn't connect with threatening letters… Or did it?

And whose bloody cottage was it, anyway?

Chapter Nineteen

The fondue was fun. Before long we were all considerably pissed, doubtless due to the charitable helpings of wine we'd drunk together with the generous amount I'd also dowsed into the melted cheese. Though the alcohol poured into the fondue had probably evaporated with the heat, I'm sure the fumes helped in getting us tipsy.

Ray kept on dropping his bread in the fondue pot and consequently suffered most of the forfeits we'd thought up. By the time we were barely halfway through the feast he had done a handstand – remarkably well, considering he's a burly fellow and that he'd lost touch with sobriety and body co-ordination at some much earlier point in the evening. He also had Tammy's pink lipstick on, and I've got to say his lips are more pleasantly shaped and sensual than a lot of girls', although it didn't seem to affect his masculinity. He'd also removed two items of his clothing (his leather belt and left shoe), but was still thankfully a long way off sitting in the nude.

My forfeit had been to kiss the person on my right, which happened to be Robbie – and which I felt was fairly embarrassing. I'd have much preferred the handstand stunt. Tammy sat with her bra over her woollen jumper. Robbie had had to attempt the splits. From the fleeting look of pain that flashed across his face, however, as he'd tried to straddle with as much ballerina grace as possible, it appeared that the only thing achieved was a rather severe pull in his hamstring.

Just as we were running out of melted cheese and toasted bread squares I became aware of a loud banging on the front door. Initially I thought I must've been imagining things, due to the generous amounts of wine I'd consumed. I simply couldn't conceive that anyone in command of his or her senses would be out and about in the driving rain, which hadn't ceased all day. But there was no doubt about it, someone was hammering on the door, someone who was doubtlessly sopping wet; in all probability someone who'd lost their way, or indeed, had mistaken the cottage for the Rural Inn as Tammy and I had on that first visit.

The others remained intent on scraping out what was left in the fondue pot as I unsteadily walked over to the front door to let whoever it was in from the downpour. It was the least I could do on such a miserable wet evening. I put the door chain on first, however, just in case. As I opened the door and peeked outside, I almost bowled over from shock. The wine was obviously playing tricks with my mind. I would have gladly suffered the world's mightiest hangover if it had been the wine causing delusions. But no, there standing on my doorstep, beside a titanic-sized suitcase, was the last person I could possibly imagine would want to visit me. I would have been less surprised, and definitely more thrilled, to see ET.

I unfastened the door chain so that I could get a better look. That was when the semi-drowned figure spoke.

"Hi Chantelle."

And there was no mistaking that screech.

***

I pulled the door open and Vivien Francis, silicone implants and all, stepped through.

As she moved into the brightly-lit living room I heard Tammy gasp in disbelief. I think she was almost more flabbergasted than I was to see the Hollywood celebrity appear in the cottage.

"Vivien," I said, trying to remain as unruffled as possible, "let me introduce you. This is Tammy, her boyfriend Ray, and that's Robbie."

As Vivien turned to Robbie, I don't know if it was from the strain of having been out in the bucketing rain together

166

with the long journey over from the States, or if she thought she was seeing a vision of Lionel, either way, the moment her eyes travelled across to Robbie, she fainted flat on her face. (Though I do believe her boobs hit the floor first and cushioned the landing, as it was quite a muffled thud. And she seemed to bounce a little, too).

Somehow we managed to get her up the stairs and on to one of the beds. I was left in charge of removing her waterlogged clothes. I didn't fancy having to do that one bit; I had no desire to view her 40DD breasts. And why did I have the underlying sense that Vivien was the cross that I was going to have to bear for ever in my quest for peace and happiness?

"What the hell are you doing here?" I hooted out loud to her unconscious body. I checked her pulse, which beat steady and strong. Her breathing was regular, too, which was a relief. I didn't fancy her fading on me. Considering her latest suicidal history, however, I wouldn't have put anything past her.

Just as I was deliberating whether or not I should call for an ambulance, she stirred and clasped my hand in her soft palm.

"I love you, Chantelle," she said. Considering that her previous words had been something along the lines of *Those diamonds are mine, you bitch*, this startled me, to say the least. I wondered if it was all just part of an intense therapy programme. In any case, despite being able to detect an improvement in attitude, I speculated on what was genuinely going through her mind. I also wondered how long she planned to stay.

I slept in the single bed opposite Vivien's. At least, I attempted to sleep, but kept on waking and straining in the dark silence to catch Vivien's shallow breathing.

Tammy and Ray slept in the double bed, though by the sound of it they did a lot more than just sleep.

Robbie remained below on the sofa.

***

The sun shone brightly the following day and I took it as a good omen. I was desperate for a good omen, I'd jolly well earned myself a good omen. I tiptoed down the stairs, not wanting to wake the others. There was no sleeping figure on the sofa. So Robbie was an early bird too, I observed, as I moved through to the kitchen.

There on the kitchen table, held down by a flower vase, was a white strip of paper. I almost swiped the vase to the floor in rage thinking that the paper was yet another poison pen note, but I halted in my tracks as I became aware that it was Tammy's writing squiggled on the sheet. She has big bubbly-girly writing that you could spot a mile off. I'd always envied her calligraphy. Mine was such a messy scrawl that at time even I struggled to decipher it. I often recalled the fact that intellectual doctors' writings are always a complete illegible scribble. But it didn't really help, because, let's be frank, there's no doctor's intellect in me whatsoever. My A in A-Level biology had been my academic peak.

I opened Tammy's note and read.

Gone on the promised kitchen appliances shopping spree. Get Vivien to leave me an autograph for Jonathan, he's a real fan of hers.

C U later sleeping beauty.

Txxx

Jonathan was Tammy's eighteen-year-old cousin. I hoped it hadn't occurred to her to call him and inform him that I had Vivien Francis over as a houseguest, as this risked having the entire adolescent male population of South London rushing to my front doorstep.

The "promised kitchen appliances shopping spree" referred to the fact that, lacking all kitchen gadgets, I'd asked Tammy if she wouldn't mind kitting out the kitchen for me that day whilst I'd planned to spend my time varnishing. That was, of course, before my unexpected houseguest had rolled up out of the blue. Or rather, out of the dark and stormy night.

It wasn't until 12.30 midday that I heard Vivien stir in the bedroom above. I was immensely curious to find out what had possessed her to fly over from the States. One thing was for sure, it wasn't for the weather. Furthermore, how on earth had she managed to locate me? The UK is small in comparison to the huge US landmass, but it's not that tiny.

In my state of paranoia and mystification, with the combination of menacing letters and Vivien's sudden appearance, I wondered if I'd been implanted with a GPS chip and had a satellite dish transmitting my whereabouts. I was also more than a little curious to know what Vivien's intentions were. I somehow doubted that her arrival was just a fleeting visit. Her case must have weighed at least 40 kilos; 40 kilos of make-up and clothes was a hell of a lot powder puff and skimpy slips to bring on a weekend break. She must have paid a fortune for excess baggage. Then again, Vivien, being who she is, had probably been given exclusive treatment the whole flight over. Moreover, I doubted she'd been body-searched the way I had suffered. There I was again, bitching behind Vivien's back like a real jealous rival.

Just as I reprimanded myself for being so spiteful, her long legs that positively went on forever appeared as she descended the stairs.

"You have a really cute house," she cooed as soon as she saw me. That left me momentarily stunned. I'd just about learned to deal with her cattiness, so her unexpected courtesy threw me somewhat.

In all truth I thought we made quite a convincing *Tom and Jerry* team – me being Jerry, of course. This new Tom in her, consequently, left me wary as hell. She would probably pull a gun or something on me the moment my back was turned. As she approached, I found myself wondering where my ice-pick was.

Vivien pulled up a chair by the kitchen table and sat down directly opposite me. For a moment we just stared at each other in awkward silence. Accustomed as we were to out-and-out slanging matches, getting a civilised conversation going was quite a challenge. I sat silent, thinking that I'd let her start the ball rolling, and depending on what she said I would decide whether to throttle her or not.

What I didn't expect was for her to turn her baby-blue eyes on me. I noticed they were brimming with unshed tears, and though she attempted to keep them at bay, it was with little success. Her chin started wobbling and her cheeks glowed from rosy pink to deep crimson. Soon the wobbling of her chin spread and her shoulders commenced to tremble.

I sat there petrified. She was obviously on the verge of some sort of spasm attack. I hadn't a clue where she kept her medication, or if she had any to start with. A Valium would come in handy. I couldn't dial 999 either, as my mobile battery, which had a life span of three hours or less, needed to be charged. My charger was in the van, and the van had been taken by Tammy to load with kitchen devices.

And, shit, I'd forgotten to phone Lionel.

My mind was in a whirl, and now I was getting as jumpy and apprehensive as she was. If I didn't soothe myself pronto, I would be in grave danger of going to pieces. And Vivien, in her disarray, was going to be no help to me.

I took a deep breath to try and control myself as I continued to witness Vivien's chronic decline. Her bright crimson cheeks had started to go blotchy and her whole body had started to judder. She'd closed her eyes momentarily. I don't want to be bitchy, but she looked truly bloodcurdling, like she was possessed or something. She looked like the girl out of *The Exorcist* – the original version – the one I've always had nightmares about.

So there was Vivien, my living nightmare, and I waited in hushed trepidation for her head to turn through 360°.

I wondered if there was a wooden cross somewhere in the house I could hold up in front of her whilst I mumbled the *Our Father* and at least six *Hail Marys* in an attempt to save myself from the crazed fiend before me. But in truth, considering I hadn't been to church in years, let alone confession, there wasn't really much hope that my lapsed Catholic faith would save me.

Vivien suddenly opened her eyes, and it was like

170

opening a sluice gate. Tears just flooded out in non-stop waves. She was leaning against the table and even this started to vibrate alongside her quivering body. I didn't know what to say to attempt to lessen her anguish. I'm always so tongue-tied in these circumstances. Eventually, in desperation, I blundered ahead and said, rather ineptly, "Is there anything wrong?"

At the rate she was going, she would surpass the previous day's rain! On hearing my words Vivien started to shake her head vigorously from side to side.

Is that a NO? I was puzzled, because I would have said that there was something very seriously wrong. My abhorrence of her started to melt away. I moved over to her side of the table and put my right arm over her shoulders protectively, as if comforting a three-year-old.

"Considering that you've just flown all the way over the Atlantic and searched me out, though God knows how, you may as well tell me what's wrong," I pressed, as I also twigged that she'd gone further out of her way to seek me out than any ex of mine ever had. This somewhat disconcerting concept was one I decided to leave to one side for the moment and think about later.

By now snot had started to dribble down from her nose. Believe me, she was not a pretty sight. She mumbled something, but between her snivelling and the hiccups which now shook her body, it was impossible to decipher what the hell she was saying.

"What was that?" I prompted as I become conscious, and considerably repulsed, that I had a slobber of phlegm rolling down my shoulder. I almost retched at the vista of the green bogie slithering down my arm. I wiped it off using the only thing I had handy: Vivien's long blonde hair.

"Freddy G," she croaked out between snivel and hiccup. She really threw me then. What did Freddy G have to do with any of this? Surely she wasn't moping over him. Saying that, small and dumpy though he was, he did have a bit of a reputation as a *Don Juan*.

"Freddy G told me where to find you," she rasped,

relatively clearly.

"Ahh!" I let out. This made a little more sense. I'd texted Freddy G my new UK location as soon as I'd arrived back in the UK in case he had to contact me and send me my next contract. Though if I'd known he planned to pass it around to the likes of Vivien, I would have given him some bogus address somewhere up in Glasgow.

"He really loves you," she blurted out.

"Who? Freddy?" I exclaimed, rather taken aback by the prospect.

Vivien actually laughed out loud at this. The mixture of laughter and sobs made me think of Doctor Jekyll and Mr Hyde.

"Lionel, you fool," she muttered, looking sad once again. Nevertheless, by calling me a fool she was obviously getting her spirit back. I took that as a good sign.

"I've loved him all my life, worshipped him ever since I was a little girl, long before he became famous. I kept hoping that one day he would stop searching for the woman of his dreams, which he'd become obsessed with finding, and realise that that woman was me. He gave up the search two years ago, which was when we finally started dating. I was so happy. My dream had come true, though I knew I was just kidding myself. I was in love with him, but not blind to the fact that he didn't love me back, at least not as I felt about him. He cares for me, always has, but as a sister, in the same way he cares for Gabby. Then it all came to an end when he saw you in that cheap film. You looked so ugly in that film. I couldn't believe that he'd become obsessed with you."

I wanted to point out that I only looked so shocking because of the horrid make-up, but decided to keep quiet as not to break Vivien's flowing confession.

"My therapist tells me it's time to move on," she sniffed.

I thoroughly agreed.

"But life without Lionel just didn't seem to have any meaning. I couldn't bear the idea, which is why I tried to commit suicide the day after the cast party. Then you, of all people, saved me. I couldn't believe it, especially after

172

putting on the spectacle that I did by hurling my handbag at you in front of all the party guests."

Your rock-filled handbag, I almost added.

"I thoroughly hated you, and made it clear from day one."

I had to agree with her there.

"And what did you do? Go and save my life." Vivien paused to regain her breath. She was still glowing pink, and I thought it best not to let my guard down in case she had a relapse into hysteria. But I was rather shocked to hear her continue, "I want to apologise for all I've put you through, and I want to thank you for giving me this second chance to start over."

She threw her arms around me then and hugged me tight. And I had to confess that her declaration had taken a lot of bottle.

"Your therapist would be proud of you," I said, smiling back and returned her warm embrace.

Vivien went on to explain that Lionel actually gave most of his money to charity, which made me, ridiculously, glow with pride. Moreover, she added that if Lionel was happy, she was happy for him. Nonetheless I believed she was only half-convinced there. She still needed a couple more therapy sessions to solidify that concept.

I suddenly remembered, once again, that I needed to call Lionel myself and was frantic for Tammy to return with the van and my charger. As I worried over the fact that I should have phoned Lionel hours earlier and that he'd probably given up on me in frustration by now, Vivien sheepishly asked, "Did I imagine it, or was there a guy here last night that looks remarkably like Lionel?"

"You didn't dream him up. He's called Robbie, and he'll be back later on."

Vivien rose to her feet in a flash. "I'd better go and make myself presentable, then." And with that she bounded up the stairs with newborn energy.

As I glanced after her as she took off to our shared bedroom, I speculated on whether I should forewarn her that

Robbie was actually a bit of a psychopath and had a tendency to leave threatening letters around the house. Then again, I reflected, perhaps it was Robbie I should warn about Vivien's rather unstable temperament.

Eventually I decided against doing either of those things. They would probably get on like a house on fire.

Chapter Twenty

Tammy, Ray and Robbie arrived with my new kitchen gear mid-afternoon. As soon as they were through the door, Vivien could be heard clattering down the stairs in three-inch stilettos. Very practical country footwear I have to say. She swished in to the living room and the others all turned to stare. She was kitted out in tiny hot pants and she had a see-through blouse on that she had tied around her waist, accentuating her slim figure. The blouse was unbuttoned to the third buttonhole, baring her generous cleavage. She looked like Miss Playboy Bunny of the Year.

I wasn't as surprised as the others by her attire, for I'd guessed she'd dress to kill and that Robbie was her target. However, considering how cool it got during the evenings, I deliberated that it was more probable that she would freeze to death before she got a chance of pouncing on her prey. I introduced her for a second time and she was all over Robbie like a rash, much to his bewilderment. I held back my mirth and watched her antics with detachment. Vivien had latched her arm through Robbie's regardless of his attempts to elude her. I don't think he had ever, on any previous occasion, been pursued with so much zeal, and he was obviously highly uncomfortable. Ray, trying to be the true gentleman and desperate not to offend Tammy, struggled not to gawk at Vivien's sexy provocative outline, which he just about achieved without breaking out in a nervous sweat. Tammy just stood open-mouthed, viewing the skimpily-dressed Vivien as if transfixed.

I winked at Tammy as I zipped past her to the van. "I'll explain later," I whispered in her ear, as I dashed to retrieve my phone charger.

I hurriedly plugged in my mobile and saw that I had five missed calls from Lionel and a couple from "Unknown number" which I imagined was probably him too. I was thrilled to see his gallant persistence in attempting to get in touch with me, although, no doubt, he thought I was a callous cow for not getting back to him. Just as I was about to dial his number the phone rang, and, of course, it was him. My heart almost lurched out of my chest. Suddenly I was in a panic at the thought of having to speak with him. For some reason, Vivien's news, which should have given me confidence and happiness, had left me a nervous wreck. It finally sunk in that Lionel was in love with me, and my voice shook uncontrollably from sheer emotion.

"Hi Lionel."

"Well I'm glad you're still alive," came his curt reply. "I'd almost got Interpol on your case." He sounded overwrought, and I wondered if there was anything else on his mind. "What with you not answering your phone, and the fact that Vivien has disappeared too, I thought someone was doing a serial kidnapping job."

"Vivien's here," I blurted out, hoping the information would calm him. It hadn't occurred to me that Vivien could have flown over without telling anyone where she was going. But obviously she had, and I'd visions of the entire California State Police and FBI out hunting for her. She was evidently in a more critical mental state than I imagined.

"She's there with you?" he gasped in shock. I wholly empathised with that, for I'd been just as stunned by her arrival the previous evening. "Is she okay?"

"Well, considering that in all my previous encounters with her she's always been somewhat insolent, I would say she's comparatively serene and affirmative. Do you want to speak to her?"

"No, no," he answered quickly. "I'll take your word for it."

I was glad he didn't want to speak to her – not for my own personal reasons (for I no longer felt envious of her), but for her own sake. If she was trying to get over Lionel, it wouldn't do any good conversing with him over the phone. In her present sensitive state she would probably have been left in floods of tears. And hysterics would only frighten off Robbie (the Menacing Letter Writer) all the more, whereas I needed him to be concentrating on her, not me.

"So what do you say?" Lionel went on.

"About what?" I hadn't a clue what he was referring to.

"About escorting me up the red carpet at the Oscars, of course," he replied exasperated, though with good humour, and obviously mindful of the fact that I must have been overwhelmed to find myself with Vivien as a houseguest, especially as we'd never been the best of bosom buddies. Not that this description of our friendship, given Vivien's rather enhanced frontage, was the best choice of words.

Believe me or believe me not, I actually paused before answering. It wasn't every day a girl got asked to the Oscars. Indeed, I was fully aware that most would have jumped at the chance blindfolded, especially if it meant being escorted by Lionel King. But, crazy though it may seem, it was not on my bucket list. In fact, the idea of willingly putting myself at the mercy of the public, the press, the paparazzi, and that entire horrific hullabaloo was something I'd always shied away from.

As if reading my mind, Lionel spoke softly down the line.

"Chantelle, I know it's asking a lot from you. I realise you have no desire to have to put up with the blinding flash bulbs, the probing questions, the gaping stares from famous and non-famous alike. I realise what a daunting experience it will be for you. But I really need you by my side. It's the first time I've ever been nominated for Best Actor, and it's the first time I've ever found someone whom I really love to share the experience with, to help me get through the evening."

What a smooth talker! Put that way there really wasn't much for me to deliberate.

"Of course I'll go to the Oscars with you!" The vision of having to fight my way through screaming crowds was cast aside by the simple, joyful fact that he'd said the words I'd been longing to hear. He loved me, and that was reason enough to dive into the lion's den.

"You'll have to fly over this week, then. We haven't got much time to get your dress sorted out."

"And my hair sorted out," I added in mirth.

"We'll let Gabby deal with that," he joked back.

I thought, gleefully, he loves me – regardless of my feral hair!

***

The following day I drove back to London with Tammy and Ray, leaving Vivien in Robbie's capable hands. He was going to have his work cut out, dealing with Vivien as well as the house restoration. Nevertheless, considering the anxiety he'd put me through over the last several days, inundating me with threatening letters, I didn't feel the slightest bit remorseful.

Vivien was all bliss and exhilaration when I told her that she could remain in the house during my absence, with the sole condition that she helped with the work. She had agreed enthusiastically. I wasn't sure if she would feel so eager at the end of the week, and several broken fingernails later. As I sped into the city I actually wondered if it had been wise to let Vivien help with the decorations. I risked returning to a pink Barbie dollshouse. I just hoped that Robbie had the good sense and male firmness to ignore her, and her colour schemes, if it came down to it.

The flight over to LA seemed to be the longest I'd ever endured. I'd managed to get a flight the very next day after speaking with Lionel. I'd turned up at the airport, luggage in hand, proposing to go on standby and, as luck would have it, the very first flight scheduled for LA had a seat available. The luck ended here, however, as the moment I sat down a chronic case of diarrhoea set in. I was out of my place every five minutes and dashing to the loo.

I asked one of the flight attendants for something to help soothe my upset stomach, but was politely informed that she was not authorised to give out medication. So I asked for a couple of adult nappies. She laughed out loud at the notion, finding the situation remarkably funny and obviously assuming that I was just pulling her leg. In fact, she had no sodding concept of how serious the situation was. I had no control over my bowels and was in agony and despair each time I scampered down the aisle to the WC as fast as my cramped-up body would allow.

On the fifth toilet stop I came face to face with a nun who was waiting her turn to use it.

"You really don't want to go in there," I said. But she obviously didn't understand English, as she took no notice of my warning and stepped inside closing the door in my face. It wasn't long before she reappeared, bright pink in the face. She'd evidently held her breath inside the cubicle and looked on the verge of hyperventilating. She made the sign of the cross as she passed me, which utterly offended me. Nevertheless, I was blessed with a brainwave and on my next loo stop I was armed with a home made *Out of Order* sign, which I proudly and promptly stuck on the outside of the door. It was with mental relief – if not stomach relief – that I saw that passengers used the other toilet during the long haul, leaving me and my out of order gut alone with the "Out of Order" loo.

I was sure that Robbie was to thank for this bout of gastritis. He'd been chef the evening before I'd left, and had impressed us all with his *cordon bleu* flair. Vivien had looked guiltily at her plate which had been piled high, but after the first mouth-watering bite she was in food paradise, as were we all: roast chicken set in a delicious herb and wine sauce, roast potatoes that just melted on the tongue, and an array of poached vegetables, all polished off with several generous goblets of red *Rias Baixas* wine.

The evil rotter had obviously gone and put rat poison in my food, or possibly a whole sachet or two of laxative in my wine. I couldn't believe that I'd been so naïve. I'd even congratulated Robbie on his cooking prowess. I could've kicked myself for my stupidity when it had been so clear for

179

so long that he was out to get me. Robbie, meanwhile, had just looked at me in sly mirth, which, at the time, I had taken for shy modesty. He really was a calculating arsehole! Having said that, he must have felt some remorse the following morning. Just as I was about to step into Tammy's Jag to return to London, he'd pulled me to one side. There'd been an anxious look in his eyes.

"There's something I've got to confess."

I was taken aback. He was obviously going to confess that he was the author of the letters. But I had neither the time nor the desire to converse with Robbie about all that just then. I wanted to leave it to one side for now and deal with it at some point in the future.

"Robbie, it's OK, I know. We'll talk about it when I get back. When we are both less emotional about the whole affair, and have had some time to reflect."

He looked rather stunned at the fact that I was aware of his conduct, though, at the same time, somewhat relieved. He looked as if a huge burden had been lifted from his shoulders.

Without another word I'd stepped into the Jag and had zipped into London, the airport, the loo – and on to the Academy of Motion Picture Awards: The Oscars.

***

I don't know how I got through passport control once I'd successfully landed in LA. For an alarming moment I thought I was going to be put into quarantine; placed under strict observation lest I was carrying some hitherto unknown and deadly bug into the States. Thankfully, they shifted me, real nippy, out into the arrivals lounge. I staggered through the sliding doors, the constant belly cramps making me double over in pain. I felt so weak, too; the only thing that actually kept me on my feet was the fact that I leaned heavily on my luggage trolley and my childlike belief that Lionel would be there at the airport to greet me with open arms.

Lionel, however, was much too famous to fight his way through mobbing crowds just to meet me at the airport.

Instead, as I tried despondently to remain lucid, I came face to face with Gabby. The moment she saw me she rushed over.

"Honey, you look absolutely shocking."

"Just as candid as ever," I managed to joke back.

"What's wrong?" she asked, concern in her voice.

"Apart from breaking the Guinness Book of Records for toilet stops over the Atlantic, I'm fine. It must be something somebody gave me to eat or drink…"

From then on everything remains rather vague. I had no recollection of the drive to Freddy G's mansion. Nor of being taken down to the cottage where I'd been accommodated during my previous stay. I had no notion of time or events.

I had visions of Lionel sponging my forehead with a damp towel, of doctors who seemed to be in and out the room like bloody yo-yos, of Gabby who looked on at me ghostly pale and fraught. As long as they don't bring in a priest, I'll be fine.

At some point, though I'd no idea if it was hours later or days, I finally felt the fever break. My entire body was sore and frail. I felt as if I'd been given a good hiding – and I guess in a way I had, by Robbie's evil cooking, or by whatever poison he'd used on me.

The diagnosis was a severe bout of salmonella, which had left me bedridden for five days. Personally, I thought I looked like I'd just stepped out of some sort of extra-severe Gabby-style fitness boot camp. My cheeks were hollow, my eyes sunken, my bust non-existent, and my bum no longer cheeky. I couldn't possibly accompany Lionel to the Oscars looking as I did.

"You look like a bloody beanpole," had been Gabby's comforting words. It looked like mission impossible. But at least it meant I was off the carrot diet for a while.

"You've got three days to recuperate before Oscar comes to call. And kid, you're gonna be ready… No shit!" said Gabby optimistically. A personal stylist was sent for, my hair was trimmed and tamed, and I had all the beauty treatments done in the cottage. Gabby even set up a portable sun-bed in the lounge.

In a frantic rush to find some elegant attire for the Oscars I was jostled in and out of at least twenty exclusively-designed evening dresses by Giorgio Armani, Dolce & Gabbana, Versace and Emanuel Ungaro, but nothing seemed to fit. The dresses were either too tight or too loose on me. Gabby insisted on an opulent lengthy red Versace dress, but it conjured up images of the red cat suit I'd been given to wear during the shooting of *The Business* and I didn't want anyone to be reminded of that ghastly film. It would not have been a good way to begin relationships with the Hollywood press. At last I saw a silver crocheted dress by Marc Bouwer that I fell in love with. It was the best fit of all the dresses and, considering that there was so little time for last minute alterations, I thought it the best choice. It was cut very low and left the midriff area almost visibly bare, except for some delicate stitching which just about covered the skin. The fine material hugged the waist and hip line and then fell straight to the floor, with a rather generous slit up the left leg.

"If you're set on wearing that dress," Gabby remarked, "you'd better put this on." She threw me a skin-coloured brassière which seemed to have a life of its own.

"What's this?" I questioned as I held it up.

"In simple terminology, it's called a wonder bra. It's the latest model on the market, and much cheaper, safer and quicker than getting a boob job. Considering that your natural bust seems to have momentarily evaporated with the salmonella, and that you're determined to wear a dress designed to flaunt a shapely bosom, you'll just have to flaunt a fake one!"

I tried it on there and then. It made a really exaggerated enlargement of my breast size. I thought it was a bit too inflated, but Gabby reassured me that it was okay. As I looked down on my overblown bosom, I mused that I could use it as a chin rest.

During all these days of recovery Lionel was my pillar of strength and security. He was the first to arrive in the mornings and stayed with me until late into the evenings. But he made no move to kiss me, or touch me in any other way than brotherly. I didn't really blame him either. I wasn't exactly Miss Desirable at the moment, rather skimpy and skinny after my bout of salmonella, and I really didn't need the added excitement of excessive physical contact with Lionel if I was to recover in time for the Oscars. I even heard one of the doctors say to Lionel, when they must have thought I was dozing, "Hands off, until she puts on at least five pounds and is on the road to recovery."

So where's that chocolate fudge cake?

Chapter Twenty-One

It was Oscar night, and boy was I impressed!

When it comes to glamour and style, being on the red carpet has been and always will be the high point. I simply couldn't believe that I was on that very carpet together with so many stars. They say that when the stars step on the red carpet they set the international standard for fashion and make style history. And there was plain old me, mingling with all the legendary celebrities. It really was quite an overwhelming experience.

It also occurred to me that I should have left my hair all frizzy in a gesture of comradeship with those who have the same mop-like hair as I do.

Being on the arm of Oscar nominee was quite an undertaking to say the least. The cameras simply seemed to zoom in on us from all angles. It was also the first time I had seen Lionel deal with the press. He effortlessly breezed through the hounding questions and daunting attention as if on a morning stroll through the park.

"Mr King, over here… Lionel, give us a wave…Who's the doll, Mr Lionel…? How do you feel about your nomination, Sir…?"

The insistent yelling went on and on and on. I do believe that one of the main factors that actually got me through the evening was the feeling that, as everything seemed so surreal, I partly believed that I was merely dreaming up the whole thing. Consequently, as occurs in dreams, I just let myself drift through the evening as if I had no real control over the proceedings, and that it was all just an impressive concoction of my over-active imagination.

Lionel finally broke free from the press. He took me by

the arm, which I was thankful for and leaned rather heavily on, and we both moved inside the Kodak Theatre. Even though Gabby had briefed me on what to expect once we were inside, nothing could have prepared me for the impressive surroundings. Wow! I was indeed thankful for Lionel's arm, which I clung to as if it was a lifejacket. The Kodak Theatre is the epitome of all things American: big, bold and brassy. As Gabby had explained to me, the seating capacity of 3,400 is on three levels, which brings the audience close to the theatre stage. The stage itself measures 113 feet wide and 60 feet deep. If she had simply said it was "bloody massive", instead of bombarding me with facts and figures, I would have got the gist.

Lionel and I had been allocated seats down by the stage, as Lionel, being an Oscar nominee, had to be close at hand. If we'd been given seating up in one of the upper tiers and Lionel was given the award (as I was sure he would be; not only was he a talented actor, I had spent the last thirty-six hours in discussion with God about the issue), it would take a good half-hour for him to simply get down and on to the stage.

As we made our way towards our seats I was impressed by the theatre interior, which was highlighted by a "tiara," a striking oval that was intertwined by smaller ovals, coated in silver leaf that endearingly matched my silver dress. I took it as a good omen.

The impact of the entire event soon surpassed the initial awe I'd felt at being surrounded by so many stars. I was struck by the impressive organisation and supervision of the affair, and wondered what I would have to do to become a member of the organising committee. I couldn't think of anything more challenging and fulfilling, and knew I would just love every moment of the demanding and taxing, but ultimately gratifying, task.

***

The ceremony started, and the biggest annual television

audience in the world tuned in. Soon, comedian Jerry Sandstone had everyone entertained, comfortable, laughing and relaxed – although that "everyone" certainly didn't include me. The foreign, technical, musical and secondary and supporting awards came and went, then the major awards began to be announced. I could feel my stomach tighten and the butterflies take wing.

Lionel laughed and clapped during the show. He frequently turned to me to whisper something – although, for the life of me, I haven't a clue what – and shouted approval when a particular favourite or friend went forward.

Then the big moment finally came. Lionel held my hand tight and I could feel his palm was damp from nerves. It was the only indication that betrayed his outward composure. Despite the cool smile and poised profile, he was even more anxious than I was – and I was, by then, a complete bundle of nerves. I appreciated how vital this moment was for him. For an actor, being honoured with the Academy Statuette, the golden trophy, the statue of merit, was the ultimate recognition.

I also reflected that it would raise his asking price, and as a considerable amount of the money he made went to various charities, I supposed they would benefit, too.

"And the Oscar goes to…" The musical voice that floated over the microphone was that of Ms Diaz, who had been given the honour of naming the Best Actor. She paused as Jerry Sandstone, who stood beside her, pretended to struggle somewhat melodramatically to open the envelope. I was vividly aware that her dress, bar the colour, was virtually the exact same model as mine. With the camera images which kept swinging from her to Lionel and me, the similarity was made all the more obvious and tremendously embarrassing.

The envelope was finally opened. In unison, Ms Diaz and Jerry Sandstone proclaimed, "Lionel King for *South of the Border*."

A tremendous roar went up and I felt one and all, near and far alike, turn to look at Lionel. He, notwithstanding, held my hand fast, seemingly overwhelmed by the outcome. The director of the film, Freddy G, and all his co-stars were up on their feet congratulating him. He was slapped on the back. Nevertheless it took him a clear five seconds to respond. He got to his feet as if in a half-trance. I rose with him, not so much by choice, but because Lionel still held my hand in a vice-like grip and seemed set on not letting go. I had images of him towing me up on to the stage and me toppling over in my neck-breaking heels.

Thankfully he relaxed his grip. But only to grasp me in a passionate embrace. He pressed his lips down on mine and for an instant I was unaware of the surrounding cameras, which were picking up an image that was being flashed around the whole world. I was just conscious of Lionel's fervent kiss, the beat of his heart that I could sense pounding in his chest and I felt myself glow with pride.

I also became acutely aware and appalled by the fact that I hadn't actually got around to watching *South of the Border*. It had been number one on my priority list. I had even got Gabby to get me a DVD copy. But my salmonella bout had left me completely and utterly wiped out. Thus, the one and only time I'd sat down to watch the film, I'd fallen into a profound sleep before the title had even hit the screen. At the time, needless to say, I'd been much too shamefaced to admit this to Gabby, let alone Lionel. I now dearly wished I'd had the guts to admit the fact to Gabby. She could at least have given me a scene-by-scene account. The chances were certain that I'd be asked, at some moment throughout the course of the night, for my opinion of the film. I hastily decided that if the situation arose I'd just have to pretend I'd drunk too much fizz to be able to give a coherent response.

Lionel was finally up on the front stage. The applause rang throughout the arena as he took the stairs two at a time. He looked so downright handsome that I really felt I was dreaming. I couldn't believe that I was with such a talented, thoughtful and positively gorgeous guy! He had on a single-breasted tuxedo, with a sharp peak lapel, while the formal trousers were slim and trim. He swung Ms Diaz around and, on having a clear view of her panties from where I was sitting, I made a mental note not to let Lionel swing me around in the same way.

Lionel briefly paused before commencing his acceptance speech. He looked around as if he was trying to memorise every fine detail of the evening and log it all into his mind so that he would never forget the moment.

"Would someone like to come up here and pinch me?" he exclaimed, and a roar of laughter went up as Ms Diaz saucily took Lionel at his word and pinched his behind.

"First, I want to thank Michael for believing in me and for giving me the opportunity to play such a challenging and colourful character. Thank you to the whole crew and cast members, too, for doing such a wonderful job. This year has been like a bed of roses for me in every possible way. Indeed, if I could spend the rest of my life with a certain 'Rose' at my side, I'd be the happiest man alive... Chantelle Rose, this," (he held up the statuette) "is for you!"

Right then would have been my ideal cue to wake from the dream. It would have been the perfect cut-off. I'd been proposed to – at least it had sounded very much like a proposal – in front of millions of people on live television, but until then I'd remained pretty much anonymous. I had quite successfully avoided the camera persecution and the media frenzy. But now, as each and every camera was turned on me to get close-ups from every possible angle, I realised that this pleasant, dream-like scenario was threatening to turn into a full-blown nightmare. There goes my anonymity.

Lionel had obviously let his emotions get the better of him. It had been a tremendous slip-up on his behalf to name me in front of the whole wide world. A snapped camera image was tolerable, but having my name declared out loud in what had sounded very much like *Chantelle, will you marry me?* was going to make an international impact. I had images of the next edition of *Trivial Pursuit* including the question: *Which year was Lionel King awarded the Oscar for Best Actor, and who or what was the Rose he referred to in his acceptance speech?*

There was no turning back now. No walking down the street unnoticed. Still, I reasoned, if I really loved Lionel and planned to be at his side for the rest of our lives, there was nothing much for it but to turn to the cameras and smile sweetly as if everything was under gratifying control. I winked at the camera lens to my left and blew a kiss at the mobile camera above.

I'll just throttle Lionel later, after I've had a drink or two to calm my shattered nerves.

***

Several drinks later, at one of the private parties, I was actually much too giddy to do anything but hold precariously onto one of Lionel's arms. Still on the road to recovery after the salmonella poisoning, I'd got pretty much legless on just a couple of glasses of champers. I had the underlying impression that everyone was scrutinising me with critical eyes, whilst thinking: *What on earth does Lionel see in her?*

Then again, I actually wondered the same thing myself.

"Lionel, you fox," called out Al P as he approached. He looked even more wasted than I was. "Congratulations, boy. And I'm not just referring to tonight's award." He winked at me and I wondered if there was a contagious eye twitch going around which was causing everyone to blink, and all at me. I didn't give it much more thought, however, as I suddenly spied Sandy, the stunt girl and my caravan-buddy in the Nevada desert, poised against the wall on the other side of the room. I slipped my arm from Lionel, who remained engrossed in conversation with legendary Al, and tottered over to where Sandy stood.

She threw her arms around me in an energetic bear-hug that almost toppled us both over. I started to wonder if someone had spiked the wine, which would explain why everyone seemed so energetically merry.

"I hope you plan to sue," she blurted with a slight slur.

"Who? Robbie?" I replied, though Christ only knew how she'd found out about the threatening letters and poisoned meal.

"Who's Robbie?" she asked back perplexed, and I didn't know who was more pissed, her or me, for the conversation was going around in circles. I certainly didn't know what the hell she was referring to, and she was obviously just as bemused by my mumblings.

"No-one," I replied back "Sue who?"

"Sue the magazine *Hollywood Blue,* of course, for publishing that article. Surely you've heard. Crystal Lee's just furious. Then again, she doesn't come across well at all. She's ridiculed as too fat-arsed to do nude scenes, whereas the mysterious Chantelle Rose, which is you of course honey, is actually the one with the exquisite figure. There are loads of stolen photos from the shoot. Real clear ones of you baring all."

Sandy suddenly paused, almost certainly on seeing my expression of utter horror. It wasn't by any means the first time she'd innocently let slip something which I simply didn't want to hear.

It came to me with shocking clarity why everyone had been looking and winking at me the whole evening, as if I was some provocative loose tramp. Not only had my anonymity been lost that evening, my integrity had gone too.

I suddenly had a vision of my mother looking down on me from the heavens above. She would be forced to use her maiden name up there from now, on I reflected despondently.

"Sorry, Mum." I whispered. To Sandy, I muttered, "I think I'm going to be sick."

I stumbled out onto the lower balcony to get some fresh air. I was in desperate need of some cooling breeze to clear my mind and my wheezy stomach. The champagne and wine mix hadn't gone down well at all, and the devastating news about *Hollywood Blue* was the decisive ingredient of a lethal concoction.

I leaned over the balcony breathing heavily. My head cleared somewhat. If it hadn't been for Lionel, and the fact that above all I didn't want to ruin his special night, I would have left there and then. A mighty leap into the gardens below would have been on the cards, except I didn't think my high heels would have taken the strain, and the dress, flimsy as it was, would probably have torn right down the back and left me nearly naked. Not that this was a novelty to anyone anymore... I'll count to one hundred, I thought, and then go back inside and face the music.

I didn't know why it bothered me as much as it did that the whole of Hollywood (and all movie fans, so we were talking of a goodly proportion of the world's total population) now knew that the girl in the nude scenes in Lionel King's latest production was me. Okay, my name had been given to the photo images of my nude behind. Then, that name had been given a face, and that face was mine. Everyone had seen it after Lionel's well-intended but regrettably untimely announcement.

When I'd decided to go ahead with the nude scenes, it was because I'd been assured that no-one would ever find out that, firstly, Crystal Lee had been in desperate need of a body double, and secondly, that the body double was me. Why was I so devastated that the information had got out? Let's face it, I'd earned more money than I'd ever dreamed of, it had been a fantastic adventure, I'd been treated like a princess by everyone – and I'd met Lionel King and he was truly, madly, deeply in love with me. Indeed, if you put the issue into perspective, what with all the starvation in the world, the terrorist attacks that were devastating the lives of so many, the hate that was evident on almost every street corner, the natural catastrophes which were just rocking the world, was it really such a big deal that everyone knew what my buttocks (and not *just* my buttocks) looked like?

In any case, the damage was done and there was sod-all I could do about it. So I decided that I'd sue the magazine and give all the money to charity.

With this decision in mind I was left feeling greatly relieved. Just as I was about to turn to brace myself for the sly looks of those inside at the party, I felt someone place strong, powerful arms around my waist. I didn't have to turn to know it was Lionel. I had breathed in his characteristic cologne and my heart starting flapping at his intimate embrace.

"What do you say," he murmured into my ear, "if we made a quick exit and left the guests to their own entertainment?"

"I couldn't agree with you more," I whispered back.

"Do you think you could jump over the wall and into the garden?" Lionel asked.

"I'm not too sure if I'll get away without a scratch, but I'll give it a shot."

It was about a metre and a half jump to the grounds below so I removed my high heels and positioned myself. After my flying leap onto the cottage garage back in England not so long ago, this jump was a piece of cake. Before I knew it both Lionel and I were scampering over the green lawn and running to the car park and freedom.

I had no idea where Lionel was planning to take me, but it wasn't a concern. I was just fully aware that, at long last, we were alone together and there was no Vivien to ruin the moment by hurling hefty items at us, and no doctors around to warn Lionel not to excite me – but in any case I was beyond being calm. Lionel drove through the darkened night in relative silence, caressing my hand that he held in his until my whole body tingled. It was just as well I wasn't driving. I was way too distracted by his tender touch to have been able to coordinate a vehicle anywhere.

Sometime later he pulled into a silent port area. It was night time but the area was familiar and with growing excitement I knew that he was taking me to his yacht, the *Chantelle*. Maybe it was destiny, him and me. I must have behaved extremely well in a previous life to deserve such good fortune in this one. We left the car in the car park and walked down the wooden walkway that led to the speedboats. Strange; Lionel's was the only one moored up and ready.

I stepped, with care, down into the vessel and positioned myself near the helm. Lionel untied the mooring rope and then stepped easily onto the boat and moved forward to start the engine. He handed me his Oscar. I gripped it hard, worried that with any slight jerk of the speedboat the bronze figure would go whirling into the water below.

It was quite creepy, at first, speeding out into the dark water. If it hadn't been that I had Lionel alongside me and assumed he knew what he was doing, I would have panicked. Racing along in the murky darkness was like driving into a black hole. The water sprayed up into my hair and I felt immensely alive and happy and excited. If we were to get lost in the immense Pacific Ocean in the dead of night, somehow I just knew that Gigi would guide us to safety.

Suddenly the *Chantelle* loomed out of the darkness, a huge silhouette on the bobbing surf. Getting from the speedboat up on deck was tricky, and I was thankful when I'd finally climbed aboard and Lionel had taken the Oscar from my hands. I'd been exhilarated by the night speedboat ride but I had not enjoyed the responsibility of holding the heavy figure the whole ride out. My arm felt dead from holding it to me in a vice-like grip. I reckoned you could probably slam someone, an intruder for example, over the head with it and they'd be out for the count without even denting the statue.

Everyone has seen pictures of it: a sort of bald, naked man holding something, but few understand its significance. The figure is of a Knight holding a Crusader's sword, standing on a reel of film with five spokes signifying the original branches of the Academy: actors, writers, directors, producers and technicians. There was a time when magazines such as *Weekly* and *Variety* had attempted to label the figure as *The Iron Man*. Thankfully that never stuck. I much preferred *The Statue of Merit* – and was glad to hand it over to its rightful owner.

Lionel handed me a drink. I had asked for something non-alcoholic, but I could smell Malibu in it. Lionel obviously planned to get me pissed so he could try to seduce me. There was really no need. If it wasn't that I would have come across as downright desperate, I would have torn my dress off there and then and pounced on him. Mind you, I was obviously all mouth, as on seeing the mattress on the deck, the same mattress we'd slept on the previous time I'd

193

been out to Lionel's yacht, I got into a state of jittering nerves.

I'd longed for this moment, dreamt of it constantly over the last months. But now the occasion had finally arrived, I was in a turmoil of utter awkwardness. I downed the cocktail in one, hoping that the alcohol would give me a brain-rush and would release all my inhibitions.

I was aware of Lionel's intense gaze and I was glad that we were standing out on deck in the darkness so that my flushed skin wasn't noticeable. This was pretty ridiculous, considering he had previously seen me standing starkers under harsh studio lights.

Standing on the swaying deck, however, it was just him and me, and it was for real. Lionel moved towards me, forward from the dancing silver shadows caused by the moon reflected on the sea, and clasped me in his arms. I felt his lips on my dark hair, my slight neck, and then on my mouth as he effortlessly swung me into his arms and strode towards the mattress, which was laden with silken cushions which I hadn't noticed before. He laid me, with ease, onto the mattress. Then he took my face in his hands and looked into my eyes with longing. With one finger he traced my eyebrows, my forehead, my nose, as if planning to sculpt my face, imprint it into his memory forever, as I too would imprint this moment forever in my mind. I felt myself shaking as Lionel slowly began to unzip my delicate silver-grey crochet dress – which had surprisingly remained intact during the adventures of the evening – and it slipped to the floor. He pulled me to him and again I felt his mouth on mine, his firm slender hands, piano hands I liked to think of them, sliding gently down to the small of my back, pressing my body against him until my whole self shook, until I could no longer withhold the rising passion.

Lionel gently unclipped the top that Gabby had given me. I wondered if he'd be in for a more than slight disappointment as the wonder bra made me look at least five sizes bigger than I actually was. Lionel, thankfully, appeared oblivious (anyway, I reminded myself again, he'd seen the

194

real me naked before) as he laid me onto the soft yielding cushions of the mattress.

Shivering with pleasure I surrendered to his touch, his mouth, his fingers. My own hands had gone into autopilot and had successfully removed Lionel's classy tux without even stumbling over the buttonholes. The alcohol had done wonders at calming my shaking hands. We were both naked and I could feel the warmth of him against me. I was overcome with a sensation that went far beyond mere carnal desire or passion.

For the first time in my whole life, as I abandoned myself to slow, sensual lovemaking, I knew that I was genuinely in love.

Chapter Twenty-Two

The following morning I woke at first light, calm and happy. I turned to face Lionel who was lying close to me, his arm wrapped around me protectively. I'd expected to feel rather vulnerable and shy, but as I turned and found Lionel's intense gaze on me I realised the one who seemed vulnerable and shy was him, as incredible as that sounds.

"Good morning, Princess," he murmured as he kissed me gently on the lips. I smiled back at him and sighed contentedly.

"How long have you been awake?" I asked.

"All night," he replied. "I was afraid that if I slept I would wake to find that this had all been a dream. That you, my darling Chantelle, had just been a figment of my imagination and that my search for you was still in vain. I know that you'll find it hard to believe, but believe me when I tell you that I've been searching for you all my life. And now that I've finally found you I don't want to let you go. I want to know that when I'm old, this same sweet face of yours will be at my side smiling back as it is now, with its added old-age wrinkles which I'll love all the more for the years we've spent together that they'll then represent. I was serious last night when I said that I would be the happiest man alive if I could spend the rest of my life with you, Chantelle Rose. I love you."

He then got me to my feet. I was butt-naked and it was all rather surreal. He in turn went down on one knee, clasped my hands in his, looked up into my face with pleading, honest, burning desire, and declared, his throaty voice quivering with passion, "Will you marry me and make me the happiest man alive?"

It was my turn to think this was all a dream. From my scant experience, the majority of men, after a night of passion, tend to scamper off as far away and as fast as possible. Lionel's reaction, however, was the reverse. He was obviously one of the few left from the old school. He, remarkably, wanted to make an "honest" woman of me, and I found the idea rather fetching.

Well, to be honest, I was absolutely thrilled, and had to refrain from throwing myself at him from sheer joy, afraid that I would probably break his neck from pure excitement. I got down on my knees level with him.

"Lionel King," I said, my voice remarkably calm. I couldn't keep the smile off my face despite trying to remain serious; it was a serious matter and required a serious reply. "Could you please pinch me, for I do believe I must be dreaming."

He squeezed my left nipple hard in reply as he laughed back in joy.

"Is that a yes?" he prompted. His green eyes sparkled in the early light, he looked so boyish and young and so utterly handsome. I couldn't believe that he, of all the men in the world, was insistent on being my future hubby. I couldn't believe my luck. Superb job, Mum, I said to myself, for only a generous helping of angel-work could have pulled this off for me.

"Of course it's a YES!" I cried out in joy.

***

It was settled. I would return to the UK to sell the cottage. Robbie could have the damn thing for all I cared. He had got his way in the end. Mind you, I guess so had I; more than got my way. Mrs King, rock on! The "Hollywood Bitch" was staying in LA.

I couldn't have been happier. I only hoped that Vivien had managed to seduce Robbie during the days she'd remained in Kent with him. I was wicked enough to calculate that if she stayed there with him, that would be another headache out of the way.

I planned to convince Gabby to set up an events organisation company with me after I married Lionel. Even if I was married to a multi-millionaire film star and we spent day and night making hot, passionate love, I knew I would still have enough restless – or perhaps reckless – energy to want to do something in my own right. I believed "Sis" Gabby and I would make a good team. I would charm the clients, and Gabby, when or if needed, would be the one sent in to kick ass. She could terrorise the clients that didn't pay on time, or intimidate sub-groups like catering or decoration staff that were slack. She would love it, and in any case she desperately needed something to occupy her mind. Otherwise, I had images of her waking both Lionel and me up at the crack of dawn for our morning runs, and scolding us for deviating from her carrot diet. Hence my proposal, in my opinion, would be ideal for everyone concerned.

It was noon by the time we docked at the pier, just two days after Oscar night. I would have loved to have stayed on the yacht for at least two or three months, but within forty-eight hours we had devoured all the food. I would've even tried fishing if I thought it would allow us a few more days together, alone in the middle of the Pacific. Food apart, Lionel, however, had several urgent press engagements he had to attend, so we reluctantly climbed back into the speedboat and headed back to shore.

I realised now why the port area looked so familiar. Next to the private boat pier area there was a slightly overgrown path that lead all the way to the very beach where Gabby had forced me to go for my sun-up dashes.

I wondered how Gabby would take to me becoming a new member of the family. I had a sense that she appreciated me more than she appreciated Vivien! There were even times when I actually found her quite a laugh, but I could never be wholly sure where I stood with her. As long as she eased off the fitness regime with me, and handed me all her spare keys to the cottage, we would continue to get on famously. I was keen to ask what she thought of my events company project.

I needed her vote of confidence, as it was a bit too much of a challenge to embark on alone. And I believed it would take her mind off trying to dominate Lionel's life – which she did, totally, though no doubt all in good faith.

Lionel left me at the gate that opened into Freddy G's quaint bungalow garden. After a passionate embrace he reassured me that he would return that evening. I just smiled blissfully back at him, content beyond words, and watched him as he retraced his steps back down the path towards the beach. Once he was out of sight, I stood a moment longer in idyllic peace, and marvelled at how wonderfully things had turned out. In a serene daze I stepped into the gardens and, humming contently to myself, made my way to the chalet. I assumed that at some future point I would have to move my stuff into Lionel's place, which I still hadn't seen or knew anything about. I couldn't abuse Freddy G's hospitality for ever, though I'd really grown to love the bungalow. It was perfect, with lush gardens and direct access to a private beach.

As I skipped along, I was startled to collide head-on wiht Gabby. I'd leapt up the terrace steps in one flying bound, kidding myself that I looked like a ballerina (though lacking all the ballerina grace, of course), just as she opened the cottage door and stepped out. Maybe I wouldn't ask her to be my business partner, I thought; she really would be too controlling and overpowering, Tammy would be much more chilled out. That was suddenly a wonderful idea. Tammy would love the California life-style. I didn't know why I hadn't thought of it before. It was about time she moved out of her parents' place, too.

"Gabby!" I exclaimed, and almost let slip, *You scared the shit out of me!* but managed to cut it down to, "Gosh, I didn't expect to find you here!" She surprised me further by picking me up and swinging me around in utter joy.

"I'm so happy for you!" she exclaimed.

Personally, I didn't know which Gabby was scarier: the military Gabby that I knew of old, or this new, utterly over-exhilarated Gabby. She was like a bouncy ball. She obviously knew that I'd spent the last two days with Lionel, but I doubted that she knew of our plans to marry. Nobody did.

"I'msoOrelievedthatyoutwofinallygotittogether." Her words came out in a single breath.

"I'm glad you're happy too," I replied, speaking slowly trying to get Gabby to calm down. If this was how hyper Gabby got with good news, how on earth would react to disagreeable or bad news? Or if she simply hadn't been keen on the idea of Lionel and me getting together?

"I'm going to tell you a secret," Gabby continued, as she led me into the cottage and sat me down at the kitchen table. I was shocked to see that she'd prepared herself a chocolate milk shake. That definitely wasn't her style. Maybe her strange mood was the result of a sugar overdose.

"When Lionel and I were younger, Lionel must have been about fourteen at the time, we escaped to New Orleans during Mardi Gras. It was the best adventure ever."

Escaped? Most kids I know escape just down the road or into the neighbour's garden. Gabby and Lionel seemingly took it that step further and escaped right across the US continent.

"During our stay in New Orleans we came across a gypsy woman fortune-teller. She didn't want money, but she insisted on reading Lionel's fortune. Everything she told him has come true. Every little detail – including, finally, the last but most important one. That's you, honey. You were foretold in Lionel's fate and this prophecy has come true."

"Gabby," I said, "that's all very interesting, but I really don't believe in fortune telling. I hate to put a damper on things, but you can't seriously think I'm going to fall for the idea that the only reason Lionel is in love with me is because some gypsy woman forecast that he would end up with someone like me."

I refused to believe that Lionel loved me for "mystic" reasons. I couldn't bear the idea that he was with me because of what some hippy woman had told him when he was a young and impressionable teenager. Surely he was with me for good old, practical, down-to-earth, reasons, such as great sex, and, of course, my never-ending intelligence and wit.

But Gabby wouldn't stop. She had to go ahead and ruin my innocent belief that Lionel loved me purely for myself. Her words were like a bucket of icy water.

"Chantelle! The gypsy woman told Lionel all those years ago that the woman of his dreams would be called Chantelle Rose; she would be dark-haired, with almond eyes, tall and slender – and only with her would he be happy, regardless of all the money and fame in the world."

Well, I had to give it to that soothsayer woman, whoever and wherever she may be; her so-called "Chantelle Rose" did sound awfully like me. And it was such a bloody let-down. The only reason that Lionel wanted to be with me was because some witch had somehow summoned up my name. Lionel had gone and fallen for her myth instead of loving me for me.

It suddenly hit me that Freddy G had nothing to do with the "I'm an agent, trust me" razzamatazz in London, or the luxurious accommodation I'd been set up in, or the film contract. It was all part of a fantastic scheme in Lionel's mind to seduce me after he'd seen me in that fucking awful film. God! The only reason he was with me was because I was called Chantelle Rose.

Chantelle Rose. Thirteen letters strung together, which, if taken apart, meant nothing at all.

Chapter Twenty-Three

It was dusk by the time Lionel arrived back at the bungalow. He let himself in. He had his own set of keys, of course, as by now it was obvious that the bungalow was his. It had all come clear to me that afternoon as I'd sat there on the sitting-room sofa, gazing out of the terrace windows and into the gardens.

I'd often wondered what Lionel's house was like, unaware that I'd actually been living in it from day one. The mansion, which I called the main house, was obviously Lionel's family home, and was where Gabby still lived. This explained why she was always so punctual and always seemed to be popping in as if it was the most natural thing in the world. It all made sense: the private beach area, and the easy access to the pier where the speedboat was moored. I couldn't believe I hadn't twigged beforehand. All the cards had been laid on the table and I hadn't seen the game. I'd naïvely keep on believing that Freddy G had been behind the whole organisation, and truly convinced myself that Lionel had fallen in love with me progressively during the time we'd spent together.

It was impossible for me to have imagined that Lionel had schemed the whole thing up from day one, and that my actual persona had nothing to do with his words of wanting, or tenderness, or passion, or love – or indeed his marriage proposal. Had I been named anything else but Chantelle Rose, he wouldn't even have blinked in my direction.

It was, to say the least, utterly disheartening.

I, on the other hand, despite my strong initial reservations about falling for a Hollywood Star, had not just side-stepped all preliminary qualms and precautions about the matter, but had, instead, bent to every whim asked of me and fallen head-over-heels in love.

I loved Lionel for himself, not for his name, his stardom or his wealth. Indeed, I saw his celebrity status as a pressure that I'd have to learn to live with because I loved him and wanted to be with him. I saw it as a barrier that my love for him would help me surmount. It would be the cross – apart from Vivien, which was bad enough – which I would have to bear if I wished to share my life with him.

I couldn't stop the thoughts that flooded through my head. I'd been in turmoil all afternoon. I loved Lionel, but who did he really love? Was it the down-to-earth, clear-cut Chantelle he'd met on the Nevada set several weeks earlier? Or was it an imaginary Chantelle who was nothing more than a vision conjured up by some strange gypsy storyteller, then embellished over the years by Lionel's own imagination and fantasy?

I had to find out.

***

Lionel slipped through the door. It was now dusk and I sat quietly in the shadows.

"Hi Princess!" he murmured quietly as he finally found me in the unlit room, and kissed me gently on the lips. He handed me an extravagant bouquet of flowers, the exact same arrangement sent to me by my "secret" admirer at the start of my American adventure. I could never have imagined then that the mighty Lionel King would have been the one behind the romantic gesture. Fool that I was! And what a whirlwind change had taken place in my life since then.

I pulled him down to sit beside me and switched on a lamp that stood beside the sofa. Blinking from the sudden brightness and the tears that pricked at the corners of my eyes, I took a deep breath and looked deep into Lionel's eyes. I needed to remain firm, but his powerful, sensual gaze was almost enough to drive all resolution to one side. He looked exhausted, too, despite the desire I could sense behind his steamy gaze. I had the overwhelming urge to hug him to me protectively. But I had to remain strong. He needed to explain why he really loved me. Was it because of *me*, or just because of my name?

"What would you say if I told you my name wasn't Chantelle Rose?"

I could see puzzlement momentarily flash across his eyes, before he light-heartedly replied, "I would hope, then, that you would say your name was Chantelle King."

"And what would you say if my name was neither Rose, nor King, nor even Chantelle?"

I desperately tried to remain calm. I'd no desire to come across as another hysterical Vivien Francis, though I could feel I was on the verge of screaming at the top of my lungs until my tonsils shook from pure frustration and tears gushed out in torrents.

"Look, Chantelle," Lionel sighed – he really was much more exhausted than I'd first grasped. "I've just sat through three studio interviews, a press conference, and had to deal with a nutty stalker who'd gone and slashed all four of Freddy G's limo tires. The only thing that has gotten me through the day is the thought that I would be with you this evening, and all through the night, and wake in the morning and start the new day with you by my side. I'm not up for any game playing. If you've got something to ask me, please go ahead and say straight out what's on your mind."

No beating about the bush, then.

Out loud, I asked bluntly, "I want to know why you truly love me. Because if what Gabby has told me is correct, the only real reason you're with me is because years ago some mystic clairvoyant gave you my name, and convinced you that you would only be happy with the girl bearing that name."

Lionel stared at me. Then, despite his weariness, let out his boisterous laugh. I actually found myself smiling back at him. I loved his laugh, and as much as I tried to remain serious, it was almost impossible with his flashing grin in my face. I felt like a complete fool.

"I'll admit that Gabby's version of the story is true. I did have my fortune told, and I was told that a certain dark-haired lady by the name of Chantelle Rose would have a great influence in my life. I'll admit that I fantasised about meeting such a mysterious and passionate woman. What I'll also admit is that the real Chantelle – that's you, my Princess – surpasses all my dreams and fantasies. Even if your name wasn't Chantelle I'd still love you just as much as I do. It's true that I sent Freddy G after you when I saw you, and your name, in that Brit film. But I never expected to feel like this about you. The vulnerability I feel when I think I may lose you. That you may return to England and leave me. The anxiety I felt throughout the days you were ill. I love you for the gutsy determination that brought you out here to face this crazy adventure in the first place. I love you because you are the first woman I've met who shows no interest in me for my money or fame. I love the fact that when I'm with you, all my worries are put to one side. I love it when you smile. I want to be the one to make you smile just as you smile now. I would love you whatever your name. I love you for you! Does that clear your doubts?"

He was kneeling before me, his clear eyes locked into mine. I just nodded meekly in reply as I had a huge lump in my throat and was beyond speaking. The earlier threatened tears were on the verge of flooding out, but now as tears of joy and pure emotion. It was such a blissful moment. I didn't want to ruin it by having mascara running down my face in unsexy black rivulets. He may love me, but I wasn't going to push things!

He held his arms open protectively, and I fell into them and rested my head on his strong chest. He held me tight and bent down to tenderly kiss my forehead.

"You silly kid," he sighed warm-heartedly as he lifted my chin and kissed me passionately on the lips.

At that point, I'm ashamed to say, the floodgates opened.

***

I remained just a couple of days longer with Lionel, in a pre-honeymoon-type bliss. For indeed it was pre-honeymoon, as we planned to marry as soon as I returned from the UK. I was to go back to England to sell the cottage, settle my affairs – which would take about half an hour – and collect all my belongings. I thought I would probably end up giving most of my clothes to an Oxfam shop as I really couldn't see that in sunny California I would have much need of my big Puffer jacket, or any of my thick itchy woollen turtle-neck jumpers, or my classy leg-warmers, earmuffs, three-metre-long scarves, mittens and sexy Wellington boots. Saying that, I wasn't sure Oxfam would be that desperate for any of those fashion statements either.

I was desperate to tell Tammy in person that I was going to get hitched. I couldn't quite believe it myself. The tabloids were going to have a field day. I hadn't even known Lionel for more than two and a half months. I was, all considered, totally ignoring every bit of guidance which had been drummed into my head for as long as I could remember: *"Don't talk to strangers… Don't walk down a dark alley at night… Don't get hitched before you're thirty… Make sure you know that 'He' doesn't like wearing your underwear… Only have kids when you're totally ready…* etc etc.

So there I was thoroughly rushing into things, jumping the gun as it were. Nevertheless, it was either marriage or living in sin, and as both appealed and the first option had been offered, there was no stopping me. If Lionel, at some future point, decided that he rather liked walking around the bungalow in my lingerie and high heels, well, I'd simply cross that bridge when and if I came to it (in any case it already seemed he had a fetish for female shades and sun hats, as I'd discovered on his yacht, so I guess I'd already been forewarned). Life was too short to be overly cautious. At least, that's what I kept telling myself. Besides, that was why some intelligent person invented the concept "Divorce." Shame on me! It was shocking that I had even thought of the D-word as I stood at the doors of matrimony.

I was thrilled by the idea of becoming Mrs King, and

was desperate to tell Tammy she was to be my Chief Bridesmaid. As my thoughts turned to England, it seemed ironic to think that my future brother-in-law would be Robbie. It was weird that one brother was obsessed with keeping me at his side, and the other hell-bent on scaring me off. I wondered if it might be something to do with nature versus nurture. Lionel and Robbie were the epitome of the saying: "It's a fine line between love and hate." On that, I had to agree.

***

Back again across the Atlantic. I was becoming quite an expert on long-haul flights, and the whole departure-arrival routine. Things always seemed to happen to me when I travelled, too. Being fair, I think it would be correct just to say that things always seemed to happen to me, full stop. I felt my life was snowballing out of my control. Of course, I was deeply in love and I did want to marry Lionel, so it wasn't as if that was beyond my control. Beyond the original scope of my imagination perhaps, but certainly not against my wishes. What was getting rather out of my control was my sudden fame and celebrity status. Lionel's public declaration of love for me at the Oscar ceremony, plus the nude pictures of me splashed around the world, had propelled me to stardom – or, depending how you look at it, to infamy. This explained why I found myself rushing through the airport to the check-in desk decked out as if I was going to a fancy-dress party. I was wearing a blonde wig (in tribute to Marilyn Monroe's golden locks), plus huge dark shades, despite the drizzling rain outside and regardless of the fact that I was actually indoors and there was no natural light.

Gabby said it was absolutely essential to wear a disguise when I was out alone and wanted to avoid attention. However, rather than making me look like a nonentity I saw myself as rather an eyesore. It didn't do the slightest bit of good anyway. Everyone saw right through the disguise – come to think of it, that's probably why celebrities use them –

and it wasn't long before I had flocks of people around me screaming for my autograph and snapping their cameras at me, whilst I, as calmly and as serenely as possible, checked in my baggage and went through passport control. I was detained even longer than usual there, of course, as the individual on duty was forced to make me remove part of my disguise, just to confirm that it really was me behind it. Finally I got myself free of fans and officials, rushed into the British Airways VIP lounge, collapsed into one of the plush armchairs, and thankfully wrenched off the itchy, hot wig. It reminded me of a poodle.

I briefly closed my eyes, trying to calm myself after fighting my way through the screaming mob of devotees. I couldn't have imagined how popular one could get overnight, though I realised that the mob that had chased after me were the regular groupies who hung out at the airport celebrity-stalking; a bit like train-spotting only slightly more energetic. I could feel a stinking headache coming on and promptly rummaged around my handbag for an ibuprofen. As I shifted through the items in my bag in vain attempt to find a painkiller, I heard a sudden gasp coming from the entrance to the VIP lounge. I looked up. Paused by the door, contemplating which would be less traumatic – sharing the lounge with me, or facing the hounding aficionados outside – was none other than the haughty Ms Crystal Lee.

As I raised my eyes to meet her deadly stare, she, realising that there was nothing for it but to enter the room, tossed her head proudly and strode in with clicking, assertive steps. She positioned herself on the far side from where I sat, held a glossy magazine up so as to obscure me from her view, and tutted with displeasure.

I was fully aware of the reasons for her unfriendly reaction. It was obvious that she assumed I had been behind the "stolen" photos. Everything considered, the nude images of myself actually showed me in a pretty favourable light – especially if one believed I'd been looking for fame and further work opportunities. Whereas Crystal, the Hollywood Queen, had not come out of it well at all. The publication of the article had been an ultimate treachery.

I sat fidgeting in my seat for a while deliberating whether I should confront the old witch and risk getting my head bitten off, or remain in my seat and pretend I was oblivious to her tittering groans and snubbing behaviour. I finally decided that by remaining in my seat in silence it was almost like admitting that I was behind the dirty deed. Moreover, I certainly wasn't going to let her go on accusing me of something I hadn't done, especially when I'd been just as angered by the article as she was.

Gathering my courage about me, I stood tall and, with more conviction than I actually felt, walked over to where she was sitting.

"Ms Lee?"

I hoped that she would at least look at me. She, however, remained with her face buried in her magazine (*1,2,3 Slim…!?*) and ignoring me completely. I couldn't believe how rude she was. I cleared my throat loudly hoping that she would remember her manners and at least acknowledge my presence. She just ruffled the pages even more rapidly and loudly, as if I was a pesky fly that had molested her but was not worthy of further attention.

I had an urge to yank the hefty fitness magazine from her hands and smack her across the head with it, but instead, I remained poised silently, hovering above her, and slowly counted to ten, convincing myself as I did so that pulling her hair out in mighty fistfulls would only lower myself to her level of behaviour. I believed that's what she wanted, because then she would've known how to react. Furthermore, I certainly didn't fancy being on the front of the tabloids for having had a catfight with the mighty Crystal Lee. Having my buttocks exposed to the world was already more than enough.

I didn't realise you were deaf as well as fat-arsed and downright rude… The words almost slipped from my lips, so I remained standing as I counted to ten once again. Crystal was obviously not used to having someone stand over her in patient silence, and I started to observe her squirm with discomfort. I'll admit I rather enjoyed the feeling of power it gave me.

"There are obviously two possible reasons why you are totally ignoring my presence," I began. My tone was calm as I spoke, hoping that if I remained unruffled Crystal would react in the same way. I had heard her whip-like tongue before, many times, and had no desire to be subjected to it myself. "The first reason," I continued, "could be that you're too conceited to talk to lesser beings such as me. The second is that your lawyers have advised you not to have any contact with me whatsoever, as you obviously believe that I'm the one behind the article in *Hollywood Blue* and that you plan to take legal action. Well, you can go ahead and prosecute, but you're wasting your time, because I had nothing to do with the publication. Believe it or not, it's not my idea of fun having my body parts, and my identity, flashed around in a glossy magazine for the whole world to stare at. The only reason I went ahead and did the scenes in the first place was because I was desperate for money, and I'd been promised that no one would even find out that a body double had been used, let alone that the body double was me. I'm truly sorry that you don't look good in all of this. But, honey, you're barking up the wrong tree if you think I had anything to do with it. In fact I would be more than happy to co-operate in bringing whoever is behind all this to justice. There are plenty of people in this world who are in need of the money I could win out of suing. I would give it to them. So stop huffing at me, you're just wasting your time."

Crystal had stopped rattling *1,2,3, Slim,* just as I was wondering if the non-stop waggling she'd kept up was some kind of upper-arm-toning exercise. Indeed she remained in total silence, and I began to wonder if, in fact, she really was hard of hearing. I stood there feeling rather perplexed, and fairly foolish. I hadn't wanted her to throw herself into a raving temper as she had done during the Nevada desert shoot. I had, however, expected to get some response from her. But she just sat there, muter than an Egyptian mummy.

She finally spoke. "Sorry for prejudging you."   This

explained a lot. She was obviously not used to apologising, and finding and using the right words must have come at a huge effort.

"No worries," I said back, and gave her a shy smile as I retraced my steps to my armchair. Just as I was settling back in the plush lounger I heard Crystal toss her 'toning' magazine aside. She clicked over to me and spoke again.

"Do you mind if I give my lawyers your number so that they can contact you to hear your side to the story?"

"Of course" I replied, quite surprised to hear her actually asking me for *my* number. I'd said I was willing to help, but I didn't think she would take me up on the offer.

She looked sad, and I found myself feeling sorry for her. She was a Hollywood star at that age where things start to sag, in an industry that worships all that is the epitome of beauty and youth; an industry which is unforgiving and strongly critical of all who do not strive for, or maintain, such an image. Growing old gracefully was going to be a tough road for Crystal. No amount of money in the world would take away her eternal obsession with her looks, her growing wrinkles, her grey hairs and her sagging bum.

So it came as no surprise to hear her ask, "Chantelle, in confidence, who's your plastic surgeon?"

I shrugged my shoulders and shook my head. "Can't help you there, I'm afraid." In my head I said a quick little prayer: *Dear God, please spare me the torment of suffering from this demoralizing obsession with one's appearance.*

I hated to think that my every waking hour could be spent fretting over cellulite and the like. I hoped that I would have something more important in my life than an ever-growing desire to remain young. There were so many other, far more important, matters to fret about.

Chapter Twenty-Four

Keeping in line with my habitual travelling mode, I slept during most of the flight over to London. This was probably just as well, as it saved me from the gawping stares of my fellow passengers, despite being in First Class. Even the cabin crew, who had to be fairly accustomed to having celebrities aboard, were flabbergasted to have me on the flight. Most famous big shots had their own private jets. I was still getting used to flying First Class.

I had a huge sparkler on my third finger which Lionel had given to me the previous night as an engagement ring. Of course I hadn't said anything to him, but to be truthful it was a bit too flashy and vulgar for my more subtle tastes. I kept my hand half-hidden; the ring may have been slightly OTT, but it was obviously worth a fortune. No more nude scenes for me. If I ever got that desperate again I could sell the ring, pay all my debts and still have enough left over to help save the rainforest.

Tammy's face lit up as soon as she saw it, once we'd managed to sidetrack a screaming mob of teen fans who recognised me as soon as I stepped through Arrivals, despite the wig, which I'd hastily replaced before disembarking. It felt a bit lopsided, indeed I think I must have put it on back to front, as I seemed to have a curtain of blonde curls obscuring my vision, which made my escape all the more tricky. Gabby's morning runs, thankfully, finally paid off; I was able to out-sprint most of the mob as we made a dash for the safety of the car, but Tammy struggled to keep up. Hence I got into the driver's seat as soon as we reached the parked car, worried that she could well hyper-ventilate and pass out somewhere along the M25. Mind, there was a chance that after the long-haul flight, I could, perhaps not hyper-ventilate, but possibly drop off to sleep (again). So relying on the fact that the constant lane changes, junction turn-offs and ongoing traffic down the M25, which is difficult enough at the best of times, would be stimulus enough for my dozy mind, I drove off.

As soon as Tammy got her breath back, not taking her eyes off the diamond ring, she exclaimed, "It's true what's all over the internet then, you're to be the future Mrs King. The most sought-after bachelor in Hollywood is finally getting hitched and you, my girl, are one lucky lady!"

I just sat there smiling in answer, like an authentic Cheshire cat. If I could've purred I would have.

We drove straight down into Kent. I wanted to sort out financial and non-financial matters there first, before returning to London to dredge up all the stuff that I'd hoarded over the last eighteen months or so in my flat in Streatham. Oddly enough, despite the offensively loud street the flat was situated in, I felt somewhat sad at the idea of leaving it all behind. Not so much the rowdy mobs that seemed to parade down the high street at all hours, but for the comfy anonymity that I'd leave behind by starting a new life as the wife (why did that word give me give me goose bumps?) of a superstar.

As we approached the dream cottage that I'd purchased, in all honesty with a bit too much zeal instead of thinking things through a little, I braced myself for my confrontation with Vivien. Despite her good intentions of putting her fixation with Lionel behind her, I wasn't sure how she would have taken the news that he was to finally marry – and that I was the lady in question.

The cottage appeared remarkably quiet on our arrival. There was no van parked. Furthermore, I'd been convinced that Vivien would've been through the front door the moment she'd heard Tammy's car pull up, demanding to know if the rumours about Lionel and me were true. The flashing engagement ring was, of course, the solid proof, and I'd prepared myself for her probable swipe for it. As I emerged from the car, however, it became clear that no one was home. I scolded myself for not having phoned or texted Robbie to inform him of my arrival. It had been very foolish of me as I realised that if neither Robbie nor Vivien were about it would also be impossible to enter the cottage, and I wasn't going to stand on Tammy's shoulders three weeks before my wedding in another attempt to scramble into the place. Tammy wouldn't have held under my weight in any case.

"Stay here for a minute, I'm just going around the back in case the kitchen door is open." Deep down I knew I was wasting my time in checking to see if I would find the kitchen door unlocked, but I'd fancied a quick scamper into the back garden, in a token gesture of farewell, before I went ahead and offered the house to Robbie.

Scarcely had I pressed my face up against the glass door that opened into the kitchen when I heard a shrill, piercing scream of terror. I thumped my head against the windowpane from shock. The cry for help, at least that's how I interpreted it, sounded like it had come from the horse barn at the back of the garden. Without giving it a second thought, I raced down the garden path as fast as I could, not blind to the fact, as I dashed along, that this was probably not the wisest or safest course of action. Instead of pausing to suss out the possible dangers, I just charged headfirst into the danger zone. The truth is I'd been spurred on because I was convinced that the voice that had screamed out in such terror was Vivien's, and I was worried about her in an almost motherly kind of way. Anyway, if it was Vivien shrieking away, the probability was that a field mouse had just run in front of her. Though I was a born and bred city girl, I figured I could handle a field mouse.

The barn was dark. I'd never actually got to see the barn before, and it was much larger than I'd imagined, and, in addition, in a much worse state. The grass on this far side of the garden was high and uncut, and I stumbled a couple of times in my haste to reach the building. The thatched roof had fallen in and the oak door hung off its hinges. I took all this in as I reached the open doorway. Then I saw Vivien's long blonde hair spread out on the floor. She was lying face down and completely still. It was the first time caution seriously entered my mind. I remained still for a brief second, trying to suppress my heavy breathing and slow my thundering heart in attempt to detect other noises which would alert me to additional danger.

Everything was silent. Even the birds seemed to have hushed their sweet melodies. I inched my way forward towards Vivien's motionless figure. At a distance, it was hard to tell to see if she was breathing or not. There was no sight of blood, which I took as a positive sign. Finally by her side, I bent over her to check her pulse – and just as I did so a shadow fell across me, blocking out the light from the half-open, broken doorway.

"Shit!" I hissed to myself in pure reflex. But before I had a chance to move, some tremendously heavy object crashed down on my head.

***

It was pitch black when I came around. I had no notion of time, except that I was aware that it must have been well into the night. I could see the moon high in the sky peeking through the clouds, and the floor was icy cold. I was shivering uncontrollably and my whole body ached. I slowly got to my feet, trying to do so without jerking and without making any sudden movements to my aching head. I felt sick and giddy and had to close my eyes a while in an attempt to fight off the wave of nausea that engulfed my whole body. I leaned against the damp wall for support, trying to get my bearings. I was abruptly alerted by something moving close by me, and on catching sight of Vivien's long blonde hair I recalled precisely where I was.

I got down by her side and helped her to sit up. As she turned to look at me, her look of puzzlement turned to fright as she recalled what had happened. She had a huge purple lump on her forehead, which looked as painful as mine felt. It crossed my mind to remark that she looked just like I had after she'd bunged her hefty handbag at me during the cast party, but I realised that this was no laughing matter. We were both in deadly danger.

"How long have we been here?" she asked in a hushed, hoarse whisper.

I shrugged my shoulders, for I had no idea. I wondered why Tammy hadn't gone for help or attempted to find me. She must have been alarmed by my disappearance. It suddenly struck me that something could well have happened to her, too. I began to feel sick again, this time with worry. I'd never forgive myself if she'd come to harm. Deep down I knew that I was the target of the attacker, and that Vivien and Tammy (if she'd also been injured) were just innocent victims who'd simply been in the wrong place at the wrong time.

"Where's Robbie?" I asked Vivien. It was hard to imagine that he'd go to such violent extremes just to get his hands on the house. I couldn't believe that he could be so brutal.

It was Vivien's turn to shrug her shoulders. "He left the house first thing in the morning to go horse riding as he's done every morning this week. He's only usually gone an hour or so, but today he just seemed to take forever. By the time it was early afternoon I was so worried for him I went along the lanes in the hope of seeing him, thinking that something must have happened to him and that he was in need of help. After walking around for about an hour I wandered down here to the barn in the hope of seeing him, or at least his horse, which he keeps in the far stall. I'd just got through the door when someone jumped me from behind. I was so shocked that I didn't even have time to react. I tried to struggle and I must have screamed really loud because the guy seemed to panic and hit out at me. I remember tripping over and must've hit my head against the wall and passed out. I can't remember anything else."

"Did the guy look familiar?"

"There was something that seemed familiar, but I can't say what. Anyway, it was dark here in the barn and the guy's face was masked under a big hooded anorak."

"Well I doubt he's still here now. We've both been lying here for ages. We should try to get out and go to the police."

As I said these words, I noticed that the oak door had been closed. And on pushing it, it became clear that it wasn't going to budge. The attacker had obviously rammed something into the other side of the door to keep it closed. It looked like the only way out was to climb up and through the half-ruined thatched roof.

Together Vivien and I piled up several bundles of hay, which we found stacked at one side of the barn. Having constructed a sort of pyramid I volunteered to climb up and over. Vivien in her high-heeled totally non-practical fashion boots wouldn't have got very far in any case. After an unsure start, I soon sat perched on what was left of the barn roof. The drop to the ground looked rather dicey, and I really didn't fancy breaking my legs with a nutty attacker on the loose. There was a sturdy chestnut tree opposite, which looked safe enough to climb down, but it seemed too far away to reach.

"Vivien," I called down, "see if you can find some rope somewhere in the barn."

She scuttled off to rummage around and a few minutes later she returned with three lengths of sturdy rope.

"That's great. Tie them together in a long line and fasten the far end to the iron bars on the window, then throw the other end up to me."

And, by God, tie them in a decent knot, or else I'll drop like a stone.

It took Vivien three attempts to successfully throw the loose end of rope high enough for me to catch as I wobbled precariously on my perch. My thumping headache wasn't any help, and I kept getting spasms of dizziness. I swung the rope over the outer wall of the barn. Without looking down (for I was a good five metres up) I grabbed the rope, worked myself off the barn roof and abseiled down the wall. As I slowly made my way down I kept saying to myself, over and over, that if I actually made it to my wedding day in one piece I would ask Lionel to take me on a really relaxing, stress-free honeymoon, to some remote corner of the planet where nothing would be required of me except to eat, drink, sleep, and have incredible sex. In fact, at this moment, just a few hours of peace and quiet anywhere would've made me more than content.

I jumped the last metre to the safety of the soft ground below and hastened over to the door of the barn. It had been tied and kept in place by a thick piece of cord, similar to the rope I'd used to make my descent. With shaking hands I fumbled with the knot to untie it. My fingers were numb and it was hard work to loosen. Finally it came undone and Vivien pushed the door open with one mighty shove. Finding herself outside the barn and safe, she pretty much fell into my arms out of sheer relief and gratitude.

Hand-in-hand like two petrified kids escaping the headmistress, we sprinted across the garden, which was quite an achievement considering Vivien's slinky-kinky footwear. Halfway across the lawn, I stopped dead in my tracks at the sight of a dark figure lying motionless on the ground like a broken doll. Vivien, who had been running blindly at my side, her hand still in mine, continued her forward charge and almost wrenched my shoulder out of its socket in her frenzied stampede across the turf.

"It's Tammy!" I cried as I broke from Vivien's grip and tore over to my best friend's immobile body. I got down at Tammy's side and rolled her over. She felt icy cold and I had to fight back the fresh waves of nausea and panic that shook my body at the thought that she might be dead. She showed no signs of physical injury, no signs of bruising from being bashed to the ground as Vivien and I had, but it took me a while to find her pulse, and her breathing was alarmingly shallow.

"I'm going to kill the fucking bastard who did this," I hissed out loud as the image of Robbie flashed in my mind. He had to be the one behind these acts of terror. Just as I spat out my words of vengeance, a fourth person unexpectedly appeared at our side.

"Thank God you girls are alright. We've just caught the guy who's been behind all this."

218

The voice was unmistakeable, and I'd either been terribly wrong about my suspicions, or it was his way of hoaxing us further. For the person who spoke was no other than Robbie himself.

Without thinking twice, I charged at him enraged.

"I'm going to kill you, you son of a bitch!" I screamed at the top of my lungs as I dived into him. Robbie, caught off guard, toppled over backwards and I landed on top of him. I started fisting him in the chest, though I was too exhausted by everything that happened in such a short period of time to cause him any harm. Nevertheless, I must have looked like some possessed nutter as I feebly kept on battering him.

I would have liked to be able to blame my odd behaviour on the fact that my mind was still pounding frenziedly in my skull, on the fact that my first evening back in the UK had been spent knocked out cold on the barn floor, on the fact that my best friend Tammy seemed more dead than alive. The truth is, however, I'd just lost it!

Robbie put his strong arms around me and held me to him, stilling my slashing fists, holding me in his warm embrace until my breathing eased. Tears of frustration and utter exhaustion started to fall down my face, tears which he tenderly wiped away, caressing my face as if caressing a lover. I lay still, on top of him, and looked into his eyes, which in the night-light reflected dark sapphire. It was the first time I read the desire flashing back at me; burning desire, which left me shaking once again.

I struggled to untangle myself from his arms. I needed to put space between Robbie and myself; not because I was afraid of him (at least, not in the same way as I'd been when I suspected he was behind the threats), but because I felt guilty that I'd totally misinterpreted his actions. It also frightened me to think that a part of me was longing to cling to him, to feel his protective arms around me, to have him in my life in a way that I could never have Lionel. A very big part of Lionel belonged to his hundreds and thousands of fans.

I now believed Robbie when he said that the person behind the menacing notes and the dreadful attacks had

219

finally been caught. Obviously it wasn't him, and I also realised that a mighty apology was called for. This was not the moment for explanations, however, as I suddenly caught sight of Tammy stirring on the ground and I rushed to her side. Robbie and I got her to her feet and half-carried her indoors.

As we entered the sitting room, Tammy almost fell from my arms as I suddenly stopped, paralysed to the spot. Before me, tied with his arms behind a chair and with Ray standing guard, was the author of the poison-pen cut-out messages and the frightening silent phone calls, the one who had caused such misery and confusion and misunderstanding. The person who had hurt Vivien and me and had almost killed Tammy.

I could hear Vivien gasp behind me on seeing who it was, and I took it that she also recognised him.

It was the man who I'd blindly driven my luggage trolley into all those weeks ago when he'd picked me up from the airport in LA the first time I'd flown over. His fancy uniform was gone, but there was no mistaking him. It was the man I knocked into at the supermarket the day it had been chucking down with rain, and had sent his baked bean tins flying. It was no wonder he didn't stop to retrieve them.

It came to me with shocking clarity. If Lionel's personal chauffer had been doing all these terrible things to drive me away from England and the cottage and back to the States, the hand which was ultimately behind everything could only be Lionel's. He was deranged, mad, *loco* with his looney obsession with 'Chantelle Rose.' *ME!* In his desperation to keep me, he'd almost killed me. I was numb with shock.

It was Vivien who broke the silence that had engulfed the room. "John!" she exclaimed, "are you okay? Untie him at once," she demanded.

Ray looked at me for guidance and slowly I nodded my head.

"It's okay Ray, you can untie him."

"Shouldn't we phone the police first?" Ray asked.

I shook my head. "There's no point. He's not the one really behind the threats, are you John?"

Although I asked the question, I really didn't want to hear the answer. I had no desire for him to confirm my realisation that my beloved Lionel could go to such extreme lengths to get his way.

I sunk into one of the sofas that furnished the newly-decorated sitting room. John had almost killed Tammy by leaving her out on the freezing ground. For this I would never forgive him, or Lionel for that matter. He'd not been directly behind that night's terror, but it had been an indirect result of his orders.

As if reading my mind, John turned to me as he spoke. "It hadn't been my intention to hurt you, Miss, but I got scared out there in the barn. I was worried that young Miss Vivien would recognise me. I only gave her a slight push so as to distract her, but then you appeared and things got a little out of control. I didn't touch your friend though; she fainted flat out when she saw me run from the back of the garden. I ran off, I know it was wrong, and wondered around for hours trying to figure out what I do. I waited till it was dark and then came back to see if the young Miss was okay and had let you out. When I saw her still lying on the ground I thought the worst; maybe she'd had a heart attack or something. I did plan to call for help, but that was when I was detained by these young gentlemen here and I was too scared to confess anything more…"

His declaration petered out. I wasn't totally following all he was saying in any case. My mind was miles away as I sat silently on the soft settee, and my heart felt like someone was wrenching it out of my very body. If Lionel was capable of organising something like this, what else would he be capable of? I couldn't believe that such a caring, considerate and loving person could be behind such dreadful, calculating actions. But what else could I believe?

"Get out of here," I hissed with intense venom. "If you're not on the next flight to LA, I'll be calling the police."

Chapter Twenty-Five

Tammy remained in hospital under observation and I remained at her side, together with Ray, and Tammy's parents who had been quick to arrive, praying for her recovery. With all the praying I was doing of late, I was on the verge of turning into a born-again Christian. I kept the notion at arm's length. I guessed if things turned really rough I could try my hand at being a nun, though I doubted if the assets I had were quite what the Church was looking for. I remained strictly at Tammy's side. I couldn't wander around the hospital in any case, as every time I did I ended up with flocks of people following me or gawping at me in wonder, for I was still, officially, Lionel's fiancée. However, instead of feeling ecstatic at the notion of being the future Mrs King, as I had been at the start, I was now engulfed by a torment of suffering, as if the person I loved most in the world had died and my heart felt literally broken in two.

Needless to say, during this period I refused all phone calls from Lionel himself. I had nothing to say to him. I was simply too upset and distraught by events in general and by Lionel's crazy behaviour in particular, as well as watching over Tammy's weak, pale, body as she slowly recovered.

The person I really needed to speak to was Robbie. I totally had to apologise for suspecting him. But I wasn't great with apologies, so it was going to be quite an effort to get the words right and make them sound as sincerely sorry and ashamed as I felt. It wasn't until late on the second day of Tammy's stay under observation in hospital that I actually found a moment to be alone with him. Ray suggested that after all the stress I'd been under it was a good idea to go home and get some proper rest. I didn't want to leave

Tammy, but I was really struggling to stay awake, the jetlag and strain taking its toll. Robbie was quick to volunteer to take me back to the cottage and see to it that I ate a hot meal and had a decent night's sleep.

I was so exhausted by worry, sorrow, emotion and physical trauma that on the drive to the cottage I started to feel a little woozy, and not quite in command of my senses. But, true to his word, Robbie did look after me. So much so that the following morning when I awoke in bed I turned to find Robbie lying peacefully asleep at my side, his thick dark hair, which fell and partially covered his handsome, chiselled face with its one-day stubble, just inches from mine.

I had to check myself so as not let out a piecing scream of horror.

There had to be some mistake. It had to be all part of a bad dream. Surely I hadn't… Surely we hadn't… I refused to believe that I could have… *Shit*, I couldn't even get the word out!

I struggled with the bedcovers as I tried to pull them off me and dash from the room as quickly and silently as possible. I had no desire to wake Robbie. I just couldn't face his azure eyes searching mine in the pale morning light. I needed to think. I needed to try to remember.

This had happened to me before. Not the sleeping with someone and not remembering, thank God – once was definitely going to be bad enough – but rather the temporary memory loss. When my mother passed away, I actually blocked out the whole incident for months. Over time, fragmented pictures started falling into place and there came a moment, with the immense help of my father and professional child psychologists, that I could remember it all.

My mother had been my absolute hero. I had, of course, loved my father dearly, but the relationship with my mother had been unique. It was as if she knew that there would come a time when she would no longer be with me. Every instant at her side was incomparable and special. She would stay with me until I slept, softy stroking my hair, and be the first to smile at me on waking. There were times, however, when I would catch her looking distracted and upset. A tear would find its way down her cheek, and not even I could bring her to smile. She was my mother, my best friend, my everything. And one day she simply wasn't there anymore, and I never got to say goodbye. I was too young to understand, and far too young to lose her.

That period of my life just seemed to disappear; it went the very day my mother left us. It was only later I was able to remember my father telling me, with tear-filled eyes and a broken voice reflecting his own broken heart, that my mother had gone and that I would never see her again. "She's gone to be with the angels," he'd tried to explain. I'd hit him and told him I didn't believe him and had run from the house and onto the main road. The cars had screeched to a stop, horns honked, but I'd kept running, blindly, tears obscuring my vision, stumbling as I ran, until my father caught up with me, picked me up and held me tight. I slumped in his arms and fainted.

The next clear moment I have is some six months later, when my father came home with a golden Labrador puppy. It was a female pup who came bounding into the sitting room and almost knocked me over in her excitement and licked my face in delight. It was the first time I laughed again. From then on, the pain started to ease and the memories gradually returned.

There are still moments, under extreme stress or anxiety, when I feel the threat of fainting. That was why I fainted when I first met Freddy G at the Ritz. The nerves, tension or excitement get too much for me, and my body reacts in a way that I haven't yet learnt to fully control.

I have improved over the years, but the risk of fainting or temporary amnesia is still there. Up until now, however, it's always been when I've been under severe pressure or distress, and nothing like how I was on losing my mother. I had no idea why this had occurred now. I know I had been under a lot of pressure, what with the whole American adventure ending in disaster and deception, together with the extreme concern I felt over Tammy's health. But surely, if

Robbie and I had actually made love, it would have been that: love. Something beautiful.

I just couldn't comprehend how I could block it out when it would have been magic. I guessed it was just too soon after Lionel. I was still officially his fiancée, after all, and deep down I felt terribly sad. From the outside it probably looked as if I was using Robbie. But I would never do that. This was just all too confusing, too much to take on in such a short space of time. This was the only explanation I could think of. It was either that, or in fact Robbie and I had actually managed to have terrible sex, and it had been enough to conk me out!

Not only was I going to have to apologise to him for believing he was originally the one behind the threatening letters, I was going to have to humiliate him by asking him if we had, or had not, had sex!

I gasped as I finally untangled myself from the bedcover, for I was totally starkers. Not even thinking to peek under the covers to check to see if Robbie was naked, too, I dashed from the room and locked myself in the bathroom. As I ran the water hot to shower myself I checked over my skin to see if there were any tell-tale signs of passionate lovemaking; if there were any love-bite marks, or scratches. Nothing, however, I was relieved to note, as I did a total body examination. I couldn't even ask Vivien what I had done the previous evening, for she'd flown back to LA with John.

As I emerged from the bathroom I had two options: one, go back into the bedroom for my clothes and risk waking Robbie up or, two, slip downstairs, fix myself some good strong coffee and think hard about what I planned to say to Robbie when he finally woke up. I decided it was best to stall for time, so I headed downstairs and into the brightly-lit kitchen, despite the looming clouds on the outside, which were, to an extent, a reflection of my alarming frame of mind.

I was finishing my second cup of coffee by the time Robbie emerged. It had probably not been the wisest idea to drink caffeine in my already accelerated mental state, but I had no decaf, and it was wiser than downing a measure or two of brandy which had been the other choice. Robbie didn't help matters at all by stepping into the kitchen with just his jeans on, his muscular, strong, torso tanned and bare. (Distracted though I was, I wondered how he was so tanned, considering the English weather!) He made his way over to me and tenderly kissed my forehead as if it was the most natural thing in the word as he said, "Morning, Princess." At that point I actually thought, these guys aren't twins – they've been cloned! It was all too uncanny and a shiver ran down my spine from the overbearing sense of *déjà vu.*

He fixed himself a cup of coffee as I sat in silence pulling my terry cloth bathrobe tighter. Coffee in hand he finally turned to me once more. I beckoned him to sit and he did so.

"I think we need to talk." I started and my voice wavered slightly from pure nerves. Robbie nodded at me as he sat in front of me. He looked suddenly sullen and I knew he wasn't going to make things easy for me. I smiled shyly at him, trying to ease the situation, thought my heart hammered from the stress of it all.

"There's so much I need to say I just don't know where to begin." I sighed. I paused a moment before continuing.

"First of all I need to thank you, Robbie, for all you've done to help me. Going back to the very start, the very first day we met when you saved me from the mud bath down by the river. I need to thank you for all your hard work on the cottage. It looks absolutely amazing." (It did too!) "I have to say you have totally transformed it in the shortest period of time. Thank you."

I was sincere in my thanks, as I would never have got it looking so homely. I actually wondered how much of Vivien had been behind the cosy change to the cottage and realised I would have to thank her too. I swallowed dryly. I'd got the easy bit out of the way. The time had come to apologise.

"I need to apologise to you, too. I'd been under the delusion that the threatening letters came from you. I can't believe now that I'd blamed you, when all you've been is a never-ending help. It's just that I couldn't possibly imagine who else could've been behind it all. At the time it made sense to blame you, as I knew that you'd always held this cottage in a special place in your heart. It was easy to imagine that the letters were your attempt to drive me away. I'm ashamed to admit that I blamed you. I'm sincerely sorry, Robbie, please forgive me."

Robbie at this point had moved over to where I sat and put his arms around me. He held me tight and rocked me slightly as if comforting a small child.

"Hush babe, it's okay. I understand," he soothed. But I hadn't finished, and I didn't think he would be quite so understanding when he heard what I still had to say. I pushed him gently, to separate us, and looked him straight in the eye.

"Robbie," I continued not wanting to leave things unresolved a moment longer. "I no longer blame you for the threats, though you have to understand that it's incredibly hard for me to believe that they come from Lionel. He's asked me to marry him. And I'd planned to, had he just trusted me to be with him out of my own desire and choice, rather than crazily pushing things to come about. I can't believe that he's been capable of going to such extremes. And it doesn't help that when I look at you I see him, just as when I look at him I see you. You are both so, so… so similar. But I need to sort things out with Lionel. So…" I'd got to the really tricky part: "What exactly happened last night?"

"You can't remember!" he exclaimed, shocked, and I didn't blame him either. I slowly shook my head, as I thought, *What a way to start and end a relationship.* I may have had no recollection of the previous evening, but I wasn't going to forget for a long, long time the look of utter regret and sorrow reflected on Robbie's face.

"If you can't remember," he repeated sadly, as he pushed his chair back, away from me, "then you have nothing to feel guilty about. If your worry is that you have been unfaithful to the very guy that's threatened your life, then I think you need to straighten out your priorities."

With that he hastily stood and made to leave the kitchen.

"Wait, Robbie," I cried out. "Let me explain." I desperately tried to detain him, but he just stormed out of the room.

"Forget it, Chantelle. This has all been a mistake."

I heard the front door slam loudly as he left.

Chapter Twenty-Six

I trudged up the stairs trying my hardest to hold it together. It wasn't the time to start bawling with self-pity, though I would've liked to. I felt thoroughly sorry for myself, selfish as it sounds, as well as guilty, sad and terribly confused.

Lethargically I changed into some jeans and a Gap jumper, trying at the same time to divert my eyes from the bed, which was still unmade, and had Robbie's boxer shorts, socks and rugby top strewn all over. In his huff, he'd left with just his jeans on. I found myself in a bit of a muddle about what I should do with his clothes. Should I wash them? Fold them up and place them on the front doorstep in case he was to return? I decided in the end to leave them be and sort them out when I returned from visiting Tammy. With this decision made, I hastened down the stairs, out of the front door and into the van.

Tammy looked much better, which was a real weight off my shoulders. At least that was one thing less to worry about. Even her parents had gone back to London, though they said they would return the following day. Tammy had been diagnosed with a mild case of pneumonia as a result of having spent such a long time outside and unconscious on the damp, cold ground. We hadn't given the doctors, or her parents, all the details as to why exactly she had spent a good few hours on the floor, and luckily nobody probed. But her cheeks had got some colour back, and she was finally out of her critical condition, though she still drifted in and out of sleep most of the time. The one who looked the worse for wear was Ray. I didn't think he'd slept or eaten anything since Tammy had been brought into the infirmary. I had pretty much to coerce him to go home for the morning and get some sleep. I told him frankly that he looked a mess and that Tammy, when she finally came round, would much more appreciate a clean-shaven fresh-looking face than the haggard one he displayed at that moment. After some hesitation he finally took the hint and left me by her side.

Holding onto Tammy's warm but limp hand, I switched on the TV. I'd hoped to distract myself by watching some cheesy chat show or soap opera – anything rather than torment myself more by thinking about my shattered love life. But, considering Lionel was a world celebrity and the most sought-after actor at this present time and, therefore, the most sought-after interview subject, channel-hopping, even in England, was perhaps not the brightest idea. There was his face staring at me, in magnified size. And instead of switching the TV off and thus avoiding all images of him, with masochistic zeal I turned the volume up and sat enraptured in my seat.

The interview seemed to be coming to an end. Lionel had just let out his characteristic boisterous laugh, and I felt a twang at my heartstrings. He smiled boyishly and it was hard to believe that such a sincere beam was just a façade which hid a dark, obsessive, shrewd and cruel side.

The chat show hostess smiled back at Lionel. She held her hand outstretched which Lionel warmly took in his.

"Say a big 'Hi' to the Queen for me; she's a great lady is Queen Elizabeth!"

With that the camera switched to Lionel as I sat there mumbling in a fluster, "What was that…? What was that joke about the Queen…?" For to me it could mean only one thing: that Lionel was on the point of flying over to the UK.

The camera then zoomed in on the hostess's smiling face as she winked into the camera lens. "Ms Rose," she said, "if you're watching over there, let me tell you you're one very lucky lady. Congratulations, you've snagged the number one bachelor in town."

Holy shit! I was suddenly frantic, for that interview had most probably been recorded a couple of days ago. Which meant, if I was right, that Lionel would be arriving in the next few hours. As soon as Ray returned I was going to have to rocket it back to the cottage. I wasn't going to have to wash Robbie's boxers, I was going to have to damn well burn them!

The moment Ray was through the door, without giving any explanation, I jumped to my feet, gave him a quick peck on the cheek and headed for the door.

"I've got to go. I'll try and be back later. If she wakes up tell her I love her." As I reached the door I quickly turned back to face Ray.

"By the way, you look much better. She'll fall in love all over again the moment she opens her eyes."

Ray blushed slightly and moved as if to say something, but I was already flying down the corridor as fast as I could. I had a horrid gut feeling that Lionel would have somehow found his way to the cottage. Despite the fact that it was he who needed to give me some explanations for having sent John to frighten me back to the States and away from pastoral dreams, it would do no good having him walk into the master bedroom with its seeming evidence of recent rampant sex.

***

I skidded the van to a halt outside the cottage gates and was out and through the front door at blinding speed. I took the stairs two at a time and tore into the main bedroom, planning to gather all Robbie's forgotten clothes and make a bonfire with them. But the moment I was through the bedroom door, I stopped dead in my tracks. The bed had been carefully made and there was no sign of discarded clothing anywhere. I assumed that Robbie had been back to collect his belongings; he still had the spare keys to the house after all. Nevertheless, I reflected, it was a bit meticulous of him to go and make the bed and tidy the room. Obviously a bit of a spick and span freak, I contemplated, as I sat down on the bed for a brief moment in order to get my breath back.

It was then that I became alarmingly aware of laughter

coming from the ground floor, from the kitchen to be precise. Loud, boisterous laughter, and there was no mistaking who that chortle belonged to. I was willing to believe that I'd imagined the sound, as there'd been no cars parked outside, no evidence of a visitor on the premises. And, in essence, I needed more time before facing Lionel. But the sound downstairs was louder and larger than life itself.

There was nothing for it but to descend and take the flak, for I wasn't jumping through the bedroom window again.

I crept downstairs. I don't know why I crept around in my own house, but somehow I felt guilty. I popped my head a little way through the archway that joined the kitchen with the sitting room and had to do a double-take. Sitting at the kitchen table, chatting as if they were the best of buddies, were Lionel and Robbie. I guess it wasn't really surprising that they seemed to get on like a house on fire considering how identical they were. It would've been incredible, I thought, to have been a fly on the wall the moment they'd met each other. The shock would have been greater for Lionel, for at least Robbie had been aware of the actor's existence. He'd even admitted to me that he'd been mistaken for him more than once. I actually wondered, for the first time, if perhaps Robbie already suspected that Lionel was his twin. He would have wondered about the possibility if he'd read about Lionel's past. Both adopted. The similarity in looks and age. I would have wondered, too, had it been me – though I'm not sure what I would have done about it.

For the second I stood unnoticed, I took in how alike they indeed were. Lionel, considering his lifestyle and who he was, was the more spruced-up of the two, with his deeper tan, flashing white teeth, finely-groomed hair and clean-shaven face. Robbie, on the other hand, had his hair standing up on end and he was still unshaven – although, thank goodness, now fully dressed. Other than that, it was like looking at a mirror image of the same person.

Robbie was the one to spot to me first. He sent me a cynical smirk as he stood.

"Chantelle! There you are. I guess you two have some

catching up to do," he remarked with a slight hint of sarcasm in his voice that only I appreciated. It was Lionel's turn to twist and face me. His eyes lit up on seeing me and it was hard to imagine that he had a calculating side to him that he'd been able to keep so well hidden. Of course, he was a bloody good actor. World-famous. But if he had to have a hidden side I would have preferred an image of him prancing about in stiletto heels clad in my pink lingerie, than him being deceitful and obsessive.

"Hi, Princess." Lionel called out in his suave, enticing voice as he, too, got to his feet.

"You know, it looks like Robbie here and I could be twins, separated at birth! How about that?"

"You don't say!" I chimed back trying to sound surprised and that I was paying attention, when in fact I was trying to figure out where Robbie had hidden his used clothing, for he was wasn't wearing the rugby shirt he'd left on the bed. What's more, his pockets didn't bulge out suspiciously like hamster's pouches stuffed with food. I rather feared that he'd strategically tidied the bedroom just to throw me, and his boxers, socks and shirt were still somewhere in the house, just waiting for Lionel to come across.

"I'll escort you to the door, Robbie." I hissed at him, looking him straight in the eye daring him to betray me. If he had whipped out his undies there and then and said something on the lines of *Fine, honey, I've collected what I left here*, that wouldn't have just betrayed me, it would have sent me straight to the guillotine. Thankfully, however, he opted to co-operate with me and moved around the table to follow me out.

"Lionel, stay there while I see Robbie off."

I addressed him over my shoulder as I hastened to the front door. I could hear the twins backslapping each other behind me in the kitchen in a brotherly farewell. "What a hypocrite," I murmured to myself. Robbie well knew that Lionel had earned himself a good clout around the ear rather than a friendly "Ho Ho."

As soon as Robbie was at my side and out of Lionel's

hearing I turned and fumed at him in a whisper.

"Where the hell have you hidden your underwear?"

"I don't know what you're talking about, sweetheart. Why on earth would I have underwear hidden in this house? Chantelle, with your memory as it is of late, you've obviously got things mixed up."

"Of course" I hissed back. "But as you don't want to listen to me and let me explain, you'll never understand."

I was working myself up into such a temper, I actually wanted to swear out loud at him. But before I could continue, he added (rather deviously and totally ignoring the fact that I could explain things given the chance), "By the way, I don't think Lionel is responsible for what's been happening. He seems a decent guy."

And with that he opened the door and was down the front steps in one energetic jump, whilst I, in frustration, slammed the door shut blocking out his mocking image.

Of course Robbie would defend Lionel. After all, there was nothing stronger than the bond of blood.

I took a deep breath and headed back to the kitchen. Robbie had got me so fired up with his mocking stance that I was ready to face Lionel, guillotine and all. The moment I passed into the kitchen I threw all the cut-out threatening letters at Lionel. I'd recovered them from their hiding place the moment I'd been aware of Lionel's laugh, and had tucked them into my waistband. They scattered to the floor, and Lionel, in his bewilderment, just looked from me to them and back to me again.

"Honey, are you okay?"

This was obviously not the welcome he'd been expecting. Robbie had probably been more enthusiastic than me to see him, and I was supposed to be his fiancée. I no longer wore the flashing diamond, and that alone should have alerted him that something was wrong. I mean, it wasn't as if you could miss the fact that the titanic jewel, which alone could have lit up Oxford Street at Christmas, was not where it should be. He bent to pick up one of the strewn pieces of paper and on reading its contents turned to me puzzled.

"What's this all about, babe?"

"For Christ's sake, Lionel, you've already won the Oscar, stop pretending you don't know what the letters are about. Quit bluffing that you're unaware of everything you've put me through."

His look of incomprehension didn't alter. What I did glimpse was a look of *Oh no, she's going to do a Vivien Francis on me!* which probably best described my mindset at that moment. I believed that I'd every right to fly off the handle, which is why I didn't think twice about picking up the china flower vase that was on the middle of the kitchen table, brimming with wild roses, and hurtling it with all my pent-up fury right at Lionel. He easily dodged the airborne missile, and it shattered straight into the wooden kitchen cupboard behind. There were place mats down on the kitchen table, which were my next string of ammunition. I flung them at him as I shrieked, "Tammy's been in intensive care for the last three days because of your idiotic scheming. It wasn't enough to let me make the decision to be with you myself, was it? You just had to have your way, no matter what, didn't you? It doesn't matter to you if you crush someone along the way, as long as in the end you get your own way. Well, let me tell you, Lionel, I'd fallen in love with you, but I can't forgive you for trying to manipulate me so. I can't believe that you could be so wicked, so selfish as to pull off a scam like you have. Sending John, your personal chauffer, over to scare me back to LA. What was it you said to me when you told me you loved me? That you worried that I may return to the UK and leave you. Well, by taking things that step too far in your attempt to control and influence me, you've gone and made sure that I never want to see you again. I'd be crazy to go back to LA with you now. You can't force people to be with you. They have to be with you because they want to, just as I did. But it's too late now."

By this point I had run out of place mats. Only one had found its target in any case, which didn't say much for my hand-eye coordination. I guess it had been a bit too much to ask; scream my head off at Lionel whilst attempting to keep the tears of frustration and woe at bay, as well as hurtle everything and anything that came to hand at him.

Lionel, in turn, just stared at me in utter confusion as he successfully dodged my flying ammunition. I think he believed that the whole scenario, all I was saying, was just part of a bad dream, a dream which he struggled to wake up from. For, if it had been just a terrible, terrible dream, then at least my final words of "Get out, I never want to see you again…" wouldn't have torn at his heart as they appeared to. I'd never seen him look so hurt and vulnerable before. I would never have believed that I could cause a grown man to break down and cry, or shake with utter remorse and sorrow. I would never have believed that I could break someone's heart, despite the fact that mine was already shattered.

Lionel left the house in silent anguish; he didn't even look me in the eye as he turned to leave. His entire body shook with grief, and I knew, implausible as it might seem, that he was crying.

I let him go. Despite the fact that his tears wrenched at my heart, they didn't absolve his manipulating and cynical behaviour.

They didn't excuse the fact that Tammy was still lying in hospital in a half-coma.

Chapter Twenty-Seven

Three days later Lionel came back. He looked an utter mess, and I'm sure I wasn't a pretty sight either. I hadn't dared to look in a mirror, but I knew my eyes were all red and puffy from crying my heart out. They felt as sore as hell. What with my unkempt hair, swollen face and runny nose, I'd really let myself go and must have looked a real picture.

Lionel wasn't that far behind me when it came to lack of personal grooming. He obviously hadn't shaved since our previous encounter. It was the first time I'd seen his hair in disarray, sticking up all over the place as if he'd just run his hand over an electric fence. His shirt was all crinkled, too, and I wondered if he'd slept rough somewhere in his day clothes. He probably hadn't eaten either. I certainly hadn't. I hadn't even been tempted by the chocolate Häagen-Dazs ice cream I'd found in the freezer, which was a real indicator of how seriously inconsolable I was.

The strange thing is that I didn't just mope around the cottage mooning over Lionel. I also found myself pining for Robbie. For the first time, I wondered what would have happened if I'd never gone over to the States to work on Lionel's film. Would things between Robbie and me have been better if we'd started dating in the good old traditional, normal and customary routine of old-fashioned courting? Let's face it, I hadn't even "gone out" with Robbie in that sense. Yet I, or simply "things," had messed everything up.

I was sure Tammy would have advised me to go on an extended holiday to the Bahamas or any Caribbean paradise to attempt to curb my heartache – and bloody well sort myself out. I, however, knew that it would take me rather more than just a few Mojitos to get over the wretchedness I felt.

I stepped aside to let Lionel through into the cottage, though I couldn't bring myself to meet his gaze. Lionel, however, didn't step inside, instead, simply remained on the doorstep. He began to speak and his voice was sad and tight with emotion.

"I'm flying back out to the States tonight. I just came by to say goodbye. I know you won't believe me when I tell you that I'm not the one behind the letters you've received. Robbie has told me everything that has happened here during the last few weeks."

I suddenly panicked and wondered precisely what it was Robbie had told Lionel concerning past and more recent events. I hoped that Robbie had had the decorum to leave a certain incident out of the story.

"It saddens me to think," Lionel went on, "that you believe with such blind venom that I could be the one behind the letters. That I could possibly want to hurt you. That I would be so cruel to play with your safety just to keep you by my side. Obviously, however, this is exactly what you think, and nothing I say now is going to change the way you feel. I hope someday you find happiness, Chantelle. And that one day you realise that all I'm saying is true, and that I could have made you very happy."

With that Lionel turned and started down the steps to the main gate. His shoulders were hunched, and from the back he looked like he'd aged ten years in the last three days.

I was totally lost for words. Of course I didn't believe him. I was angered that he couldn't admit to me that the letters had been a part of his ruthless plan to keep me at his side. I couldn't believe that he could be so proud; that he couldn't tell me he was sorry for all he'd put me through over the last weeks. He couldn't even tell me that he was sorry Tammy was still hospital-bound due to his foolishness. He hadn't just come to say goodbye. His last words were simply to make me feel even worse; blaming me for not trusting him, when I'd given him all of me, not only my trust but my very heart and soul.

I slammed the door on his retreating figure and ran up the stairs into my bedroom. I rummaged around under the wardrobe until I came across the piece of wrapping paper I'd stuck to the base with cellotape. My hands fumbled as I tore the paper from its hiding place and ran into one of the guest rooms that overlooked the front garden. I opened the window wide and shouted down at Lionel who was just about to drive off in his rented Mercedes.

I flung right at him, with all my might, the precious diamond engagement ring he'd given me. The moment it was out of my hands, I could hear Tammy's voice in my mind cry out, *You daft cow, there goes your pass to early retirement and your ticket to the Bahamas!*

The diamond flashed in the morning light as it spun in the air and I was almost out of the window and after it, with sudden second thoughts. I couldn't believe I'd hurtled something of such value into the wild outdoors, as if it was just a worthless piece of glass. I'd wanted to hurt Lionel, give him back everything he'd given me, in the hope that it hurt him as much as I hurt, deep to my very core. I realised, however, as Lionel looked up at me whilst I leaned precariously out of the window and our eyes locked that he was indeed hurting, possibly even more than me.

Without even pausing to gather the jewel, he stepped into his car and drove off. I, of course, was down the stairs and out of the front door in a jiffy. It had started drizzling but this was of little concern now, for I had an absolute fortune's worth of precious stone somewhere in my front garden and I'd be damned if I was going to let a little spot of rain deter me. I couldn't believe I was actually giving something of materialistic value more importance than pining over my broken heart. I simply concluded that the instinct for survival is definitely the greatest of all, and that the diamond was, at this moment, the only thing I had to treasure; the one thing that would see me through a cold harsh winter – a life's worth of winters, come to think of it. I would have settled for love, like the love I'd felt for Lionel, but considering how fleeting and treacherous love can be, I opted for the diamond. I suddenly understood why they say *Diamonds are a girl's best friend*. Because they can cut through glass, but not through your heart.

In any case, hunting around the front garden for the precious stone was a winner at keeping my mind off my heartache.

***

Two hours later, and with it utterly pissing down with rain, I was still down on my hands and knees ploughing through the front garden in vain search of the ring. I couldn't believe I hadn't watched to see where it had landed. I'd been too busy at the time gazing at Lionel's heartbroken face. I wondered, and not for the first time, if Lionel had caught the ring in mid-flight before driving off, as there was no sign of flashing stone anywhere on the front lawn.

I sat back on my haunches for a moment, wondering for the umpteenth time where on earth the ring could have landed, when suddenly a magpie appeared from out of nowhere. It soared down onto the grass area right up by the house and started pecking at something on the ground. It amused me to think that the bird had braved the rain to fish a worm or two out of the damp soil. Then I caught sight of the sparkling object the magpie was busy trying to uncover and I almost keeled over in anguish at the thought that some feathered thief was about to fly off with my life savings. I charged over to it throwing several pebbles I'd scooped up in an attempt to scare it away. But the stubborn fowl didn't budge; it just looked at me with bright, defiant eyes before becoming airborne with my engagement ring flashing in its beak. I lunged for it, thinking that if I didn't knock it down, the next few weeks would be spent scouring the neighbouring woods in search for my treasured jewel.

The magpie let out a harsh "caw" in anger and the ring dropped to the ground. I was down on the jewel like a woman possessed, breathing heavily, hair stuck down on my face from the relentless rain, clothes sodden and soiled. But I

240

had my ring back, and all paled in comparison. The magpie turned on me and swooped down in attack and pecked my head hard. I was so surprised I let the ring slip from my grip in my attempt to thrash off the aggressive bird. It flashed through my mind that I'd heard of cases in Australia of magpies who tended to take out their venom on the poor postmen. But Aussie magpies are renowned for being more aggressive than their UK cousins, which brought me to the general notion, even as I was wildly waving my arms about, that they obviously grow their crops big and strong down under!

I finally had the diamond ring safely in my palm, but the ring was so huge I couldn't close my fist properly, so I placed my other hand under it in protection. As I scurried up the front steps I remembered the times I'd teased Lionel about all the luxurious things he had, such as his lavish caravan and opulent yacht, the cars and the helicopter. Now there was no more Lionel in my life. Just me battling it out with a magpie over my precious stone; all I had left of my memories. The ring seemed to have the same effect on me and my winged foe as the ring from the *Lord of the Rings* did over Gollum. Poor fellow.

Just as I turned the door handle to let myself into the cottage, I became aware of the sound of horse's hooves crashing down along the lane in a wild gallop. I couldn't believe that Robbie was foolish enough to be out in such dire weather. At the same time I slicked my hair back off my face, so that if he saw me he would simply assume I'd just stepped out of the shower, rather than spent two hours on my hands and knees outside in the torrential rain. Galloping so fast, I didn't think he would notice how soiled my clothes were. I also wondered why I should be bothered about what Robbie thought of me. The concept he already had of me couldn't possibly sink any lower.

The black stallion charged past at alarming speed, but what concerned me more was that there was no rider. Robbie was either lying on the ground somewhere after being thrown from his saddle, or would soon appear dashing down the lane after his mount. I stood and waited in anticipation. The thought of seeing his face after such a humiliation would have been quite a treat; anything to take my mind off current events.

Five minutes passed and I found myself trudging down the country lane in the hope of coming across Robbie. Ten minutes later, just as I was about to retrace my steps in order to restart my hunt for Robbie in the van, armed with my mobile in case I had to call for an ambulance, I became aware of a low moan. At first it was hard to decipher where exactly it had come from as it was muffled by the falling rain, and the surrounding dense woods obscured my vision. The moan came again, and this time I located it to my right. I stepped into the undergrowth that grew wild along the roadside and accidentally slipped some paces down a muddy slope that had been concealed from my vision, catching myself on some thorny brambles as I did so.

"For fuck's sake!" I grumbled to myself as I picked a thorn out of my now ripped tracksuit bottoms. They say unlucky events occur in threes. Someone had obviously lost count at number three with me, for I was having a never-ending run of bad luck.

The grunt suddenly came much closer and much louder, which wasn't really surprising considering I'd just rammed my heel down on Robbie's hand. I was quickly off his hand and down beside him. All things considered I wasn't too sure if he would be too thrilled to see me, but I was a better option than being left out all day and night in the pelting rain, so that alone had to be of some comfort to him.

"Chantelle" he croaked out, trying to muffle the pain in his voice, "What are you doing here?"

"I have a fetish for mud baths. I thought you knew that!"

I thought a little light humour might help. It was obvious that he was in excruciating pain and had counted on someone responsible finding him. I didn't know if he counted me as responsible; little me, who couldn't even keep track of my nocturnal habits or bed partners, but I did notice what looked like a slight smile play on his lips on hearing my crack about

242

my sludge mania. Perhaps he didn't totally hate me after all.

"Do you think you could stand if I help you?" I asked, determined to get Robbie to his feet and prove to him that I was of some worth and not, as he probably thought, just a slapper. On catching his feeble nod, I got him to a sitting position and then, with his arm around my shoulder I gradually got him to his feet. His hand somehow brushed against my breast and I wondered, for a split second, if it had been intentional. I gave him the benefit of the doubt. Who would want to flirt in the condition he was in? And after me saying I couldn't remember sleeping with him anyway.

His left leg had obviously been quite badly injured during the fall, as Robbie was unable to place any weight on it at all. His clothes were all torn as if he had been pulled through a holly bush. To save his manly pride I didn't ask any questions. Finally on his feet and leaning heavily on me, we somehow made it up the muddy slope and level with the country lane. It took us a good half hour to get back to the cottage. I thought my back would snap somewhere down the lane as I struggled under Robbie's increasingly heavy weight. I could hardly stand up straight when we finally got to the cottage door and I fumbled to find the key to the lock. I remained stooped over like the Hunchback of Notre Dame as I ultimately opened the front door and shuffled through, Robbie hobbling beside me.

The only good omen was finding Robbie's stallion lazily grazing on the grass in the front garden. The black horse raised its head ever so slightly on seeing Robbie and me approach, but soon resumed its steady chomping at my precious lawn. If it hadn't been that I couldn't stand straight I would have picked up something and hurtled it at the beast. Not only was he dangerously close to my roses, but he'd also thrown Robbie, which was animal treachery in my books. Robbie, however, was thrilled to see his stallion safe and sound and whistled joyfully at him. What a forgiving guy, I thought. I didn't think I would have been quite so charitable if I'd been in Robbie's shoes. The action, nevertheless, gave me hope. Possibly I would be forgiven, too. If, of course, he gave me the opportunity to explain everything to him.

Robbie refused to be taken to the hospital to have his battle wounds tended to, so I decided the best thing was to run a hot bath and attempt first aid myself. He'd obviously landed right in the middle of a bramble bush, as there were fine scratches all over his arms and his whole back was covered in thorns. I got my tweezers out and started to extract the sharp spikes that were visible. Some of the scratches looked quite deep and painful. I was aware that if I didn't clean the wounds properly they could possibly get infected. The problem was, I had no medical alcohol in the house and I couldn't waste time driving into town and back. As I wondered what to do it suddenly struck me that there was something I could use, even if it wasn't the most appropriate substance.

"I'll be back in a second," I shouted to Robbie as I dashed down into the kitchen. As I stepped back into the bathroom, which was rapidly turning into a steam-room as the warm bathwater vaporised into the cool surrounding air, Robbie, without even looking at me, sullenly declared, "You knew he was my brother, didn't you?"

I was totally caught off guard, but there was no point in pretending I hadn't twigged to what he meant. The question had been inevitable sooner or later. I moved to look him in the eye and nodded as he continued.

"I've always suspected it anyway. There were too many coincidences. I even foolishly tried to contact him once." He let out a harsh laugh as he said this. "Lionel probably receives hundreds of fan letters a day, and mine was probably just one of many, with the added inconvenience that it looked as if I was looking for fame or fortune. But all I was looking for was for a brother."

He choked on this last word.

"But why didn't *you* tell me?" he went on, as he held my gaze steady. His brow was creased with concern, his eyes melancholy. I returned his gaze, but it was impossible for me to answer. How did he think I could tell him, then or ever, that whilst he didn't even have enough money to buy this small cottage, he had a twin brother who was one of the wealthiest actors in the world? Not only that, his brother Lionel had everything else too: elegance, class, charm, fame.

I hesitated a moment longer before I mumbled, "I was waiting for the right moment… Robbie, I'm sorry. I realise I should have told you. I just never found the occasion."

It was an unconvincing, half-hearted lie, and I knew Robbie had seen straight through it. As if reading my mind, there was a slight pitch of dejection in his voice as he softly whispered, "It's okay, I understand why. He has everything, and I have nothing. And I'm nobody. I'm not blind." He gave a slight cynical chuckle before adding, "He even had The Girl."

For a split second he held my gaze steady, intently searching my face as if probing for an answer that would prove otherwise. For I knew, as big-headed as it sounded, that "The Girl" in question was me. Though it was quite hard to believe that I, with my impulsive attitude and somewhat reckless behaviour could attract anyone, let alone two wonderful men. Well, at least Robbie was a true gentleman. I didn't even want to word what I thought Lionel was after his treachery. We remained staring at each other, and I realised that Robbie, like me, didn't hanker after fame and fortune, for we both knew they were not the keys to happiness. The only thing we both searched for was true love, as love and love alone is what, in turn, leads to fulfilling peace and happiness. And it was about time I realised that there were no riches in the world that could give that kind of love.

The room suddenly felt exceedingly steamy and hot – and it was not just from the sweltering bathwater. In an attempt to change the conversation and overcome the charged atmosphere that was rapidly building up between us, I felt I needed to lower the temperature and be decidedly practical by attempting some sort of first aid on Robbie's back. It was not a pretty sight.

In my attempt to bring myself back to reality and avoid at all costs Robbie's penetrating gaze, I handed him a shot glass full to the brim with brandy.

"If I were you," I said, "I'd down that in one." Taking my own advice, I gulped down a generous measure straight from the bottle that I'd uncovered in the kitchen cupboard. I took a couple more swigs of the strong and warming spirit in an attempt to still my shaking hands. I had no idea if I was shaking from trying to pass myself off as Florence Nightingale or because of Robbie's nude torso sitting in my bathtub and our recent intense conversation. I decided it was best not to ponder the matter and, feeling the liquor rush through my veins, I held my breath in hushed anticipation before splashing the remaining brandy down Robbie's back as a form of antiseptic. There was a moment of silence and just as I was breathing a sigh of relief, Robbie yelled out in shock, "*FOR CHRIST'S SAKE, WOMAN!* You could have at least warned me…"

"I thought I did." I slurred back bemused, as, at the same time, I let out a loud, irrepressible hiccup.

***

I locked the door to my bedroom that night. It wasn't in order to keep Robbie out, rather to keep me in. It would do no good to go wandering around in the middle of the night, as I knew I would probably end up in his bed. I still had some dignity and self-control left, I thought. At least I was trying to recover what I once had. But my head was in a terrible muddle, to say the least, and there was no point blaming the generous amounts of brandy I'd gulped down.

How was it possible that each brother, each in his own charming way, had been capable of seeping into my heart until I no longer knew what was what and who was who? There was no point pretending that I no longer loved Lionel. I did love him, deeply. I just felt tremendous anger towards him at this instant because of his lunatic, manipulating behaviour. Nevertheless, though I still loved him, I also knew that after his show of possessiveness I could never quite trust him again. I would never be sure how far he would go in his desire to control me, and I had no intention of hearing the dreaded words: *If I can't have you, no one will!*

Then there was Robbie. Kind, considerate Robbie. Robbie whom I'd so misunderstood from the start. Robbie who was a pillar of strength at the end of a long day. Robbie who, if I was honest, deserved someone so much better than me; someone responsible like he was, someone more reliable and less reckless. Someone who would bestow on him peace and happiness – together with a half dozen kids! I didn't know if I could ever aspire to these solid principles, though I would like to think that I could.

Everything seemed such a shambles at this moment. I would certainly need to get a grip on myself and the situation. But before I tried to do anything, I felt that I needed to get away for a while; to disappear until the whole affair had blown over and until my mind and heart settled. It was weak of me, I knew, to want to run away instead of facing up to things – but I just didn't want to mess up again, as I probably would if I stayed around.

I certainly didn't want to start something on the rebound; that wouldn't be fair on anyone. Anyway, as they say, *Let the bird fly free; if it returns, it's yours forever*. And I needed to spread my wings and find my real self again.

But I also realised that if I did go away for I while, I would be taking a huge risk. I couldn't ask Robbie to wait for me; that would just be too selfish. I simply hoped that if he truly loved me, he would be patient with me.

Apart from Robbie and my uncertain heart – and mind! – I also dreaded the thought of having to go through the hell of persecution when the media found out that Lionel and I were no longer together – especially if Lionel looked as bad when he got back to the States as he did when he'd left England. To a great many, Lionel was not only a star with that rare quality of being a nice guy with it, he was a hero who helped the less fortunate. That I knew him to be an obsessive nutter didn't matter. In this particular drama I'd be cast as the heartless, scheming, cheap tart. I'd be hounded for days, weeks, maybe months. This rural idyll would become a madhouse if I stayed.

Chapter Twenty-Eight

I did stay, though – but only because Robbie and I spent the next couple of days dallying around the cottage both with stinking colds as a result of our prolonged jaunts out in the hammering rain. I wasn't too sure who was the worse for wear. I was so bunged-up that I couldn't breathe properly, whilst Robbie also had a really bad cough. His back was sore from the tumble through the bramble bushes, and his ankle was so swollen that he could barely walk. Needless to say, in our present state all notion of hanky-panky was out of the question. For me, that was a great relief.

On the second day of our recuperation, I summoned enough courage to try and explain to Robbie, once again, what had happened to me. I'd desperately tried to remember that night we'd spent together, but the more I tried, the more confused things seemed to get. As I'd experienced from childhood, the flashback usually came when I least expected, and I relied on the fact that at some point soon I would remember. Until now, the whole incident had been left unspoken as if it had never happened. We were lounging in the sitting room, the afternoon light filtered through the windows, setting off the copper gleam of the wooden floorboards. I was wearing my Dalmatian spotted onesie, and was very glad that I hadn't bought a unicorn or crocodile one. I didn't need to get things more comic than they already were; with my hair in a frizz and my "Rudolph the Red-nosed Reindeer" nose, I looked rather clownish as it was.

Robbie had just been telling me about his rather solitary youth living in the middle of the British countryside, with the stress of city life unthinkable. He believed that life was too short to waste time commuting for hours just to get to work

248

and be hassled by people all pushing to get ahead. He believed that life should be kept as simple as possible, for the simplest things are often the greatest, and without a doubt usually the most peaceful. He'd looked at me then and smiled shyly and held my gaze as if to say "*This* is what I can offer."

I was the first to break eye contact. I suddenly felt terribly hot with my onesie on, and started fanning myself with a magazine that Tammy had left lying around the house on her first visit.

"Robbie," I murmured, and had to clear my voice as it sounded all croaky – and it wasn't just because of the cold. I was feeling extremely emotional and my voice wavered. "I lost my mother when I was very young. I couldn't cope or accept it, and blanked the whole period out of my mind. I was diagnosed with temporary amnesia. It took me months to remember. And not just to remember what happened, but to remember *her*. There was a time I couldn't even bring to mind her beautiful face, her sweet smile, or anything about her."

By this point Robbie had attempted to move close to me, but I waved him away. I didn't think I could cope by having him move closer. There was a chance that I could have a relapse into oblivion, and now that I had his attention I needed to finish.

"I haven't had one of these memory lapses in years, until the other night when you brought me home from the hospital. I don't know what happened. As much as I try I just can't remember."

Robbie looked at me tenderly. "What do you think happened?" he whispered.

"I'm not sure" I said, rapidly picking up the magazine again and fanning myself. God, it was hot!

"What would you have liked to have happened?"

"Errrr…." Christ! Was this necessary? I was trying to avoid getting myself more confused than I already was, and Robbie's pressing certainly wasn't helping.

"Can't you just tell me what happened?" I pleaded, stalling to reply properly.

"Would you remember it if it was magical? If it was the most amazing night of your life?" he asked.

"Yes." There was a lump in my throat and I couldn't trust myself to say much more.

"Then I'll wait for you to remember."

And with that he stood and walked over to where I was sitting, took hold of my hands and pulled me to my feet, holding me tight in his arms for what felt like an eternity. Neither of us spoke or made an attempt to move. Finally he bent and kissed me gently on one cheek and brushed away a tear that was trickling down my face.

"I think I'd better go."

And with that he left, closing the front door softly behind him.

***

The following morning, after a restless night, I went to visit Tammy. I was relieved that Robbie now knew what had happened to me, and that he didn't seem to mind waiting until I remembered, but I still felt terribly anxious. So it was a huge relief to find Tammy almost fully recovered. There was so much I wanted to tell her, too, but I thought it best to ease all of my latest gossip and goings on to her bit by bit. I didn't know how much she remembered about the night of the attack, and I didn't want to risk giving her a relapse. Thus, when she turned her pale face to me, with dark circles under her eyes, and asked me how I was doing, I just smiled at her and told her I was great. I added that when she fully recovered I was taking her on holiday. And Ray too, if she wished. She looked slightly puzzled at this notion; after all she still thought I was on the brink of my wedding day. In an attempt to lull her look of perplexity I just smiled back at her in my carefree way and reached out to hold her hand tight.

I spent the whole day at Tammy's side. However, as she was still weak, she fell in and out of sleep a couple of times whilst I was talking. It was hard not to feel slightly offended by her sudden snoring whilst I found myself in mid-sentence, but, of course, it wasn't that important. What was imperative was that she continued to progress well. Once she was allowed to go home, that alone would be a real weight off my mind.

It was dark when I arrived back at the cottage. As I stepped into the front room. I paused for a brief moment as I'd picked up on a light scent of musky perfume. There was something tremendously familiar about the soft fragrance, and I closed my eyes trying to pinpoint where I'd come across this scent before. Just as I did so I was aware that the lamp in the front room was switched on. Instinctively I dived behind the sofa.

"It's OK," called a voice. "It's only me…"

I poked my head around the armrest to verify the voice with my own eyes.

"For crying out loud, Gabby!" I exclaimed, in part relief and part fury. "You've given me the shock of my life. How the hell did you get in?" There was no point asking her how she'd found me, for everyone (except for the stalking paparazzi, thank goodness) seemed to know my whereabouts.

"I have my ways," she replied smoothly.

Hadn't anyone ever told her that it was illegal to break into homes? I honestly wasn't sure if I was glad to see her or not. For starters, she'd have me awake at sun-up and sprinting down the lane and back at least a dozen times before breakfast. I wasn't too sure how she would take to seeing Robbie either. And where was Lionel in all of this?

"I don't have much time," she began and motioned me to sit. I did so, but rather hesitantly as I actually preferred to keep the sofa between us as a sort of shield. There was something about Gabby that just didn't seem right. At first I thought she was drunk, or maybe high on something. But as both notions were just so "un-Gabby" I just had to assume that she was naturally this scary and I'd never fully twigged before.

"I'm flying back to the States first thing tomorrow morning."

Phew!!

"I've just come over to tell you in person that Lionel had nothing whatsoever to do with the letters you received. I was the one behind the incidents all along. I was the one who send John over here to spy on you and unsettle you."

Gabby paused for a moment, whilst I, realising what a bloody fruit cake she really is, started to slowly inch myself towards the edge of the settee in order to be able to shoot behind it if she really lost her wits and I had to defend myself against her in hand-to-hand combat. If it came to that, of course, the odds were firmly against me. As I sustained my subtle bum shifting across the sofa, Gabby continued her confession in her usual cold, clipped tones.

"I originally thought I was doing the correct thing. All I've achieved, however, is breaking Lionel's heart. He will never forgive me, and I doubt you will either. All I can hope for is that by flying over here to tell you, somehow things between Lionel and you will work out, and at least then my conscience will be eased a little. Please believe me when I tell you that my intentions were to help keep you guys together. I thought that if you received signs of hostility here, you would return even quicker to be by Lionel's side and resign yourself to the idea of being the wife of a superstar. I even passed on the nude photos of you to the magazine, thinking that if everything about you was exposed," (she couldn't have chosen a more apt term) "then there would be no need for you to hide in the shadows. I believed that if everyone knew who you were, there would no longer be a reason for you to reject Lionel's celebrity lifestyle and try to remain anonymous, as you, yourself, would be a star in your own right."

Gabby hesitated a moment to get her breath back, and, with all probability, to attempt to assess my possible reaction. I was fuming. I couldn't believe it; my love life was in a total mess, and all because of her.

"*Why?*" I cried out in hopeless bewilderment. It was the only word that I could think of uttering aloud which wasn't a downright obscenity. Angered as I was, I didn't want to fly off the handle. It wouldn't achieve anything, other than, perhaps, a black eye (and it was my eyes I was worried about).

"The gypsy woman in New Orleans told me, after she had read Lionel's fortune, that I would never find the love of my life until Lionel was happily married…"

Well, that certainly explained things – as well as the fact that Gabby obviously had no common sense whatsoever to have fallen for that string of lies and rubbish and gone to the extremes she had. To follow through on a mystic tale like that she must be barking mad… She is barking mad!

We remained a moment in silence before Gabby got up and walked towards the front door.

"Where are you going?" I asked, as I realised that Gabby was about to let herself out of the cottage and into the dark night. She looked across at me, her expression miserable and overwrought. I realised that even if Lionel and I did ever manage to forgive her, I doubted she would ever forgive herself.

"I've got a plane to catch," she stated flatly, and with that stepped outside and closed the door silently behind her.

Chapter Twenty-Nine

The other person who had a plane to catch was, of course, me.

I wasn't too sure how things would pan out, and I had no plan of action. No A, let alone B or C strategy to fall back on. All I knew was that it was crucial for me to see Lionel again. I had a lot of explaining to do. I felt it was only fair to both of us to give each other a moment together to talk things through; to somehow try to unravel the mess we (I!) found ourselves in. I didn't know if he would forgive me for not trusting him and not believing in him. I cringed at the recollection of my manic outburst when I'd chucked all the menacing letters at him, followed by my other bout of hysteria when I'd hurtled the engagement ring at him. It was very probable that he wouldn't forgive me.

All the same, I had to see him and tell him I was sorry.

There was an available seat on a Virgin Atlantic flight scheduled to fly out to LA forty-eight hours after Gabby's confession. I'd just about enough time to say a quick farewell to Tammy. I didn't explain everything to her then, as it would have taken me longer than the forty-eight hours I had before my flight. I just promised her that I would return as soon as I could. After all, we still had a "girly" holiday together to look forward to.

The other person I searched high and low to say goodbye to, was, unsurprisingly, Robbie.

But there was no sign of him anywhere, and even Ray had no idea where he was. I hadn't seen Robbie since the day before I'd visited Tammy; the day before Gabby appeared out of the blue – well, darkness, actually – and pleaded guilty to the whole sad, sorry, sordid affair. I wondered if Robbie had been somewhere in the house during the encounter and had overheard everything, and decided it was best to disappear until I got my wits together. I could think of no other reason. His horse wasn't even in the paddock. No one in the village knew where he was either. I found myself panicking that something serious had happened to him. Maybe he'd been thrown from his horse again and was lying abandoned and injured somewhere along the country lane. The very idea terrified me.

The minutes ticked by and soon it was time for me to leave. I started the van and sat in the driver's seat, letting the engine purr away softly, trying to think where I could possibly find Robbie in one last frantic search before I headed into the city. Following a last-minute gut feeling I turned the van down the country lane and parked off the main track by the crossroads which Tammy and I had come across the very first time we'd ventured here: the time when Tammy foolishly decided to manoeuvre her precious Jag down the muddy trail that led to the river. Leaving the van safely at the start of the track, I slowly and cautiously made my way down to the river on foot.

There were imprints of horse's hooves on the damp, muddy ground. Keenly I followed them, sure that they belonged to Robbie's black hunter. They led me down to the riverbank, and there, with its head down quenching its thirst, was the magnificent jet-black horse. He raised his head on hearing me and let out a soft neigh in recognition, which was truly touching. I whistled back in response, searching at the same time for signs of Robbie.

It took me a while to spot the figure that sat hunched someway further up the river. But, on approaching, there was no doubt that it was Robbie. Before I had a chance to say anything he turned to me with a sad half-smile.

"I told you Lionel wasn't the one behind the letters."

I nodded back at him in answer. I didn't ask him how he knew, assuming, as I had from the start, that he'd obviously overheard Gabby's disclosure. It was ironic that Robbie had had more faith in Lionel than I did. At the time I'd just assumed that Robbie defended his brother, protected blood of his blood, in order to enrage me. I couldn't have been more wrong.

"You're leaving, then…?" He sighed as he turned his gaze back to the river, leaving it impossible for me to read anything from his eyes.

I was lost for words. What could I say? It was true, I was leaving. For how long…? Not even I knew for sure. I stood for a moment in silence listening to the wind whistle through the surrounding woodland and rippling through the leaves that hung from the trees. It would be autumn soon, and those very leaves would fall lightly, at Mother Nature's call, onto the forest floor in shades of russet and gold.

"Every time I come down here to the river, I can't help but think of you. Of the way you looked that day when you and Tammy got stuck in the mud."

He chuckled slightly at the memory whilst I in turn glowed scarlet.

"You were covered in mud, but all I could see were your shining almond eyes, and how beautiful you looked to me. I fell in love with you from the very instant I set my eyes on you."

He hesitated a moment as he turned to look at me. Our eyes locked and I had to struggle to keep my emotions still. My breathing became shallow and my heart hammered in my chest. He loved me? After all I had put him through? Moreover, though I'd selfishly longed to hear these words, I realised that things would have been much easier if they'd been left unsaid. For I was on my way to catch a plane across the Atlantic, and after hearing this tender, sincere, loving admission it was going to be impossible to say goodbye. I felt a tear of sorrow and grief slowly trail down my cheek. Robbie was quick to reach my side and tenderly wiped it away.

"Promise me," he whispered, "that if you're not happy, you'll come back."

I wondered, not for the first time, as I stood there with his penetrating eyes locked into mine, what it was that I'd done to deserve the love of such an unselfish and great man. Indeed, what had I done to deserve the love of two such wonderful men? Both special, each in their own, endearing way. I felt awful. Sick. I wouldn't envy anyone in this situation. If anyone ever confessed to me that they found themselves caught between two loves, I'd say a prayer for them. It was a bloody nightmare.

***

Somehow I left. I don't know how – and I don't know how I didn't kill myself on the drive back to London. I don't remember anything at all about the journey.

Robbie's soft murmur as he'd whispered his feelings to me, tugged at my heart, as I'd climbed back into the van and had driven off. He felt that the rural cottage was our destiny. It was as if the cottage had played some magical trick on us to draw us together. And I think he was right, the house had bewitched me from the very beginning. I had even wished for it and to have Robbie in my life at the very start of my Hollywood venture. I'd never imagined it would end like this though.

On the whole flight across the Atlantic, his words *I'll be waiting for you...* repeated in my head over and over like a stuck gramophone record. I remembered my mum had a Barry Manilow record which she just loved, and played over and over until it scratched and we were left with just *Bermuda Tri-an-gle.... Bermuda Tri-an-gle....* which drove the next-door neighbours crazy. They would thump on the dividing wall. These days you would probably get a machine gun rammed through the letterbox...

I felt really queasy throughout the flight, too. The airline meals didn't go down well at all, though there was nothing extraordinary about that. What really concerned me was Lionel's possible reaction. How would he take to seeing me again? I was preparing myself for the worst, for his probable words of *Go to hell*. And I wouldn't blame him in the least.

As I sat there on that long-haul flight, I tried to

concentrate and mentally string a few lines together to form some sort of apology which I could rehearse and get word perfect before having to speak to Lionel. But before I got any further than "Hi Lionel…" I was overcome with waves of nausea. I really fought to calm myself. I couldn't afford another memory lapse now.

Somehow I made it through passport control, immigration and customs without throwing up or fainting, and grabbed a cab. It wasn't long before I was charging down the garden path of the big house, which I'd always believed to be Freddy G's, and into the private grounds that encircled Lionel's bungalow – the bungalow that had been my home during the course of much of the summer. A summer that had been filled with so much: a journey from unknown "extra" to surprise, adventure, love, and… what now?

The door was wide open and I dashed through. My heart was in my throat at the thought of seeing Lionel again, and I was swamped by both anticipation and trepidation. The second I was through the door, however, I stopped dead as I became aware of a happy female voice chirpily singing away. And the melody came directly from the bedroom.

I believe I momentarily stopped breathing, and I felt sure that my heart had stopped beating. I held fast to the doorframe in an attempt to steady my suddenly weak knees. It served me right if Lionel had substituted me so quickly, after all it was me who had driven him away. But still, he'd obviously not wasted any time, and I was tremendously offended. As I attempted to gather my wits and do a quick cut-and-paste job to my prepared words of apology, changing them into words of anger, little Sav, the Mexican maid, sambaed through from the bedroom, brandishing a huge feather duster. Her big brown eyes got even larger when she saw me. I don't think she'd ever before seen someone so pleased and relieved to see her as I was at that moment. And I don't think I'd ever been so pleased to see a feather duster.

"*El Señorito…?*" I questioned in an attempt to discover where Lionel was. But it was a mistake to have risked my crummy Spanish, as the young girl, encouraged by my attempts to communicate in her language, simply let out a string of rapid Spanish which flew right over my head. I looked at her in confusion and shrugged my shoulders. Sav sighed at my obvious incomprehension, paused for a moment and then smiled coyly at me before energetically flapping her arms by her side. I stood for a moment perplexed.

"Bird." I said in an attempt to decipher her sign language. She shook her head slightly and started flapping away again.

"Fly." I cried out, as I suddenly realised what the arm flutter was all about. Sav nodded her head enthusiastically before she commenced the same movement, but with the added extra of turning in circles at the same time. It was my turn to sigh; I'd never been any good at charades. I tried to concentrate.

"Ok, first word 'fly,' second word…'dizzy,' 'spin'…?" Sav stopped turning for a moment and I don't know how she didn't keel over from all that energetic twirling. She shook her head and paused for a tick before she held three fingers up. I nodded.

"Third word…" I prompted, and she raised her hands level with her face, bent the fingers of her left hand into a circle which she held up over her right eye as if peering through a telescope, and with her right hand, fist closed, she started moving it in small circles as if reeling something. I gasped. I'd got it.

"Camera, film…" I cried out enthusiastically, as Sav nodded vigorously. She suddenly started spinning in circles with the arm flutter once again, and though she didn't bear any resemblance whatsoever to a helicopter, I suddenly clicked.

"Lionel's down by the helicopter pad because he's about to fly off to film his next movie." I exclaimed. Sav beamed back at me in joy as she threw her arms around me in pride. How we'd done all this without knowing much of each other's language must have been, as the Mexicans say, *un milagro*. And a bloody amazing miracle at that.

As soon as I'd untangled myself from her elated embrace

I was out the door and down the path that led to the beach, racing along as if I had a swarm of killer bees after me. Despite the fact that I could hear my gasping breath loud inside my head, I was vividly aware of the sound of helicopter blades cutting through the air as they rotated for take-off. I stumbled a couple of times on the soft sand as I ran, and realised that if I made it to the take-off pad before the helicopter soared away, I would actually be too out of breath to utter a single word, let alone the whole discourse I'd so painstakingly prepared.

I finally had the helicopter in sight, and battled against the gusts of air that were battering in every direction as the blades picked up speed.

"Lionel…" I shrieked out at the top of my lungs, but the wind just blew my words futilely back at me. I sank to my knees in despair. It was agonising to watch how the helicopter slowly took off. I'd so wanted to tell Lionel that I was sorry for not trusting in him. But it was too late. He would be away for months, and I'd been unable to make it in time to tell him how sorry I was.

I remained hunched over, oblivious to my surroundings. It took me a while to realise that the wind had suddenly dropped and that the humming engine had stilled. It was only when I heard my name being called over and over that I realised that the helicopter had landed again and that Lionel was running towards me. We would have made the perfect final scene to a soppy romance, for, on hearing my name called and seeing the image (or rather, blurred vision) of Lionel sprinting towards me, I was up and skipping in joy across the ground and into his strong embrace. He swung me around in delight and I held onto him tight. He was breathless as he turned to me.

"My little Chantelle, I can't believe you're here. Gabby told me everything, but I never believed I'd have you back."

He looked intently at me as if I was some simple figment of his imagination. I smiled back at him, but my voice was serious.

"I'm so sorry Lionel for blaming you, for believing that

you could have risked my safety for your own gains. You asked me once if I trusted you. I should have done, but I let you down. I let us both down. Even if you can't forgive me, I just wanted you to know how sorry I am. Sorry to have messed everything up. To have behaved as childishly as I did…"

Lionel held his fingers to my lips as he hushed me.

"Forget about it, the important thing is you're here now. I would love to stay, but I've been called out on location. This is a big, big movie and I've got thousands of crew and cast waiting. I can't just leave them. I'll be gone for three weeks or so. Stay here, we'll talk about it all when I get back. OK?"

I nodded gratefully at him. (If I analysed it, my place at the aisle had been substituted by a multi-million dollar shoot, but all considered I didn't think I was in a position to grumble). He briefly bent down and tenderly kissed my lips, so delicately it was as if he believed they might crumble. As quickly as he had appeared by my side he was gone. The sand swirled at my feet as the helicopter swished off, and I raised my hand above my head and waved until the aircraft was just a small spot in the far distance.

***

I slowly ambled back along the soft sand, but instead of turning to take the path that led up to the cottage, I kept going along the beach. Barefoot, I let the tide gently lap over my toes as I paused to breathe in the salty Ocean air. The sun was low over the horizon, and as the gulls squawked overhead I was filled with a sensation of utter peace and harmony.

I'd been blessed with three weeks all to myself; three weeks to think things through. To try and decide what I really wanted – and, more importantly, who I really wanted to be. I'd been lucky. I'd been given the love of two incredible men and both had selflessly offered me a future. Which path I chose would be light years away from whichever one I left behind. I also realised that once I'd reached a decision, there would be no turning back. Whatever I decided would be forever, with all the consequences.

I sat down for a moment on the warm, golden dune and briefly closed my eyes. I was unexpectedly overcome by that queasy sensation again. And I was suddenly filled with panicky dread. I did a quick calculation in my head as I tried to keep the waves of nausea at bay.

Could it be? I mentally checked the dates again in panic. My period had been due at least three days ago, and I was as regular as clockwork. *Holy shit!* I was pregnant – and I didn't know who the hell the father was!

"*Oh, Jesus!*" I exclaimed out aloud. I had an abrupt image of my poor mother in the heavens above swoon at my sudden realisation as she looked down on me: *That's scandalous behaviour, Chantelle, just scandalous. And your language, young lady, is just shocking!*

Heavens, what a relief that both Lionel and Robbie looked so similar!

It also ironically came to mind, as I sat there feeling sick and suddenly holding my stomach, that I owed Tammy fifty quid. For, let's face it, I had a fifty-fifty chance of providing solid proof that Robbie definitely wasn't gay!

Moments later I was overcome by a fervent craving for a tuna pate and peanut butter sandwich – the soft spread, you know, not the lumpy kind. That, plus a really thick and creamy banana milkshake... Or maybe two.

My, I thought, if the following nine months were going to be filled with cravings like this, I was going to get huge! So I had three weeks to sort out my life and my future. First of all, I had to make absolutely sure that I was indeed pregnant. I certainly wasn't anticipating, or needing, this added drama.

I breathed in slowly. "Come on Chantelle," I said out loud. Calling myself by my own name was a sure sign of trouble. "You're one tough cookie. And anyway, who the hell got you into this mess?"

Now *that* was a bloody good question. Because, let's face it, it takes two to tango. Or, in this case, three.

I exhaled slowly. I was going to be OK. If I have to do

this on my own, I'll be just fine. It takes more than a pregnancy scare to bowl me over. I can sort this out. I will sort this out. It's not the ending I was expecting, but then, who has the fairy tale?

I smiled to myself. "You can do it, Chantelle. You can take what life throws at you, turn it around and make it your unique tale."

And, come what may, I was determined to find my happy ever after.

But that's another story...

Epilogue

As I sit here wondering and planning my (our!) future, I've just remembered some words of wisdom that I was once told, a long time ago, and only now fully appreciate. Words I now wish to share with all who've followed this little bit of my story. It feels like a lifetime, but in truth, only a few months have gone past since this adventure started. It's my way of saying thank you. It's my way to help bring a little smile.

Chantelle Rose xxx.

I love you not because of who you are, but because of who I am when I am with you. (Lionel and Robbie… For making me the woman I am)

A true friend is someone who reaches for your hand and touches your heart. (Tammy, thanks babe)

The worst way to miss someone is to be sitting right beside them knowing you can't have them. (Vivien, pass this one to your therapist)

Never frown, even when you are sad, because you never know who is falling in love with your smile. (Crystal, honey, I think you'll like this one)

No man or woman is worth your tears, and the one who is won't make you cry. (Sandy, stick this on the next producer who asks you to do something crazy)

Don't cry because it's over; simply smile because it happened. (Mum, Dad... simply, thank you!)

Live and let live. (Gabby, thinking of you).

To the world you may be one person, but to one person you may be the world. (To my future baby, I hope I can live up to the demands of motherhood!)

Make yourself a better person and know who you are before you try to know someone else and expect them to know you. (I think this one is for me)

Don't try so hard; the best things come when you least expect them. (This one's for you...)

THE END

Fantastic Books
Great Authors

CROOKED
CAT

Meet our authors and discover
our exciting range:

- Gripping Thrillers
- Cosy Mysteries
- Romantic Chick-Lit
- Fascinating Historicals
- Exciting Fantasy
- Young Adult and Children's
  Adventures

Printed in Great Britain
by Amazon